NO-NO BOY

CLASSICS OF ASIAN AMERICAN LITERATURE

With a New Foreword by **RUTH OZEKI**

Introduction by **LAWSON FUSAO INADA**

Afterword by **FRANK CHIN**

NO-NO BOY

JOHN OKADA

UNIVERSITY OF WASHINGTON PRESS
Seattle and London

Original cloth editions published by Charles E. Tuttle,
Rutherford, Vermont, and Tokyo, Japan, 1957

First paperback edition published by the Combined Asian-American
Resources Project, Inc., Seattle and San Francisco, 1976;
distributed by the University of Washington Press

Printed in the United States of America
Design by Thomas Eykemans
Cover illustration by Jillian Tamaki
Composed in Chaparral, typeface designed by Carol Twombly
Display type set in Futura, typeface designed by Paul Renner
18 17   5 4 3 2

UNIVERSITY OF WASHINGTON PRESS
www.washington.edu/uwpress

LIBRARY OF CONGRESS CATALOGING-IN-PUBLICATION DATA
Okada, John.
No-no boy / John Okada ; with a new foreword by Ruth Ozeki ;
introduction by Lawson Fusao Inada ; afterword by Frank Chin.
    pages cm
ISBN 978-0-295-99404-8 (pbk. : alk. paper)
I. Title.
PS3565.K33N6 2014   813'.54—dc23   2014009214

The paper used in this publication meets the minimum requirements
of American National Standard for Information Sciences—Permanence
of Paper for Printed Library Materials, ANSI Z39.48-1984.∞

TO MY WIFE,
DOROTHY

FOREWORD

DEAR JOHN OKADA,

I'm writing to you across time, as one writer to another, to congratulate you on the reissue of your groundbreaking novel, *No-No Boy*. The University of Washington Press has done me the honor of asking me to write a new foreword to your book, and to tell you the truth, I'm nervous. I wish I could consult with you, or visit you and ask you for your blessing, but I can't.

You probably don't even know that your novel was groundbreaking. When it was published, back in 1957, you probably thought it was a colossal failure. It's hard enough to write a novel, and harder still to get one published, but then to have it so completely ignored—this must have been crushing. Your original publisher, Charles E. Tuttle, was based in Tokyo, which I'm sure didn't help your chances for success in North America. The few critics here who bothered to review it pretty much panned it. They bitched about your "bad English" and said it wasn't literature. Even Japanese Americans shunned it. It seems they were embarrassed by it, which sounds crazy now, but in retrospect I suppose I understand why. In *No-No Boy* you wrote unflinchingly about the scarring experience of being a Japanese American on the West Coast during World War II, but that war had only ended twelve years earlier, and twelve years is no time at all. When your book came out, Japanese Americans were busy keeping their heads down, assimilating, and working on becoming the model minority of 1950s America. It's understandable. They had been rounded up and sent to prison camps in the desert. They had lost their homes and businesses and communities. They had suffered, and they wanted to move on. *No-No Boy* was radical, but it was ahead of its time. It was angry and raw. It touched nerves and opened wounds. It reminded them of a past they wanted to forget, and so they rejected it. Your book disappeared almost overnight.

Of course, you don't need me to tell you all this. You probably spent those years after publication thinking about what had happened, turning it over in your mind, trying to understand why your book had failed to find readers. To some extent, it must have broken your heart, and I'm guessing this is so because you never wrote another.

But what you don't know is this: twelve years after its initial publication, a guy named Jeff Chan found a copy of your book in a Japantown bookstore in San Francisco, and he started passing it around to his Chinese American and Japanese American literary buddies, and little by little, they grew passionate about it. They formed a group called CARP, the Combined Asian-American Resources Project, and finally, in 1976, they reissued your book. And this time, people paid attention.

Two decades had passed, and the world had changed. The civil rights movement had made huge gains. Americans were talking about racism and discrimination. Japanese Americans were starting to speak out against the internment and criticize the United States government for its unconstitutional policies during the war. There was even the beginning of a reparations movement for internees. By 1976, people were ready for your book, and they read it and loved it and were inspired by it. And this should have been a wonderful moment for you, seeing your book republished and appreciated, and your passion for writing vindicated at last, but sadly it was not as wonderful as it should have been because you were dead.

When you died in 1971 of a heart attack, at the age of forty-seven, you still thought your novel was a failure, and I'm truly sorry about that, and I'm writing this now to tell you that it wasn't. *No-No Boy* has the honor of being the first Japanese American novel, and among the first of what has become an entire literary canon of Asian American literature. You broke the ground for us, John Okada, and now, in 2014, we're celebrating you again. I just wish you were alive to enjoy this moment.

Your book and I are about the same age. I was born a year before *No-No Boy* was published, and I hope you'll forgive me for not reading it then, but I had only just turned one and wasn't reading yet, and the book disappeared from the bookshops pretty quickly. When your novel was reissued in 1976, I was twenty and quite a good reader, but I'm afraid I still didn't read it. This is harder to explain, but the fact is that I wasn't very interested in the Japanese American cultural movement at the time. I didn't think of myself as Japanese American, even though my mother was Japanese and my father was Anglo American. I saw myself as mixed race, "half," or "half-Japanese" instead, and I was growing up in New England, where there were relatively few Asians. The whole Japanese American cultural movement seemed like a west coast thing, heavily defined by the internment experience, and while my grandfather had been interned and my mother put under house arrest, all those World War II stories just seemed like ancient history to me. Now that I'm older, I have a different perspective on time, but when we're young, we think time starts with us.

When I finally did read your book, at the age of forty-something, I was stunned. I'd grown up in the shadow of World War II. I knew about the internment, and I had a general sense of the world you describe in the novel, but I'd never *felt* it before. Your novel made me feel it. The way you told Ichiro Yamada's story shocked me into realizing how profoundly shaped I'd been by the normative postwar assimilationist values that were so prevalent among people of Japanese heritage living in America, including my own family. This may sound unbelievable, but I'd never realized, until I read your novel, that a Japanese American could be angry. Mad with rage, or just plain crazy! I thought the Japanese American emotional palette comprised more neutral shades: resignation, obedience, forbearance, sadness, nostalgia, regret.

Reading *No-No Boy* reminded me that history—and in this case, a history I thought I knew—is so much more than just facts.

For example, I knew that after the Japanese navy attacked Pearl Harbor, more than 110,000 persons of Japanese ancestry were rounded up and incarcerated for up to four years, without trial or charge, in remote desert concentration camps. Over 60 percent of them were American citizens like Ichiro—Nisei, born in America of Japanese parents—but that didn't matter. As Lieutenant General John L. DeWitt, head of the Western Defense Command, famously said, "A Jap's a Jap. It makes no difference if he's an American citizen or not." DeWitt was in charge of designating the areas from which people would be taken—Washington, Oregon, Idaho, Montana, California, Nevada, and Utah—and his sentiment determined the policy for the internment: Since we can't tell them apart, imprison them all.

I knew that the War Department required Nisei males like Ichiro to fill out a questionnaire and answer two "loyalty" questions:

No. 27   Are you willing to serve in the armed forces of the United
         States on combat duty, wherever ordered?
No. 28   Will you swear unqualified allegiance to the United States
         of America and faithfully defend the United States from
         any or all attack by foreign or domestic forces, and for-
         swear any form of allegiance or obedience to the Japa-
         nese emperor, or any other foreign government, power,
         or organization?

But I didn't know that while many of the young men answered yes-yes to these two questions, some, like Ichiro, did not. I'd never thought about it until I read your book, but of course they had their reasons, which were various and complex. Some had family in Japan and did not want to have to kill a brother or a cousin in combat. Others were tripped up by semantics: they were Americans, so how could they forswear an allegiance to a foreign emperor they'd never pledged to begin with? And still others didn't understand why they should give their lives for a country that had branded them "enemy aliens," stripped them of all rights of citizenship, herded up their families, corralled them like cattle, and forced them to submit to the draft.

And I didn't know that those who refused, the boys who answered no-no, were found guilty of draft evasion, arrested, and taken first to jail and then to a maximum security segregated detention facility for the final years of the war.

When the war ended and the camps closed, many of the displaced internees returned to the West Coast to try to rebuild their lives. The no-no boys, too, were released from prison, but when they tried to go home, their reception was mixed. Reviled and shunned, or sometimes lauded, they became the target of the Japanese American community's agonizing ambivalence about the war.

This is the gritty, postwar world of rifts and schisms that you paint so brilliantly. It's Japantown noir, a demimonde of broken dreams, fallen heroes and brawling drunks at the Club Oriental, threaded together by the urgent jazz riff of Ichiro's perseverations. Obsessive, tormented, his voice is a threnody of guilt, rage, and blame, as he tries to negotiate his reentry into a shattered world. Some of his friends, and even his younger brother, despise him for the decision he made. Others, who fought to prove themselves loyal Americans, are able to embrace his confusion. And still others, like his mother, will never forgive him for his doubt. Unswervingly devoted to the emperor, Mrs. Yamada lives inside the delusion that Japan has won the war, and she is waiting for the day when the Japanese ships will come for her and return her to her homeland.

I didn't know how fractured the Japanese American communities were, how riven with divided allegiances. I didn't understand the internment's legacy of anger, self-hatred, and shame. I'd never thought to imagine what fanatical patriotism might *feel* like, until I read your descriptions of Ichiro's mad and twisted mother. And I never knew that any Japanese American had ever said no. This was new to me. I didn't realize that no was even an option.

Because, in some deep, unquestioned, and unconscious way, I had bought the propaganda, too. I had swallowed the stereotypes. I thought all "Japs" were alike, docilely compliant to authority, suffering the indignities of the internment until our uncomplaining stoicism and industrious forbearance would pay off. And it did pay off, further entrenching the myth of the model minority. This was the model I grew up with, the myth that had shaped me. In 1966, ten years after I was born and your book came out, an article entitled "Success Story: Japanese American Style" was published in the *New York Times Magazine*. I wonder if you read it. The author, William Petersen, a sociologist at the University of California, Berkeley, wrote,

> Barely more than 20 years after the end of the wartime camps, this is a minority that has risen above even prejudiced criticism. By any criterion of good citizenship that we choose, the Japanese Americans are better than any other group in our society, including native-born whites. They have established this remarkable record, moreover, by their own almost totally unaided effort. Every attempt to hamper their progress resulted only in enhancing their determination to succeed. Even in a country whose patron saint is the Horatio Alger hero, there is no parallel to this success story.

Oh, yes! How proud we were, even those of us too young to understand. The emerging stereotype affirmed all of our cultural values:

the Japanese virtues of stoicism and hard work, as well as those bootstrap virtues of the American meritocracy. It gently exonerated America's human rights abuses during the internment, even while it was held up as an example to undermine the claims of the African American civil rights movement. Who would dare challenge American mythmaking like this?

Well, you would. Your book subverted this stereotype by complicating the issue. That took real courage, and now, almost sixty years later, we applaud you, but at the time, nobody wanted to read it.

You were not a no-no boy yourself. Quite to the contrary, you appear to have been a model member of the model minority, and although information about your life is scant, there are moments when I catch a glimpse of you, the writer, lurking behind the thin scrim of facts. You were born in 1923 in Seattle's Pioneer Square, in a hotel managed by your father. You went to elementary school and high school in Seattle, but in 1942, halfway through your second year at the University of Washington, you and your family were caught up in the evacuation dragnet and sent to the Puyallup Assembly Center, a makeshift detention camp built on the county fairgrounds, and from there shipped off to the War Relocation Center in Minidoka, Idaho. My grandfather was in a similar camp in Santa Fe, and I've seen pictures. They were prisons, surrounded by barbed wire and guard towers, manned by armed soldiers, but you must have settled in well, because you were one of the first to be allowed out to attend classes at a junior college in Lincoln, Nebraska. Then, when the draft was reinstated for Nisei, you didn't wait. You volunteered. You served in the South Pacific as a member of the Eighth Army Air Forces Radio Squadron Mobile, also known as the "Flying 8 Ball," stationed in Guam. As an interpreter, you volunteered to fly dangerous reconnaissance missions over Japanese-held territory, listening in on Japanese air-to-ground military transmissions and translating these into English. You even went to Japan after the surrender, as a member of the U.S. occupation forces.

You earned the rank of sergeant and were, in your own words, a "good Japanese-American."

After the war, too, you continued to be an exemplar of the model, at least by outward appearances. You returned to Seattle and finished college. You got a BA from the University of Washington and later an MA from Teachers College at Columbia University, where you met your wife, Dorothy. You married her and within the next two years had two children, a boy and a girl. Your first two degrees were in English, which indicates to me that you were already interested in writing fiction, but in classic Asian American overachiever style, you went back to the University of Washington and earned a practical second BA in library science. Then, in 1953 or 1954, you moved to Detroit and got a job, first as a librarian and later as a technical writer for Chrysler Missile Operations, and this is where you started writing *No-No Boy*.

The move to Detroit was interesting. Your brother, Frank Okada, said in an interview once that you loved living in Seattle.[1] You loved the town and you loved your friends. You used to fish with them and go on picnics, and although you enjoyed all this, you knew that if you stayed there, you'd never write your novel, and so you moved to Detroit in order to isolate yourself from your friends and community. Frank, who became quite a well-known painter himself, said he found your decision inspiring. He said it taught him that if you're going to do something, and by this I think he meant something creative, you have to be able to isolate yourself and "see the situation objectively."

Frank's story gave me a small window onto who you were as a writer. I've had to isolate myself in order to write, too, and I wonder if this isn't particularly true for Japanese American writers, growing up in a culture that values conformity to the group

1 "Oral History Interview with Frank S. Okada, 1990 Aug. 16–17." Interview by Barbara Johns. Archives of American Art. http://aaa.si.edu/collections/interviews/oral-history-interview-frank-s-okada-11693.

norm. Fiction writers need the freedom to deviate, the space to speculate and license to transgress, and these are hard to find in a tight community. But Frank also said that your family was very proud of you for writing and publishing your book, however controversial it proved to be. He said you were "a hell of a role model" for him, and he was grateful to you for that.

After *No-No Boy* was published in 1957, you moved again, this time to Los Angeles, where you took another job as a technical writer for the Hughes Aircraft Company, which, I was interested to learn, was the aerospace and defense contractor founded by the iconic American industrialist Howard Hughes. In that same interview, Frank said that around the time of your move, you made a decision to take time off from writing to enjoy your family, and I can't help but wonder if this decision had anything to do with your disappointment over the reception of your book. Still, you must have recovered, because at the time of your death you were researching and possibly writing another novel.

There's some discrepancy in the accounts of what became of this unfinished novel. Your champions tell one story. Lawson Fusao Inada and Frank Chin, two writers from CARP who wrote the introduction and the afterword to the 1976 reissue of *No-No Boy*, went to interview your widow, Dorothy, in Los Angeles. According to their accounts, she told them that you'd almost finished the second novel, and that she had offered the manuscript, along with all your papers, to the Japanese American Research Project at UCLA after your death. In his Afterword, Frank Chin writes that they refused to look at the papers and encouraged her to destroy them. Whether or not that is true, it does seem clear that Dorothy thought nobody was interested, and she needed to move and didn't know what to do with them, and so she burned the lot. "I wanted to kick her ass around the block," Frank Chin wrote. "I wanted to burn UCLA down."

Your brother tells a slightly different story and a more measured one. He'd heard that UCLA was accepting material only from Issei, first-generation immigrants from Japan, written in

Japanese, and so your papers fell outside their curatorial mandate. He also insisted that you hadn't started writing the new novel yet, although you'd started researching it.

Does it matter? It's easy to vilify large educational institutions, or wives, and your brother admits that "Frank [Chin] can be a little dramatic." What's clear is that there is no surviving manuscript, and that's a shame, for so many reasons.

You died just on the cusp what we are now calling the Information Age. There's an emerging branch of scholarship, which I find particularly interesting, and which I think you would have found interesting, too. You were a trained librarian, after all. The field is called agnotology. Agnotology is the study of ignorance, how it is produced and maintained, what is lost and forgotten, and most importantly, why. What drops—or is dropped—from the historical record? What has gone missing, and whose agenda do those gaps and holes serve? You could say that agnotology is the study of what isn't.

Your novel, *No-No Boy*, almost wasn't. It wouldn't have been if you, a "good Japanese American," hadn't thought to ask the kinds of questions that novelists and agnotologists ask: What would it have felt like to say no? What would it have felt like to remain loyal to a different set of ideals and values? What would it have felt like to buck the tide? To be vilified? To disappear?

If you hadn't found the courage to isolate yourself and to resist the pressures of the Japanese American community to conform and adapt, you might never have written *No-No Boy*. And if Jeff Chan and Frank Chin and Lawson Inada hadn't rediscovered and reissued it in the 1970s, it might have disappeared completely.

In 1956, around the time of the original publication of *No-No Boy*, you wrote a letter to your publisher, Charles Tuttle, in which you describe your hopes for the second novel:

> I am now at work on a second [novel] which will have for its
> protagonist an immigrant Issei rather than a Nisei. When
> completed, I hope that it will to some degree faithfully describe

the experiences of the immigrant Japanese in the United States. This is a story which has never been told in fiction and only in fiction can the hopes and fears and joys and sorrows of people be adequately recorded. I feel an urgency to write of the Japanese in the United States for the Issei are rapidly vanishing and I should regret if their chapter in American history should die with them.

Where did your sense of urgency go? Fifteen years passed between the time you wrote this letter and your death in 1971. Why did it take you so long to reengage with your writing? Why did you have to die so young? Of course, there are no answers to these questions. There's just a novel-shaped hole in the historical record, filled with untold stories of your parents' generation.

A lot has changed since you were alive. The world is a different place—or then again, perhaps it's not so different. When you talked about "the War," the phrase meant only one thing: World War II. Now when I use this same phrase, people look at me, blankly. *What war? Which?* There have been so many—Vietnam, Afghanistan, Iraq, just to name a few. The university students I teach in 2014 were five years old on September 11, 2001, when suicide bombers flew planes into the World Trade Center. At the time, the news media compared them to the Japanese kamikaze during World War II. They compared the tragedy to the Japanese sneak attack on Pearl Harbor, and Arab Americans suffered a racist backlash in its wake. Different, yes, but also not. My students, many of them, have never heard of the internment of Japanese Americans, and yet they have never known a time without a war.

In that letter to your publisher, the one you wrote in 1956, you said "only in fiction can the hopes and fears and joys and sorrows of people be adequately recorded." I love this, and I agree with it completely. It points to the truth that the historical record is more than just facts. The dense emotional textures of a time, the layered, nuanced feelings of an age, these are the vital bits of information that drop quickly away. Only fiction has the power to ask the questions that bring the past to life and to record it in all its vibrant confusion and complexity. You have done that, John Okada. By filling in these gaps in the past, you have helped complete the present. In this way, with this one book, you have served to rectify the world.

Sincerely yours,
Ruth Ozeki
Seattle, 30 April 2014

INTRODUCTION

WE WERE TALKING ABOUT THE BOOK. WE HAD *BEEN* TALKING about the book, it seemed, for a very long time, ever since Jeff Chan discovered it in some J-Town San Francisco bookstore in 1970. The book had been published in 1957 and gone practically unnoticed. We "discovered" it, then, and were passing it on.

Tonight, it would reach my hand, my life, and the story would continue. So we were talking about the book, in the long Oregon dusk, over a bucket of steamed clams Frank Chin and David Ishii brought down from Seattle. With the book. This was before Frank would take "The Chickencoop Chinaman" to New York to be the first Asian-American drama produced by the "legitimate" theater. This was before David would open his landmark Seattle bookstore. This was before I drove up to Seattle with my wife and children just to see the book in context.

The book, you see, had something to do with all of that.

Somehow, after each ensuing one of us would read it—those of us who eventually formed the Combined Asian-American Resources Project, CARP, committed to the living tradition of Asian-American thought and action—the unspoken commitment would grow between us: we were going to do something about the book.

We knew, we felt, we owed it to us, to John: the world had been deprived too long. A book this true and strong was our very substance. So we got as many copies as we could and spread the word, bringing the book to campuses and communities. Jeff, Frank, Shawn Wong, and myself, we featured an excerpt from the book in our collection of Asian-American writing, *Aiiieeeee!*, and dedicated it to John, along with Louis Chu, a story in himself. Many more stories, I'm sure, will happen.

I could tell about how we tried to locate John, his family; I could tell about letters to his publisher, Charles Tuttle; I could tell about the hows and whys of the book's almost total lack of reception. Suffice to say that, after we "found" it, the book gained an immediate and receptive audience and went quickly out of print.

But that was before this part of the story. Frank and I left San Francisco on a late spring afternoon heading for L.A. We stopped off for a moment at my parents' home in Fresno before dinner at Richard Wing's Imperial Dynasty in the storied China Alley of Hanford. Phillip Ahn, the actor, was there, and we said hello. Richard greeted us as though we were on a mission, which we were: we were going to meet Dorothy Okada.

A lot of important stories happened in the next few days. We taped an interview with George Takei, later to be the incredible lead in Frank's "The Year of the Dragon," the first Asian-American play on national television. We spoke to Franklin Odo's Asian-American Studies class at UCLA, with Gordon Hirabayashi, who made *his* story in Seattle for courageous opposition to "evacuation." Then we all had dinner at Harry Kitano's, where Harry told a great story about "passing" for Chinese so he could get out of the Camps to play dixieland trombone. More stories, more warmth, more feelings, sharing our collective experience.

Later on we gave a benefit reading for Amerasia Bookstore at the Senshin Buddhist Church. Frank read from "The Chickencoop Chinaman," Warren Furutani sang strong songs, and I read "Asian Brother, Asian Sister" with Dan and June Kuramoto on flute and koto. Altogether a beautiful evening.

Then it turned out that our car had been broken into.

We lost some tapes, the recorder, found Frank's briefcase in an alley, but by then it really didn't matter that much because we knew there was much more material to be gotten, and we had *met* Dorothy Okada.

Dorothy is a truly wonderful person. It hurt to have her tell us that "John would have liked you." It hurt to have her tell us that "you two are the first ones who ever came to see him about his work." It hurt to have her tell us that she recently burned his "other novel, about the Issei, which we both researched, and which was almost finished." It hurt to have her tell us that "the people I tried to contact about it never answered, so when I moved I burned it, because *I have him in my heart*." It hurt to have her tell us that all she had to show of his "other work" were a few technical brochures for business corporations, which is how he made his living. It hurt to have her tell us that "you really didn't miss meeting him by very long."

You could say that John was "ahead of his time," that he was born too early and died too young. That was back in the days when a man like him was an "Oriental," and you worked hard for your family, for what you believed in. That was back in the days of "humble beginnings," before "ethnic" literature, before "ethnic" programs on campuses, before "Asian-America," even. That was back in the days when a Jap was just a Jap.

You could say all that about John and be wrong. That doesn't fit his measure. You don't measure a man like that, not in those terms, not with all his power and stature. John Okada was a magnificent man, a huge man who lived a full life of love and action. Most certainly he had difficulties—he *was*, after all, a Jap in America, who lived through America, through the War—but what he brought through the beauty of his soul is a tribute to us all. John Okada was a man with a *vision*, and he saw it through.

So John was really there with us, all along. You could feel him in the presence of Dorothy, so very proud and warm. You could feel him in the way she spoke of their children—a daughter and son in college, both devoted to music. You can feel him as you read this book, the very *heart* of the man, throbbing, within you, making you stand up and move to others, filled with the passion and compassion of being.

Such is the man John was, and is. And of all his family we have been proud to meet, of all his friends, the one thing that stands out when they speak of him is *love*. Love, and the pride that goes with it—for him, and from him. Love. This is what you will feel, too, beneath the unanimity of brilliance: love. This is the gift and measure of the man: a legacy of love. This is what sustains us, gives us hope and vision, ennobles our lives.

And as proud as we are to make this book available again, as our fittingly initial publication, the privilege is really ours: take it, and give it, from John.

Whoever reads this book will be a bigger person for it. Whoever reads this book will never be the same. Whoever reads this book will see, and be, with greater strength and clarity. And in this way does the world begin to change.

For as with Carlos Bulosan's *America Is in the Heart,* as with Louis Chu's *Eat a Bowl of Tea,* and as with Toshio Mori's *Yokohama, California,* John Okada's *No-No Boy* is much more than a great and lasting work of art. It is a *living* force among us. And it is just one of the many beautiful and courageous stories of the continuing story of what we know as Asian-America.

Lawson Fusao Inada
La Grande, Oregon
July 29, 1976

PREFACE

DECEMBER THE SEVENTH OF THE YEAR 1941 WAS THE DAY
when the Japanese bombs fell on Pearl Harbor.

As of that moment, the Japanese in the United States became,
by virtue of their ineradicable brownness and the slant eyes
which, upon close inspection, will seldom appear slanty, animals
of a different breed. The moment the impact of the words solemnly being transmitted over the several million radios of the
nation struck home, everything Japanese and everyone Japanese
became despicable.

The college professor, finding it suddenly impossible to meet
squarely the gaze of his polite, serious, but now too Japanese-ish
star pupil, coughed on his pipe and assured the lad that things
were a mess. Conviction lacking, he failed at his attempt to be
worldly and assuring. He mumbled something about things turning out one way or the other sooner or later and sighed with relief
when the little fellow, who hardly ever smiled and, now, probably
never would, stood up and left the room.

In a tavern, a drunk, irrigating the sponge in his belly, let it
be known to the world that he never thought much about the
sneaky Japs and that this proved he was right. It did not matter
that he owed his Japanese landlord three-weeks' rent, nor that
that industrious Japanese had often picked him off the sidewalk
and deposited him on his bed. Someone set up a round of beer for

the boys in the place and, further fortified, he announced with patriotic tremor in his alcoholic tones that he would be first in line at the recruiting office the very next morning. That night the Japanese landlord picked him off the sidewalk and put him to bed.

Jackie was a whore and the news made her unhappy because she got two bucks a head and the Japanese boys were clean and considerate and hot and fast. Aside from her professional interest in them, she really liked them. She was sorry and, in her sorrow, she suffered a little with them.

A truck and a keen sense of horse-trading had provided a good living for Herman Fine. He bought from and sold primarily to Japanese hotel-keepers and grocers. No transaction was made without considerable haggling and clever maneuvering, for the Japanese could be and often were a shifty lot whose solemn promises frequently turned out to be groundwork for more extended and complex stratagems to cheat him out of his rightful profit. Herman Fine listened to the radio and cried without tears for the Japanese, who, in an instant of time that was not even a speck on the big calendar, had taken their place beside the Jew. The Jew was used to suffering. The writing for them was etched in caked and dried blood over countless generations upon countless generations. The Japanese did not know. They were proud, too proud, and they were ambitious, too ambitious. Bombs had fallen and, in less time than it takes a Japanese farmer's wife in California to run from the fields into the house and give birth to a child, the writing was scrawled for them. The Jap-Jew would look in the mirror this Sunday night and see a Jap-Jew.

The indignation, the hatred, the patriotism of the American people shifted into full-throated condemnation of the Japanese who blotted their land. The Japanese who were born Americans and remained Japanese because biology does not know the meaning of patriotism no longer worried about whether they were Japanese-Americans or American-Japanese. They were Japanese, just as were their Japanese mothers and Japanese fathers and Japanese brothers and sisters. The radio had said as much.

First, the real Japanese-Japanese were rounded up. These real Japanese-Japanese were Japanese nationals who had the misfortune to be diplomats and businessmen and visiting professors. They were put on a boat and sent back to Japan.

Then the alien Japanese, the ones who had been in America for two, three, or even four decades, were screened, and those found to be too actively Japanese were transported to the hinterlands and put in a camp.

The security screen was sifted once more and, this time, the lesser lights were similarly plucked and deposited. An old man, too old, too feeble, and too scared, was caught in the net. In his pocket was a little, black book. He had been a collector for the Japan-Help-the-Poor-and-Starving-and-Flooded-Out-and-Homeless-and-Crippled-and-What-Have-You Fund. "Yamada-san, 50 American cents; Okada-san, two American dollars; Watanabe-san, 24 American cents; Takizaki-san, skip this month because boy broke leg"; and so on down the page. Yamada-san, Okada-san, Watanabe-san, Takizaki-san, and so on down the page were whisked away from their homes while weeping families wept until the tears must surely have been wept dry, and then wept some more.

By now, the snowball was big enough to wipe out the rising sun. The big rising sun would take a little more time, but the little rising sun which was the Japanese in countless Japanese communities in the coastal states of Washington, Oregon, and California presented no problem. The whisking and transporting of Japanese and the construction of camps with barbed wire and ominous towers supporting fully armed soldiers in places like Idaho and Wyoming and Arizona, places which even Hollywood scorned for background, had become skills which demanded the utmost of America's great organizing ability.

And so, a few months after the seventh day of December of the year nineteen forty-one, the only Japanese left on the west coast of the United States was Matsusaburo Inabukuro who, while it has been forgotten whether he was Japanese-American or American-

Japanese, picked up an "I am Chinese"—not American or American-Chinese or Chinese-American but "I am Chinese"—button and got a job in a California shipyard.

Two years later a good Japanese-American who had volunteered for the army sat smoking in the belly of a B-24 on his way back to Guam from a reconnaissance flight to Japan. His job was to listen through his earphones, which were attached to a high-frequency set, and jot down air-ground messages spoken by Japanese-Japanese in Japanese planes and in Japanese radio shacks.

The lieutenant who operated the radar-detection equipment was a blond giant from Nebraska.

The lieutenant from Nebraska said: "Where you from?"

The Japanese-American who was an American soldier answered: "No place in particular."

"You got folks?"

"Yeah, I got folks."

"Where at?"

"Wyoming, out in the desert."

"Farmers, huh?"

"Not quite."

"What's that mean?"

"Well, it's this way . . ." And then the Japanese-American whose folks were still Japanese-Japanese, or else they would not be in a camp with barbed wire and watchtowers with soldiers holding rifles, told the blond giant from Nebraska about the removal of the Japanese from the Coast, which was called the evacuation, and about the concentration camps, which were called relocation centers.

The lieutenant listened and he didn't believe it. He said: "That's funny. Now, tell me again."

The Japanese-American soldier of the American army told it again and didn't change a word.

The lieutenant believed him this time. "Hell's bells," he exclaimed, "if they'd done that to me, I wouldn't be sitting in the belly of a broken-down B-24 going back to Guam from a reconnaissance mission to Japan."

"I got reasons," said the Japanese-American soldier soberly.

"They could kiss my ass," said the lieutenant from Nebraska.

"I got reasons," said the Japanese-American soldier soberly, and he was thinking about a lot of things but mostly about his friend who didn't volunteer for the army because his father had been picked up in the second screening and was in a different camp from the one he and his mother and two sisters were in. Later on, the army tried to draft his friend out of the relocation camp into the army and the friend had stood before the judge and said let my father out of that other camp and come back to my mother who is an old woman but misses him enough to want to sleep with him and I'll try on the uniform. The judge said he couldn't do that and the friend said he wouldn't be drafted and they sent him to the federal prison where he now was.

"What the hell are we fighting for?" said the lieutenant from Nebraska.

"I got reasons," said the Japanese-American soldier soberly and thought some more about his friend who was in another kind of uniform because they wouldn't let his father go to the same camp with his mother and sisters.

NO-NO BOY

1

TWO WEEKS AFTER HIS TWENTY-FIFTH BIRTHDAY, ICHIRO got off a bus at Second and Main in Seattle. He had been gone four years, two in camp and two in prison.

Walking down the street that autumn morning with a small, black suitcase, he felt like an intruder in a world to which he had no claim. It was just enough that he should feel this way, for, of his own free will, he had stood before the judge and said that he would not go in the army. At the time there was no other choice for him. That was when he was twenty-three, a man of twenty-three. Now, two years older, he was even more of a man.

Christ, he thought to himself, just a goddamn kid is all I was. Didn't know enough to wipe my own nose. What the hell have I done? What am I doing back here? Best thing I can do would be to kill some son of a bitch and head back to prison.

He walked toward the railroad depot where the tower with the clocks on all four sides was. It was a dirty looking tower of ancient brick. It was a dirty city. Dirtier, certainly, than it had a right to be after only four years.

Waiting for the light to change to green, he looked around at the people standing at the bus stop. A couple of men in suits, half a dozen women who failed to arouse him even after prolonged good behavior, and a young Japanese with a lunch bucket. Ichiro studied him, searching in his mind for the name that went with the round, pimply face and the short-cropped hair. The pimples were gone and the face had hardened, but the hair was still cropped. The fellow wore green, army-fatigue trousers and an Eisenhower jacket—Eto Minato. The name came to him at the same time as did the horrible significance of the army clothes. In panic, he started to step off the curb. It was too late. He had been seen.

"Itchy!" That was his nickname.

Trying to escape, Ichiro urged his legs frenziedly across the street.

"Hey, Itchy!" The caller's footsteps ran toward him.

An arm was placed across his back. Ichiro stopped and faced the other Japanese. He tried to smile, but could not. There was no way out now.

"I'm Eto. Remember?" Eto smiled and extended his palm. Reluctantly, Ichiro lifted his own hand and let the other shake it.

The round face with the round eyes peered at him through silver-rimmed spectacles. "What the hell! It's been a long time, but not that long. How've you been? What's doing?"

"Well . . . that is, I'm . . ."

"Last time must have been before Pearl Harbor. God, it's been quite a while, hasn't it? Three, no, closer to four years, I guess. Lotsa Japs coming back to the Coast. Lotsa Japs in Seattle. You'll see 'em around. Japs are funny that way. Gotta have their rice and saké and other Japs. Stupid, I say. The smart ones went to Chicago and New York and lotsa places back east, but there's still plenty coming back out this way." Eto drew cigarettes from his breast pocket and held out the package. "No? Well, I'll have one. Got the habit in the army. Just got out a short while back. Rough time, but I made it. Didn't get out in time to make the quarter, but I'm planning to go to school. How long you been around?"

Ichiro touched his toe to the suitcase. "Just got in. Haven't been home yet."

"When'd you get discharged?"

4

A car grinding its gears started down the street. He wished he were in it. "I . . . that is . . . I never was in."

Eto slapped him good-naturedly on the arm. "No need to look so sour. So you weren't in. So what? Been in camp all this time?"

"No." He made an effort to be free of Eto with his questions. He felt as if he were in a small room whose walls were slowly closing in on him. "It's been a long time, I know, but I'm really anxious to see the folks."

"What the hell. Let's have a drink. On me. I don't give a damn if I'm late to work. As for your folks, you'll see them soon enough. You drink, don't you?"

"Yeah, but not now."

"Ahh." Eto was disappointed. He shifted his lunch box from under one arm to the other.

"I've really got to be going."

The round face wasn't smiling any more. It was thoughtful. The eyes confronted Ichiro with indecision which changed slowly to enlightenment and then to suspicion. He remembered. He knew.

The friendliness was gone as he said: "No-no boy, huh?"

Ichiro wanted to say yes. He wanted to return the look of despising hatred and say simply yes, but it was too much to say. The walls had closed in and were crushing all the unspoken words back down into his stomach. He shook his head once, not wanting to evade the eyes but finding it impossible to meet them. Out of his big weakness the little ones were branching, and the eyes he didn't have the courage to face were ever present. If it would have helped to gouge out his own eyes, he would have done so long ago. The hate-churned eyes with the stamp of unrelenting condemnation were his cross and he had driven the nails with his own hands.

"Rotten bastard. Shit on you." Eto coughed up a mouthful of sputum and rolled his words around it: "Rotten, no-good bastard."

Surprisingly, Ichiro felt relieved. Eto's anger seemed to serve as a release to his own naked tensions. As he stooped to lift the suitcase a wet wad splattered over his hand and dripped onto the

5

black leather. The legs of his accuser were in front of him. God in a pair of green fatigues, U.S. Army style. They were the legs of the jury that had passed sentence upon him. Beseech me, they seemed to say, throw your arms about me and bury your head between my knees and seek pardon for your great sin.

"I'll piss on you next time," said Eto vehemently.

He turned as he lifted the suitcase off the ground and hurried away from the legs and the eyes from which no escape was possible.

Jackson Street started at the waterfront and stretched past the two train depots and up the hill all the way to the lake, where the houses were bigger and cleaner and had garages with late-model cars in them. For Ichiro, Jackson Street signified that section of the city immediately beyond the railroad tracks between Fifth and Twelfth Avenues. That was the section which used to be pretty much Japanese town. It was adjacent to Chinatown and most of the gambling and prostitution and drinking seemed to favor the area.

Like the dirty clock tower of the depot, the filth of Jackson Street had increased. Ichiro paused momentarily at an alley and peered down the passage formed by the walls of two sagging buildings. There had been a door there at one time, a back door to a movie house which only charged a nickel. A nickel was a lot of money when he had been seven or nine or eleven. He wanted to go into the alley to see if the door was still there.

Being on Jackson Street with its familiar store fronts and taverns and restaurants, which were somehow different because the war had left its mark on them, was like trying to find one's way out of a dream that seemed real most of the time but wasn't really real because it was still only a dream. The war had wrought violent changes upon the people, and the people, in turn, working hard and living hard and earning a lot of money and spending it on whatever was available, had distorted the profile of Jackson Street. The street had about it the air of a carnival without quite succeeding at becoming one. A shooting gallery stood where once had been a clothing store; fish and chips had replaced a jewelry shop; and a bunch of Negroes were horsing around raucously in front of a pool parlor. Everything looked older and dirtier and shabbier.

He walked past the pool parlor, picking his way gingerly among the Negroes, of whom there had been only a few at one time and of whom there seemed to be nothing but now. They were smoking and shouting and cussing and carousing and the sidewalk was slimy with their spittle.

"Jap!"

His pace quickened automatically, but curiosity or fear or indignation or whatever it was made him glance back at the white teeth framed in a leering dark brown which was almost black.

"Go back to Tokyo, boy." Persecution in the drawl of the persecuted.

The white teeth and brown-black leers picked up the cue and jigged to the rhythmical chanting of "Jap-boy, To-ki-yo; Jap-boy, To-ki-yo . . ."

Friggin' niggers, he uttered savagely to himself and, from the same place deep down inside where tolerance for the Negroes and the Jews and the Mexicans and the Chinese and the too short and too fat and too ugly abided because he was Japanese and knew what it was like better than did those who were white and average and middle class and good Democrats or liberal Republicans, the hate which was unrelenting and terrifying seethed up.

Then he was home. It was a hole in the wall with groceries crammed in orderly confusion on not enough shelving, into not enough space. He knew what it would be like even before he stepped in. His father had described the place to him in a letter, composed in simple Japanese characters because otherwise Ichiro could not have read it. The letter had been purposely repetitive and painstakingly detailed so that Ichiro should not have any difficulty finding the place. The grocery store was the same one the Ozakis had operated for many years. That's all his father had had to say. Come to the grocery store which was once the store of the

Ozakis. The Japanese characters, written simply so that he could read them, covered pages of directions as if he were a foreigner coming to the city for the first time.

Thinking about the letter made him so mad that he forgot about the Negroes. He opened the door just as he had a thousand times when they had lived farther down the block and he used to go to the Ozakis' for a loaf of bread or a jar of pickled scallions, and the bell tinkled just as he knew it would. All the grocery stores he ever knew had bells which tinkled when one opened the door and the familiar sound softened his inner turmoil.

"Ichiro?" The short, round man who came through the curtains at the back of the store uttered the name preciously as might an old woman. "Ya, Ichiro, you have come home. How good that you have come home!" The gently spoken Japanese which he had not heard for so long sounded strange. He would hear a great deal of it now that he was home, for his parents, like most of the old Japanese, spoke virtually no English. On the other hand, the children, like Ichiro, spoke almost no Japanese. Thus they communicated, the old speaking Japanese with an occasional badly mispronounced word or two of English; and the young, with the exception of a simple word or phrase of Japanese which came fairly effortlessly to the lips, resorting almost constantly to the tongue the parents avoided.

The father bounced silently over the wood flooring in slippered feet toward his son. Fondly, delicately, he placed a pudgy hand on Ichiro's elbow and looked up at his son who was Japanese but who had been big enough for football and tall enough for basketball in high school. He pushed the elbow and Ichiro led the way into the back, where there was a kitchen, a bathroom, and one bedroom. He looked around the bedroom and felt like puking. It was neat and clean and scrubbed. His mother would have seen to that. It was just the idea of everybody sleeping in the one room. He wondered if his folks still pounded flesh.

He backed out of the bedroom and slumped down on a stool. "Where's Ma?"

"Mama is gone to the bakery." The father kept his beaming eyes on his son who was big and tall. He shut off the flow of water and shifted the metal teapot to the stove.

"What for?"

"Bread," his father said in reply, "bread for the store."

"Don't they deliver?"

"Ya, they deliver." He ran a damp rag over the table, which was spotlessly clean.

"What the hell is she doing at the bakery then?"

"It is good business, Ichiro." He was at the cupboard, fussing with the tea cups and saucers and cookies. "The truck comes in the morning. We take enough for the morning business. For the afternoon, we get soft, fresh bread. Mama goes to the bakery."

Ichiro tried to think of a bakery nearby and couldn't. There was a big Wonder Bread bakery way up on Nineteenth, where a nickel used to buy a bagful of day-old stuff. That was thirteen and a half blocks, all uphill. He knew the distance by heart because he'd walked it twice every day to go to grade school, which was a half-block beyond the bakery or fourteen blocks from home.

"What bakery?"

The water on the stove began to boil and the old man flipped the lid on the pot and tossed in a pinch of leaves. "Wonder Bread."

"Is that the one up on Nineteenth?"

"Ya."

"How much do you make on bread?"

"Let's see," he said pouring the tea, "Oh, three, four cents. Depends."

"How many loaves does Ma get?"

"Ten or twelve. Depends."

Ten loaves at three or four cents' profit added up to thirty or forty cents. He compromised at thirty-five cents and asked the next question: "The bus, how much is it?"

"Oh, let's see." He sipped the tea noisily, sucking it through his teeth in well regulated gulps. "Let's see. Fifteen cents for one

9

time. Tokens are two for twenty-five cents. That is twelve and one-half cents."

Twenty-five cents for bus fare to get ten loaves of bread which turned a profit of thirty-five cents. It would take easily an hour to make the trip up and back. He didn't mean to shout, but he shouted: "Christ, Pa, what else do you give away?"

His father peered over the teacup with a look of innocent surprise.

It made him madder. "Figure it out. Just figure it out. Say you make thirty-five cents on ten loaves. You take a bus up and back and there's twenty-five cents shot. That leaves ten cents. On top of that, there's an hour wasted. What are you running a business for? Your health?"

Slup went the tea through his teeth, slup, slup, slup. "Mama walks." He sat there looking at his son like a benevolent Buddha.

Ichiro lifted the cup to his lips and let the liquid burn down his throat. His father had said "Mama walks" and that made things right with the world. The overwhelming simplicity of the explanation threatened to evoke silly giggles which, if permitted to escape, might lead to hysterics. He clenched his fists and subdued them.

At the opposite end of the table the father had slupped the last of his tea and was already taking the few steps to the sink to rinse out the cup.

"Goddammit, Pa, sit down!" He'd never realized how nervous a man his father was. The old man had constantly been doing something every minute since he had come. It didn't figure. Here he was, round and fat and cheerful-looking and, yet, he was going incessantly as though his trousers were crawling with ants.

"Ya, Ichiro, I forget you have just come home. We should talk." He resumed his seat at the table and busied his fingers with a box of matches.

Ichiro stepped out of the kitchen, spotted the cigarettes behind the cash register, and returned with a pack of Camels. Lighting a match, the old man held it between his fingers and waited until the son opened the package and put a cigarette in his mouth. By then the match was threatening to sear his fingers. He dropped it hastily and stole a sheepish glance at Ichiro, who reached for the box and struck his own match.

"Ichiro." There was a timorousness in the father's voice. Or was it apology?

"Yeah."

"Was it very hard?"

"No. It was fun." The sarcasm didn't take.

"You are sorry?" He was waddling over rocky ground on a pitch-black night and he didn't like it one bit.

"I'm okay, Pa. It's finished. Done and finished. No use talking about it."

"True," said the old man too heartily, "it is done and there is no use to talk." The bell tinkled and he leaped from the chair and fled out of the kitchen.

Using the butt of the first cigarette, Ichiro lit another. He heard his father's voice in the store.

"Mama. Ichiro. Ichiro is here."

The sharp, lifeless tone of his mother's words flipped through the silence and he knew that she hadn't changed.

"The bread must be put out."

In other homes mothers and fathers and sons and daughters rushed into hungry arms after week-end separations to find assurance in crushing embraces and loving kisses. The last time he saw his mother was over two years ago. He waited, seeing in the sounds of the rustling waxed paper the stiff, angular figure of the woman stacking the bread on the rack in neat, precise piles.

His father came back into the kitchen with a little less bounce and began to wash the cups. She came through the curtains a few minutes after, a small, flat-chested, shapeless woman who wore her hair pulled back into a tight bun. Hers was the awkward, skinny body of a thirteen-year-old which had dried and toughened through the many years following but which had developed

11

no further. He wondered how the two of them had ever gotten together long enough to have two sons.

"I am proud that you are back," she said. "I am proud to call you my son."

It was her way of saying that she had made him what he was and that the thing in him which made him say no to the judge and go to prison for two years was the growth of a seed planted by the mother tree and that she was the mother who had put this thing in her son and that everything that had been done and said was exactly as it should have been and that that was what made him her son because no other would have made her feel the pride that was in her breast.

He looked at his mother and swallowed with difficulty the bitterness that threatened to destroy the last fragment of under-standing for the woman who was his mother and still a stranger because, in truth, he could not know what it was to be a Japanese who breathed the air of America and yet had never lifted a foot from the land that was Japan.

"I've been talking with Pa," he said, not knowing or caring why except that he had to say something.

"After a while, you and I, we will talk also." She walked through the kitchen into the bedroom and hung her coat and hat in a wardrobe of cardboard which had come from Sears Roebuck. Then she came back through the kitchen and out into the store.

The father gave him what was meant to be a knowing look and uttered softly: "Doesn't like my not being in the store when she is out. I tell her the bell tinkles, but she does not understand."

"Hell's bells," he said in disgust. Pushing himself out of the chair violently, he strode into the bedroom and flung himself out on one of the double beds.

Lying there, he wished the roof would fall in and bury forever the anguish which permeated his every pore. He lay there fighting with his burden, lighting one cigarette after another and drop-ping ashes and butts purposely on the floor. It was the way he felt, stripped of dignity, respect, purpose, honor, all the things which added up to schooling and marriage and family and work and happiness.

It was to please her, he said to himself with teeth clamped together to imprison the wild, meaningless, despairing cry which was forever straining inside of him. Pa's okay, but he's a nobody. He's a goddamned, fat, grinning, spineless nobody. Ma is the rock that's always hammering, pounding, pounding, pounding in her unobtrusive, determined, fanatical way until there's nothing left to call one's self. She's cursed me with her meanness and the hatred that you cannot see but which is always hating. It was she who opened my mouth and made my lips move to sound the words which got me two years in prison and an emptiness that is more empty and frightening than the caverns of hell. She's killed me with her meanness and hatred and I hope she's happy because I'll never know the meaning of it again.

"Ichiro."

He propped himself up on an elbow and looked at her. She had hardly changed. Surely, there must have been a time when she could smile and, yet, he could not remember.

"Yeah?"

"Lunch is on the table."

As he pushed himself off the bed and walked past her to the kitchen, she took broom and dustpan and swept up the mess he had made.

There were eggs, fried with soy sauce, sliced cold meat, boiled cabbage, and tea and rice. They all ate in silence, not even disturbed once by the tinkling of the bell. The father cleared the table after they had finished and dutifully retired to watch the store. Ichiro had smoked three cigarettes before his mother ended the silence.

"You must go back to school."

He had almost forgotten that there had been a time before the war when he had actually gone to college for two years and studiously applied himself to courses in the engineering school. The

13

statement staggered him. Was that all there was to it? Did she mean to sit there and imply that the four intervening years were to be casually forgotten and life resumed as if there had been no four years and no war and no Eto who had spit on him because of the thing he had done?

"I don't feel much like going to school."

"What will you do?"

"I don't know."

"With an education, your opportunities in Japan will be unlimited. You must go and complete your studies."

"Ma," he said slowly, "Ma, I'm not going to Japan. Nobody's going to Japan. The war is over. Japan lost. Do you hear? Japan lost."

"You believe that?" It was said in the tone of an adult asking a child who is no longer a child if he really believed that Santa Claus was real.

"Yes, I believe it. I know it. America is still here. Do you see the great Japanese army walking down the streets? No. There is no Japanese army any more."

"The boat is coming and we must be ready."

"The boat?"

"Yes." She reached into her pocket and drew out a worn envelope.

The letter had been mailed from Sao Paulo, Brazil, and was addressed to a name that he did not recognize. Inside the envelope was a single sheet of flimsy, rice paper covered with intricate flourishes of Japanese characters.

"What does it say?"

She did not bother to pick up the letter. "To you who are a loyal and honorable Japanese, it is with humble and heartfelt joy that I relay this momentous message. Word has been brought to us that the victorious Japanese government is presently making preparations to send ships which will return to Japan those residents in foreign countries who have steadfastly maintained their faith and loyalty to our Emperor. The Japanese government regrets

14

that the responsibilities arising from the victory compels them to delay in the sending of the vessels. To be among the few who remain to receive this honor is a gratifying tribute. Heed not the propaganda of the radio and newspapers which endeavor to convince the people with lies about the allied victory. Especially, heed not the lies of your traitorous countrymen who have turned their backs on the country of their birth and who will suffer for their treasonous acts. The day of glory is close at hand. The rewards will be beyond our greatest expectations. What we have done, we have done only as Japanese, but the government is grateful. Hold your heads high and make ready for the journey, for the ships are coming."

"Who wrote that?" he asked incredulously. It was like a weird nightmare. It was like finding out that an incurable strain of insanity pervaded the family, an intangible horror that swayed and taunted beyond the grasp of reaching fingers.

"A friend in South America. We are not alone."

"We *are* alone," he said vehemently. "This whole thing is crazy. You're crazy. I'm crazy. All right, so we made a mistake. Let's admit it."

"There has been no mistake. The letter confirms."

"Sure it does. It proves there's crazy people in the world besides us. If Japan won the war, what the hell are we doing here? What are you doing running a grocery store? It doesn't figure. It doesn't figure because we're all wrong. The minute we admit that, everything is fine. I've had a lot of time to think about all this. I've thought about it, and every time the answer comes out the same. You can't tell me different any more."

She sighed ever so slightly. "We will talk later when you are feeling better." Carefully folding the letter and placing it back in the envelope, she returned it to her pocket. "It is not I who tell you that the ship is coming. It is in the letter. If you have come to doubt your mother—and I'm sure you do not mean it even if you speak in weakness—it is to be regretted. Rest a few days. Think more deeply and your doubts will disappear. You are my son, Ichiro."

No, he said to himself as he watched her part the curtains and start into the store. There was a time when I was your son. There was a time that I no longer remember when you used to smile a mother's smile and tell me stories about gallant and fierce warriors who protected their lords with blades of shining steel and about the old woman who found a peach in the stream and took it home and, when her husband split it in half, a husky little boy tumbled out to fill their hearts with boundless joy. I was that boy in the peach and you were the old woman and we were Japanese with Japanese feelings and Japanese pride and Japanese thoughts because it was all right then to be Japanese and feel and think all the things that Japanese do even if we lived in America. Then there came a time when I was only half Japanese because one is not born in America and raised in America and taught in America and one does not speak and swear and drink and smoke and play and fight and see and hear in America among Americans in American streets and houses without becoming American and loving it. But I did not love enough, for you were still half my mother and I was thereby still half Japanese and when the war came and they told me to fight for America, I was not strong enough to fight you and I was not strong enough to fight the bitterness which made the half of me which was you bigger than the half of me which was America and really the whole of me that I could not see or feel. Now that I know the truth when it is too late and the half of me which was you is no longer there, I am only half of me and the half that remains is American by law because the government was wise and strong enough to know why it was that I could not fight for America and did not strip me of my birthright. But it is not enough to be American only in the eyes of the law and it is not enough to be only half an American and know that it is an empty half. I am not your son and I am not Japanese and I am not American. I can go someplace and tell people that I've got an inverted stomach and that I am an American, true and blue and Hail Columbia, but the army wouldn't have me because of the stomach. That's easy and I would do it,

16

only I've got to convince myself first and that I cannot do. I wish with all my heart that I were Japanese or that I were American. I am neither and I blame you and I blame myself and I blame the world which is made up of many countries which fight with each other and kill and hate and destroy but not enough, so that they must kill and hate and destroy again and again and again. It is so easy and simple that I cannot understand it at all. And the reason I do not understand it is because I do not understand you who were the half of me that is no more and because I do not understand what it was about that half that made me destroy the half of me which was American and the half which might have become the whole of me if I had said yes I will go and fight in your army because that is what I believe and want and cherish and love . . .

Defeatedly, he crushed the stub of a cigarette into an ash tray filled with many other stubs and reached for the package to get another. It was empty and he did not want to go into the store for more because he did not feel much like seeing either his father or mother. He went into the bedroom and tossed and groaned and half slept.

Hours later, someone shook him awake. It was not his mother and it was not his father. The face that looked down at him in the gloomy darkness was his brother's.

"Taro," he said softly, for he had hardly thought of him.

"Yeah, it's me," said his brother with unmistakable embarrassment. "I see you got out."

"How've you been?" He studied his brother, who was as tall as he but skinnier.

"Okay. It's time to eat." He started to leave.

"Taro, wait."

His brother stood framed in the light of the doorway and faced him.

"How've you been?" he repeated. Then he added quickly for fear of losing him: "No, I said that before and I don't mean it the

17

way it sounds. We've got things to talk about. Long time since we saw each other."

"Yeah, it's been a long time."

"How's school?"

"Okay."

"About through with high school?"

"Next June."

"What then? College?"

"No, army."

He wished he could see his face, the face of the brother who spoke to him as though they were strangers—because that's what they were.

"You could get in a year or two before the draft," he heard himself saying in an effort to destroy the wall that separated them. "I read where you can take an exam now and get a deferment if your showing is good enough. A fellow's got to have all the education he can get, Taro."

"I don't want a deferment. I want in."

"Ma know?"

"Who cares?"

"She won't like it."

"Doesn't matter."

"Why so strong about the army? Can't you wait? They'll come and get you soon enough."

"That isn't soon enough for me."

"What's your reason?"

He waited for an answer, knowing what it was and not wanting to hear it.

"Is it because of me? What I did?"

"I'm hungry," his brother said and turned into the kitchen.

His mother had already eaten and was watching the store. He sat opposite his brother, who wolfed down the food without looking back at him. It wasn't more than a few minutes before he rose, grabbed his jacket off a nail on the wall, and left the table. The bell tinkled and he was gone.

18

"Don't mind him," said the father apologetically. "Taro is young and restless. He's never home except to eat and sleep."

"When does he study?"

"He does not."

"Why don't you do something about it?"

"I tell him. Mama tells him. Makes no difference. It is the war that has made them that way. All the people say the same thing. The war and the camp life. Made them wild like cats and dogs. It is hard to understand."

"Sure," he said, but he told himself that he understood, that the reason why Taro was not a son and not a brother was because he was young and American and alien to his parents, who had lived in America for thirty-five years without becoming less Japanese and could speak only a few broken words of English and write it not at all, and because Taro hated that thing in his elder brother which had prevented him from thinking for himself. And in his hate for that thing, he hated his brother and also his parents because they had created the thing with their eyes and hands and minds which had seen and felt and thought as Japanese for thirty-five years in an America which they rejected as thoroughly as if they had never been a day away from Japan. That was the reason and it was difficult to believe, but it was true because he was the emptiness between the one and the other and could see flashes of the truth that was true for his parents and the truth that was true for his brother.

"Pa," he said.

"Ya, Ichiro." He was swirling a dishcloth in a pan of hot water and working up suds for the dishes.

"What made you and Ma come to America?"

"Everyone was coming to America."

"Did you have to come?"

"No. We came to make money."

"Is that all?"

"Ya, I think that was why we came."

"Why to make money?"

19

"There was a man in my village who went to America and made a lot of money and he came back and bought a big piece of land and he was very comfortable. We came so we could make money and go back and buy a piece of land and be comfortable too."

"Did you ever think about staying here and not going back?"

"No."

He looked at his father, who was old and bald and washing dishes in a kitchen that was behind a hole in the wall that was a grocery store. "How do you feel about it now?"

"About what?"

"Going back."

"We are going."

"When?"

"Oh, pretty soon."

"How soon?"

"Pretty soon."

There didn't seem to be much point in pursuing the questioning. He went out to the store and got a fresh pack of cigarettes. His mother was washing down the vegetable stand, which stood alongside the entrance. Her thin arms swabbed the green-painted wood with sweeping, vigorous strokes. There was a power in the wiry, brown arms, a hard, blind, unreckoning force which coursed through veins of tough bamboo. When she had done her work, she carried the pail of water to the curb outside and poured it on the street. Then she came back through the store and into the living quarters and emerged once more dressed in her coat and hat.

"Come, Ichiro," she said, "we must go and see Kumasaka-san and Ashida-san. They will wish to know that you are back."

The import of the suggested visits made him waver helplessly. He was too stunned to voice his protest. The Kumasakas and the Ashidas were people from the same village in Japan. The three families had been very close for as long as he could recall. Further, it was customary among the Japanese to pay ceremonious visits upon various occasions to families of close association. This was particularly true when a member of one of the families either departed on an extended absence or returned from an unusually long separation. Yes, he had been gone a long time, but it was such a different thing. It wasn't as if he had gone to war and returned safe and sound or had been matriculating at some school in another city and come home with a sheepskin *summa cum laude*. He scrabbled at the confusion in his mind for the logic of the crazy business and found no satisfaction.

"Papa," his mother shouted without actually shouting.

His father hastened out from the kitchen and Ichiro stumbled in blind fury after the woman who was only a rock of hate and fanatic stubbornness and was, therefore, neither woman nor mother.

They walked through the night and the city, a mother and son thrown together for a while longer because the family group is a stubborn one and does not easily disintegrate. The woman walked ahead and the son followed and no word passed between them. They walked six blocks, then six more, and still another six before they turned into a three-story frame building.

The Ashidas, parents and three daughters, occupied four rooms on the second floor.

"Mama," screamed the ten-year-old who answered the knock, "Mrs. Yamada."

A fat, cheerful-looking woman rushed toward them, then stopped, flushed and surprised. "Ichiro-san. You have come back."

He nodded his head and heard his mother say, with unmistakable exultation: "Today, Ashida-san. Just today he came home."

Urged by their hostess, they took seats in the sparsely furnished living room. Mrs. Ashida sat opposite them on a straight-backed kitchen chair and beamed.

"You have grown so much. It is good to be home, is it not, Ichiro-san?" She turned to the ten-year-old who gawked at him from behind her mother: "Tell Reiko to get tea and cookies."

"She's studying, Mama."

"You mustn't bother," said his mother.

"Go, now. I know she is only listening to the radio." The little girl fled out of the room.

"It is good to see you again, Ichiro-san. You will find many of your young friends already here. All the people who said they would never come back to Seattle are coming back. It is almost like it was before the war. Akira-san—you went to school with him I think—he is just back from Italy, and Watanabe-san's boy came back from Japan last month. It is so good that the war is over and everything is getting to be like it was before."

"You saw the pictures?" his mother asked.

"What pictures?"

"You have not been to the Watanabes'?"

"Oh, yes, the pictures of Japan." She snickered. "He is such a serious boy. He showed me all the pictures he had taken in Japan. He had many of Hiroshima and Nagasaki and I told him that he must be mistaken because Japan did not lose the war as he seems to believe and that he could not have been in Japan to take pictures because, if he were in Japan, he would not have been permitted to remain alive. He protested and yelled so that his mother had to tell him to be careful and then he tried to argue some more, but I asked him if he was ever in Japan before and could he prove that he was actually there and he said again to look at the pictures and I told him that what must really have happened was that the army only told him he was in Japan when he was someplace else, and that it was too bad he believed the propaganda. Then he got so mad his face went white and he said: 'How do you know you're you? Tell me how you know you're you!' If his mother had not made him leave the room, he might even have struck me. It is not enough that they must willingly take up arms against their uncles and cousins and even brothers and sisters, but they no longer have respect for the old ones. If I had a son and he had gone in the American army to fight Japan, I would have killed myself with shame."

"They know not what they do and it is not their fault. It is the fault of the parents. I've always said that Mr. Watanabe was a stupid man. Gambling and drinking the way he does, I am almost ashamed to call them friends." Ichiro's mother looked at him with a look which said I am a Japanese and you are my son and have conducted yourself as a Japanese and I know no shame such as other parents do because their sons were not really their sons or they would not have fought against their own people.

He wanted to get up and dash out into the night. The madness of his mother was in mutual company and he felt nothing but loathing for the gentle, kindly-looking Mrs. Ashida, who sat on a fifty-cent chair from Goodwill Industries while her husband worked the night shift at a hotel, grinning and bowing for dimes and quarters from rich Americans whom he detested, and couldn't afford to take his family on a bus ride to Tacoma but was waiting and praying and hoping for the ships from Japan.

Reiko brought in a tray holding little teacups and a bowl of thin, round cookies. She was around seventeen with little bumps on her chest which the sweater didn't improve and her lips heavily lipsticked a deep red. She said "Hi" to him and did not have to say look at me, I was a kid when you saw me last but now I'm a woman with a woman's desires and a woman's eye for men like you. She set the tray on the table and gave him a smile before she left.

His mother took the envelope from Sao Paulo out of her dress pocket and handed it to Mrs. Ashida.

"From South America."

The other woman snatched at the envelope and proceeded to read the contents instantly. Her face glowed with pride. She read it eagerly, her lips moving all the time and frequently murmuring audibly. "Such wonderful news," she sighed breathlessly as if the reading of the letter had been a deep emotional experience. "Mrs. Okamoto will be eager to see this. Her husband, who goes out of the house whenever I am there, is threatening to leave her unless she gives up her nonsense about Japan. Nonsense, he calls it. He is no better than a Chinaman. This will show him. I feel so sorry for her."

"It is hard when so many no longer believe," replied his mother, "but they are not Japanese like us. They only call themselves such.

23

It is the same with the Teradas. I no longer go to see them. The last time I was there Mr. Terada screamed at me and told me to get out. They just don't understand that Japan did not lose the war because Japan could not possibly lose. I try not to hate them but I have no course but to point them out to the authorities when the ships come."

"It's getting late, Ma." He stood up, sick in the stomach and wanting desperately to smash his way out of the dishonest, warped, and uncompromising world in which defeated people like his mother and the Ashidas walked their perilous tightropes and could not and would not look about them for having to keep their eyes fastened to the taut, thin support.

"Yes," his mother replied quickly, "forgive us for rushing, for you know that I enjoy nothing better than a visit with you, but we must drop in for a while on the Kumasakas."

"Of course. I wish you could stay longer, but I know that there will be plenty of opportunities again. You will come again, please, Ichiro-san?"

Mumbling thanks for the tea, he nodded evasively and hurried down the stairs. Outside, he lit a cigarette and paced restlessly until his mother came out.

"A fine woman," she said without stopping.

He followed, talking to the back of her head: "Ma, I don't want to see the Kumasakas tonight. I don't want to see anybody tonight. We'll go some other time."

"We won't stay long."

They walked a few blocks to a freshly painted frame house that was situated behind a neatly kept lawn.

"Nice house," he said.

"They bought it last month."

"Bought it?"

"Yes."

The Kumasakas had run a dry-cleaning shop before the war. Business was good and people spoke of their having money, but they lived in cramped quarters above the shop because, like most of the other Japanese, they planned some day to return to Japan and still felt like transients even after thirty or forty years in America and the quarters above the shop seemed adequate and sensible since the arrangement was merely temporary. That, he thought to himself, was the reason why the Japanese were still Japanese. They rushed to America with the single purpose of making a fortune which would enable them to return to their own country and live adequately. It did not matter when they discovered that fortunes were not for the mere seeking or that their sojourns were spanning decades instead of years and it did not matter that growing families and growing bills and misfortunes and illness and low wages and just plain hard luck were constant obstacles to the realization of their dreams. They continued to maintain their dreams by refusing to learn how to speak or write the language of America and by living only among their own kind and by zealously avoiding long-term commitments such as the purchase of a house. But now, the Kumasakas, it seemed, had bought this house, and he was impressed. It could only mean that the Kumasakas had exchanged hope for reality and, late as it was, were finally sinking roots into the land from which they had previously sought not nourishment but only gold.

Mrs. Kumasaka came to the door, a short, heavy woman who stood solidly on feet planted wide apart, like a man. She greeted them warmly but with a sadness that she would carry to the grave. When Ichiro had last seen her, her hair had been pitch black. Now it was completely white.

In the living room Mr. Kumasaka, a small man with a pleasant smile, was sunk deep in an upholstered chair, reading a Japanese newspaper. It was a comfortable room with rugs and soft furniture and lamps and end tables and pictures on recently papered walls.

"Ah, Ichiro, it is nice to see you looking well." Mr. Kumasaka struggled out of the chair and extended a friendly hand. "Please, sit down."

"You've got a nice place," he said, meaning it.

"Thank you," the little man said. "Mama and I, we finally decided that America is not so bad. We like it here."

Ichiro sat down on the sofa next to his mother and felt strange in this home which he envied because it was like millions of other homes in America and could never be his own.

Mrs. Kumasaka sat next to her husband on a large, round hassock and looked at Ichiro with lonely eyes, which made him uncomfortable.

"Ichiro came home this morning." It was his mother, and the sound of her voice, deliberately loud and almost arrogant, puzzled him. "He has suffered, but I make no apologies for him or for myself. If he had given his life for Japan, I could not be prouder."

"Ma," he said, wanting to object but not knowing why except that her comments seemed out of place.

Ignoring him, she continued, not looking at the man but at his wife, who now sat with head bowed, her eyes emptily regarding the floral pattern of the carpet. "A mother's lot is not an easy one. To sleep with a man and bear a son is nothing. To raise the child into a man one can be proud of is not play. Some of us succeed. Some, of course, must fail. It is too bad, but that is the way of life."

"Yes, yes, Yamada-san," said the man impatiently. Then, smiling, he turned to Ichiro: "I suppose you'll be going back to the university?"

"I'll have to think about it," he replied, wishing that his father was like this man who made him want to pour out the turbulence in his soul.

"He will go when the new term begins. I have impressed upon him the importance of a good education. With a college education, one can go far in Japan." His mother smiled knowingly.

"Ah," said the man as if he had not heard her speak, "Bobbie wanted to go to the university and study medicine. He would have made a fine doctor. Always studying and reading, is that not so, Ichiro?"

He nodded, remembering the quiet son of the Kumasakas, who never played football with the rest of the kids on the street or appeared at dances, but could talk for hours on end about chemistry and zoology and physics and other courses which he hungered after in high school.

"Sure, Bob always was pretty studious." He knew, somehow, that it was not the right thing to say, but he added: "Where is Bob?"

His mother did not move. Mrs. Kumasaka uttered a despairing cry and bit her trembling lips.

The little man, his face a drawn mask of pity and sorrow, stammered: "Ichiro, you—no one has told you?"

"No. What? No one's told me anything."

"Your mother did not write you?"

"No. Write about what?" He knew what the answer was. It was in the whiteness of the hair of the sad woman who was the mother of the boy named Bob and it was in the engaging pleasantness of the father which was not really pleasantness but a deep understanding which had emerged from resignation to a loss which only a parent knows and suffers. And then he saw the picture on the mantel, a snapshot, enlarged many times over, of a grinning youth in uniform who had not thought to remember his parents with a formal portrait because he was not going to die and there would be worlds of time for pictures and books and other obligations of the living later on.

Mr. Kumasaka startled him by shouting toward the rear of the house: "Jun! Please come."

There was the sound of a door opening and presently there appeared a youth in khaki shirt and wool trousers, who was a stranger to Ichiro.

"I hope I haven't disturbed anything, Jun," said Mr. Kumasaka.

"No, it's all right. Just writing a letter."

"This is Mrs. Yamada and her son Ichiro. They are old family friends."

Jun nodded to his mother and reached over to shake Ichiro's hand.

The little man waited until Jun had seated himself on the end of the sofa. "Jun is from Los Angeles. He's on his way home from the army and was good enough to stop by and visit us for a few days. He and Bobbie were together. Buddies—is that what you say?"

"That's right," said Jun.

"Now, Jun."

"Yes?"

The little man looked at Ichiro and then at his mother, who stared stonily at no one in particular.

"Jun, as a favor to me, although I know it is not easy for you to speak of it, I want you to tell us about Bobbie."

Jun stood up quickly. "Gosh, I don't know." He looked with tender concern at Mrs. Kumasaka.

"It is all right, Jun. Please, just this once more."

"Well, okay." He sat down again, rubbing his hands thoughtfully over his knees. "The way it happened, Bobbie and I, we had just gotten back to the rest area. Everybody was feeling good because there was a lot of talk about the Germans' surrendering. All the fellows were cleaning their equipment. We'd been up in the lines for a long time and everything was pretty well messed up. When you're up there getting shot at, you don't worry much about how crummy your things get, but the minute you pull back, they got to have inspection. So, we were cleaning things up. Most of us were cleaning our rifles because that's something you learn to want to do no matter how anything else looks. Bobbie was sitting beside me and he was talking about how he was going to medical school and become a doctor—"

A sob wrenched itself free from the breast of the mother whose son was once again dying, and the snow-white head bobbed wretchedly.

"Go on, Jun," said the father.

Jun looked away from the mother and at the picture on the mantel. "Bobbie was like that. Me and the other guys, all we talked about was drinking and girls and stuff like that because it's important to talk about those things when you make it back from

28

the front on your own power, but Bobbie, all he thought about was going to school. I was nodding my head and saying yeah, yeah, and then there was this noise, kind of a pinging noise right close by. It scared me for a minute and I started to cuss and said, 'Gee, that was damn close,' and looked around at Bobbie. He was slumped over with his head between his knees. I reached out to hit him, thinking he was fooling around. Then, when I tapped him on the arm, he fell over and I saw the dark spot on the side of his head where the bullet had gone through. That was all. Ping, and he's dead. It doesn't figure, but it happened just the way I've said."

The mother was crying now, without shame and alone in her grief that knew no end. And in her bottomless grief that made no distinction as to what was wrong and what was right and who was Japanese and who was not, there was no awareness of the other mother with a living son who had come to say to her you are with shame and grief because you were not Japanese and thereby killed your son but mine is big and strong and full of life because I did not weaken and would not let my son destroy himself uselessly and treacherously.

Ichiro's mother rose and, without a word, for no words would ever pass between them again, went out of the house which was a part of America.

Mr. Kumasaka placed a hand on the rounded back of his wife, who was forever beyond consoling, and spoke gently to Ichiro: "You don't have to say anything. You are truly sorry and I am sorry for you."

"I didn't know," he said pleadingly.

"I want you to feel free to come and visit us whenever you wish. We can talk even if your mother's convictions are different."

"She's crazy. Mean and crazy. Goddamned Jap!" He felt the tears hot and stinging.

"Try to understand her."

Impulsively, he took the little man's hand in his own and held it briefly. Then he hurried out of the house which could never be his own.

His mother was not waiting for him. He saw her tiny figure strutting into the shadows away from the illumination of the street lights and did not attempt to catch her.

As he walked up one hill and down another, not caring where and only knowing that he did not want to go home, he was thinking about the Kumasakas and his mother and kids like Bob who died brave deaths fighting for something which was bigger than Japan or America or the selfish bond that strapped a son to his mother. Bob, and a lot of others with no more to lose or gain then he, had not found it necessary to think about whether or not to go in the army. When the time came, they knew what was right for them and they went.

What had happened to him and the others who faced the judge and said: You can't make me go in the army because I'm not an American or you wouldn't have plucked me and mine from a life that was good and real and meaningful and fenced me in the desert like they do the Jews in Germany and it is a puzzle why you haven't started to liquidate us though you might as well since everything else has been destroyed.

And some said: You, Mr. Judge, who supposedly represent justice, was it a just thing to ruin a hundred thousand lives and homes and farms and businesses and dreams and hopes because the hundred thousand were a hundred thousand Japanese and you couldn't have loyal Japanese when Japan is the country you're fighting and, if so, how about the Germans and Italians that must be just as questionable as the Japanese or we wouldn't be fighting Germany and Italy? Round them up. Take away their homes and cars and beer and spaghetti and throw them in a camp and what do you think they'll say when you try to draft them into your army of the country that is for life, liberty, and the pursuit of happiness? If you think we're the same kind of rotten Japanese that dropped the bombs on Pearl Harbor, and it's plain that you do or I wouldn't be here having to explain to you why it is that I won't go and protect sons-of-bitches like you, I say you're right and *banzai* three times and we'll sit the war out in a nice cell, thank you.

And then another one got up and faced the judge and said meekly: I can't go because my brother is in the Japanese army and if I go in your army and have to shoot at them because they're shooting at me, how do I know that maybe I won't kill my own brother? I'm a good American and I like it here but you can see that it wouldn't do for me to be shooting at my own brother; even if he went back to Japan when I was two years old and couldn't know him if I saw him, it's the feeling that counts, and what can a fellow do? Besides, my mom and dad said I shouldn't and they ought to know.

And after the fellow with the brother in the army of the wrong country sat down, a tall, skinny one sneered at the judge and said: I'm not going in the army because wool clothes give me one helluva bad time and them O.D. things you make the guys wear will drive me nuts and I'd end up shooting bastards like you which would be too good but then you'd only have to shoot me and I like living even if it's in striped trousers as long as they aren't wool. The judge, who looked Italian and had a German name, repeated the question as if the tall, skinny one hadn't said anything yet, and the tall, skinny one tried again only, this time, he was serious. He said: I got it all figured out. Economics, that's what. I hear this guy with the stars, the general of your army that cleaned the Japs off the coast, got a million bucks for the job. All this bull about us being security risks and saboteurs and Shinto freaks, that's for the birds and the dumbheads. The only way it figures is the money angle. How much did they give you, judge, or aren't your fingers long enough? Cut me in. Give me a cut and I'll go fight your war single-handed.

Please, judge, said the next one. I want to go in your army because this is my country and I've always lived here and I was all-city guard and one time I wrote an essay for composition about what it means to me to be an American and the teacher sent it into a contest and they gave me twenty-five dollars, which proves that I'm a good American. Maybe I look Japanese and my father and mother and brothers and sisters look Japanese, but we're better Americans than the regular ones because that's the way it has to be when one looks Japanese but is really a good American. We're not like the other Japanese who aren't good Americans like us. We're more like you and the other, regular Americans. All you have to do is give us back our home and grocery store and let my kid brother be all-city like me. Nobody has to know. We can be Chinese. We'll call ourselves Chin or Yang or something like that and it'll be the best thing you've ever done, sir. That's all, a little thing. Will you do that for one good, loyal American family? We'll forget the two years in camp because anybody can see it was all a mistake and you didn't really mean to do it and I'm all yours.

There were others with reasons just as flimsy and unreal and they had all gone to prison, where the months and years softened the unthinking bitterness and let them see the truth when it was too late. For the one who could not go because Japan was the country of his parents' birth, there were a thousand Bobs who had gone into the army with a singleness of purpose. In answer to the tall, skinny one who spouted economics, another thousand with even greater losses had answered the greetings. For each and every refusal based on sundry reasons, another thousand chose to fight for the right to continue to be Americans because homes and cars and money could be regained but only if they first regained their rights as citizens, and that was everything.

And then Ichiro thought to himself: My reason was all the reasons put together. I did not go because I was weak and could not do what I should have done. It was not my mother, whom I have never really known. It was me, myself. It is done and there can be no excuse. I remember Kenzo, whose mother was in the hospital and did not want him to go. The doctor told him that the shock might kill her. He went anyway, the very next day, because though he loved his mother he knew that she was wrong, and she did die. And I remember Harry, whose father had a million-dollar produce business, and the old man just boarded everything up because he said he'd rather let the trucks and buildings and warehouses rot than sell them for a quarter of what they were worth.

Harry didn't have to stop and think when his number came up. Then there was Mr. Yamaguchi, who was almost forty and had five girls. They would never have taken him, but he had to go and talk himself into a uniform. I remember a lot of people and a lot of things now as I walk confidently through the night over a small span of concrete which is part of the sidewalks which are part of the city which is part of the state and the country and the nation that is America. It is for this that I meant to fight, only the meaning got lost when I needed it most badly.

Then he was on Jackson Street and walking down the hill. Through the windows of the drugstore, the pool hall, the cafés and taverns, he saw groups of young Japanese wasting away the night as nights were meant to be wasted by young Americans with change in their pockets and a thirst for cokes and beer and pinball machines or fast cars and de luxe hamburgers and cards and dice and trim legs. He recognized a face, a smile, a gesture, or a sneer, but they were not for him, for he walked on the outside and familiar faces no longer meant friends. He walked quickly, guiltily avoiding a chance recognition of himself by someone who remembered him.

Minutes later he was pounding on the door of the darkened grocery store with home in the back. It was almost twelve o'clock and he was surprised to see his father weave toward the door fully dressed and fumble with the latch. He smelled the liquor as soon as he stepped inside. He had known that his father took an occasional drink, but he'd never seen him drunk and it disturbed him.

"Come in, come in," said the father thickly, moments after Ichiro was well inside. After several tries, his father flipped the latch back into place.

"I thought you'd be in bed, Pa."

The old man stumbled toward the kitchen. "Waiting for you, Ichiro. Your first night home. I want to put you to bed."

"Sure. Sure. I know how it is."

33

They sat down in the kitchen, the bottle between them. It was half empty. On the table was also a bundle of letters. By the cheap, flimsy quality of the envelopes, he knew that they were from Japan. One of the letters was spread out before his father as if he might have been interrupted while perusing it.

"Ichiro." His father grinned kindly at him.

"Yeah?"

"Drink. You have got to drink a little to be a man, you know."

"Sure, Pa." He poured the cheap blend into a water glass and took a big gulp. "God," he managed to say with the liquor burning a deep rut all the way down, "how can you drink this stuff?"

"Only the first one or two is bad. After that, it gets easier."

Ichiro regarded the bottle skeptically: "You drink all this?"

"Yes, tonight."

"That's quite a bit."

"Ya, but I finish."

"What are you celebrating?"

"Life."

"What?"

"Life. One celebrates Christmas and New Year's and Fourth of July, that is all right, but life I can celebrate any time. I celebrate life." Not bothering with a glass, he gurgled from the bottle.

"What's wrong, Pa?"

The old man waved his arm in a sweeping gesture.

"Nothing is wrong, Ichiro. I just celebrate you. You are home and is it wrong for me to be happy? Of course not. I am happy. I celebrate."

"Things pretty tough?"

"No. No. We don't get rich, but we make enough."

"What do you do with yourself?"

"Do?"

"Yeah. I remember you used to play Go with Mr. Kumasaka all the time. And Ma was always making me run after you to the Tandos. You were never home before the war. You still do those things?"

34

"Not so much."

"You go and visit them?"

"Once in a while."

He watched his father, who was fiddling with the letter and avoiding his gaze. "Many people think Japan won the war?"

"Not so many."

"What do you think?"

"No."

"Why?"

"I read, I hear, I see."

"Why don't you tell Ma?"

The old man looked up suddenly and Ichiro thought that he was going to burst out with laughter. Just as quickly, he became soberly serious. He held up the thick pile of letters. "Your mama is sick, Ichiro, and she has made you sick and I am sick because I cannot do anything for her and maybe it is I that is somehow responsible for her sickness in the first place. These letters are from my brothers and cousins and nephews and people I hardly knew in Japan thirty-five years ago, and they are from your mama's brother and two sisters and cousins and friends and uncles and people she does not remember at all. They all beg for help, for money and sugar and clothes and rice and tobacco and candy and anything at all. I read these letters and drink and cry and drink some more because my own people are suffering so much and there is nothing I can do."

"Why don't you send them things?"

"Your mama is sick, Ichiro. She says these letters are not from Japan, that they were not written by my brothers or her sisters or our uncles and nephews and nieces and cousins. She does not read them any more. Propaganda, she says. She won't let me send money or food or clothing because she says it's all a trick of the Americans and that they will take them. I can send without her knowing, but I do not. It is not for me to say that she is wrong even if I know so."

The father picked up the bottle and poured the liquor into his throat. His face screwed up and tears came to his eyes.

35

"I'm going to sleep, Pa." Ichiro stood up and looked for a long time at his drunken father who could not get drunk enough to forget.

"Ichiro."

"Yeah?"

His father mumbled to the table: "I am sorry that you went to prison for us."

"Sure. Forget it." He went to the bedroom, undressed in the dark, and climbed into bed wondering why his brother wasn't sleeping.

2

THERE IS A PERIOD BETWEEN EACH NIGHT AND DAY WHEN one dies for a few hours, neither dreaming nor thinking nor tossing nor hating nor loving, but dying for a little while because life progresses in just such a way. From that sublime depth, a stranger awakens to strain his eyes into focus on the walls of a strange room. Where am I? he asks himself. There is a fleeting sound of lonely panic as he juggles into order the heavy, sleep-laden pieces of his mind's puzzle. He is frightened because the bed is not his own. He is in momentary terror because the walls are clean and bare and because the sounds are not the sounds of home, and because the chill air of a hotel room fifteen stories above the street is not the same as the furry, stale warmth of a bedroom occupied by three and pierced by the life-giving fragrance of bacon and eggs sizzling in a pan down below. Then he remembers that he is away from home and smiles smugly as he tells himself that home is there waiting for him forever. He goes to the window, expands his chest, and stretches his arms to give vent to the magnitude of his joys upon being alive and happy and at home in a hotel room a hundred miles away, because home is as surely there as if he had never left it.

For Ichiro, there was no intervening span of death to still his great unrest through the darkness of night. It was nine o'clock when he woke up and the bitterness and profanity and hatred and fear did not have to be reawakened. He did not have to ask himself where he was or why because it did not matter. He was Ichiro who had said no to the judge and had thereby turned his back on the army and the country and the world and his own self. He thought only that he had felt no differently after spending his first night in prison. On that morning, when he woke up and saw the bars, it had not mattered at all that the bars were there. This morning, for the first time in two years, there were no bars, but the fact left him equally unimpressed. The prison which he had carved out of his own stupidity granted no paroles or pardons. It was a prison of forever.

"Ahhhhhh." Out of the filth of his anguished soul, the madness welled forth in a sick and crazy scream, loud enough to be heard in the next room.

"What is it, Ichiro, what is it?" His father hovered hesitantly in the doorway, peering into the blind-drawn gloom of the bedroom with startled eyes.

"Nothing." He felt like crying.

"You are not ill?"

"No."

"Not sick someplace for sure?"

"No, goddammit, I'm fine, Pa, fine."

"That is all right then. I thought something was wrong."

Poor, miserable old fool, he thought. How in the world could he understand? "I'm okay, Pa," he said kindly, "hungry, that's all, hungry and . . . and glad to be home."

"Ya, you get used to it. I cook right away." He smiled, relief flowing to his face, and he turned back hastily into the kitchen.

When he dressed and went through the kitchen to the bathroom, it was his father who stood beside the stove with frying pan in hand. When he came back out and sat at the table, his mother was there.

"Good morning, Ichiro. You slept well?" She sounded cheerful.

The eggs were done the way he liked them, sunny side up with the edges slightly browned. He felt grateful to his father for remembering. "Yeah, I slept pretty good," he answered as he broke the yolks.

"You are pleased to be at home and I am pleased that you are here."

"Sure. I feel like singing."

She sat rigidly with hands palms-down on her lap. "I did not tell you about Kumasaka-san's boy because it was not important."

"Yes, I know."

"Then you understand. It is well."

"No, I don't understand, but it doesn't matter."

"Oh?" Her mouth pressed into a tight little frown. "What is it you do not understand?"

"A lot of things, a whole lot of things."

"I will tell you. The Germans did not kill Kumasaka-san's boy. It was not he who went to war with a gun and it was not he who was shot by the Germans—"

"Of course not. You heard last night when the fellow told about it. It was an accident."

Patiently, she waited until he had spoken. "Germans, Americans, accident, those things are not important. It was not the boy but the mother who is also the son and it is she who is to blame and it is she who is dead because the son did not know."

"I just know that Bob is dead."

"No, the mother. It is she who is dead because she did not conduct herself as a Japanese and, no longer being Japanese, she is dead."

"And the father? What about Mr. Kumasaka?"

"Yes, dead also."

"And you, Ma? What about you and Pa?"

"We are Japanese as always."

"And me?"

"You are my son who is also Japanese."

"That makes everything all right, does it? That makes it all right that Bob is dead, that war was fought and hundreds of thousands killed and maimed, and that I was two years in prison and am still Japanese?"

"Yes."

"What happens when I'm no longer Japanese?"

"How so?"

"Like Bob, I mean. What happens if I sign up and get shot up like him?"

"Then I will be dead too."

"Dead like me?"

"Yes, I will be dead when you go into the army of the Americans. I will be dead when you *decide* to go into the army of the Americans. I will be dead when you begin to cease to be Japanese and entertain those ideas which will lead you to your decision which will make you go into the army of the Americans. I will be dead long before the bullet strikes you. But you will not go, for you are my son."

"You're crazy." He said it softly and deliberately, for he wanted her to know that he meant it with all the hatred in his soul.

Underneath the table her hands stiffened and jerked a few inches above her lap. Her face revealed only the same little tight frown that he had seen many times before. He waited, hoping that she would scream and rant and cry and denounce him, tearing asunder with fury the slender bond that held them together still, and set him free.

"Ah, Ichiro. I thought for a moment that you meant it."

"I do. I do."

She shrugged without actually moving. "That is what they all say. They who claim to be Japanese. I see it in their faces and I feel it on their lips. They say I am crazy, but they do not mean it. They say it because they are frightened and because they envy my strength, which is truly the strength of Japan. They say it with the weakness which destroyed them and their sons in a traitorous cause and they say it because they see my strength which was vast enough to be your strength and they did not have enough for themselves and so not enough for their sons."

"Balls!" He leaned across the table, letting the ugliness twist his lips and fill his voice with viciousness. "Balls! Balls!" he shrieked, his face advancing steadily upon hers.

A flicker of surprise, then fear. Yes, he saw it in her eyes in the fraction of an instant before her hands covered them. To the hands which had come forever between them he continued to shriek: "Not your strength, crazy woman, crazy mother of mine. Not your strength, but your madness which I have taken. Look at me!" He gripped her wrists and wrenched them away from her face. "I'm as crazy as you are. See in the mirror the madness of the mother which is the madness of the son. See. See!"

He was halfway to the bathroom door with her when the father rushed in to intervene. "Ichiro, Ichiro," he gasped excitedly as he extended a feeble hand.

With his fury at a sickening peak, Ichiro released the skinny wrists and arced his arm in a wild swing at his father. The mother collapsed limply to the floor and the father, propelled by the painful blow, collided against the wall.

For long moments he stood between them as the anger drained out of his body. He watched his mother rise and go out to the store, her face once again calm and guileless.

"Pa. I'm sorry, Pa." He put his arm around his father, wanting to hug him like a baby.

"Ya, Ichiro," the old man uttered shakily, "I am sorry too."

"Lost my head, Pa."

"Ya, ya. I know." He got a bottle from the cupboard and drank greedily. Then he sat down and offered the bottle to Ichiro.

The whisky was ugly tasting but it helped to relax him. He looked at his father, who seemed about to cry. "Ah, Pa, Pa. Forget it, won't you? I'm sorry. It just happened."

"Ya, sure." He smiled.

Ichiro felt better. "I've got to do something, Pa. I'll go nuts sitting around."

"Whatever you wish, Ichiro. It will take time. I know."

"Where's Freddie?"

"Freddie?"

"Yeah, Akimoto-san's boy. Where do they live?"

"Oh. Freddie. He was . . . yes. On Nineteenth. Small, yellow apartment house on the south side."

"I'll go see him. I can talk to him."

"Here, Ichiro," said his father, placing a twenty-dollar bill on the table.

"But that's a lot of money, Pa. I won't need all that."

"Take. Take. Go to a movie with Freddie. Eat someplace nice. Have a good time."

"Okay, Pa. Thanks." He pocketed the money and went through the store and on out without looking at his mother.

The small apartment house on the south side was not far from the bus stop. He saw it the minute he got off the bus. He climbed up the shaky stairs and consulted the mailboxes, which told him that the Akimotos occupied 2-B. Although there were only two units on each floor, six in all, he had to light a match in the dark hallway to see the faded 2-B on the door to the right of the stairway. He knocked softly and waited. When no one answered, he pounded more heavily.

It was the door to 2-A that opened. A plump, young Japanese woman peered into the hall and asked not unkindly: "What you want?"

"I'm looking for Fred Akimoto. He lives here, doesn't he?"

The woman opened the door wider, inspecting him in the added light. Her housecoat was baggy and dirty and unzipped down to her waist. A baby cried far inside. "Freddie's sleeping. He always sleeps late. You can pound on the door until he hears you, or," she grinned at him, "you're really welcome to come sit in my place and wait. Freddie's a good friend of mine."

"Thanks just the same, but I'm kinda anxious to see him."

"Tell Freddie I'll have breakfast for him. You come with him, okay?"

"I'll tell him." He waited until she had closed the door before he

42

started to pound on 2-B again.

Finally he heard noises deep inside the apartment. Footsteps padded reluctantly toward the door and the latch snapped.

"Who is it, for crissake, who is it?" Freddie's lean, sleepy face peered up at him through the crack.

"Hello, Shorty. It's Itchy."

"Itchy boy! They let you out! About time, I say, about time, I say, about time." The door swung wide open and revealed Freddie, small and wiry and tough. He wore a rumpled T-shirt and nothing else.

Ichiro took the other's hand and they shook warmly.

"What time is it?" asked Freddie as they went through the living room and past the kitchen into a bedroom in the back.

"Ten o'clock or thereabouts, I guess."

"No wonder I'm sleepy. How've you been, huh? Whatcha been doin'?"

"Just got home yesterday, Shorty. What have you been doing? Been out pretty near a month, haven't you?"

"Five weeks tomorrow." Freddie dressed hurriedly and sat on the bed beside his guest.

"How's it been?" He was disturbed by Freddie's nonchalance, his air of insuppressible gaiety.

"What's what been?"

"Things. You know what I mean. I've been worried."

Standing up, Freddie whisked through his pockets and found an empty cigarette pack. "Out. Nuts. Got some?"

Ichiro handed over cigarettes and matches and waited until Freddie had lighted up. "Tell me, Shorty. I've got to know."

"Crap! That's what I've been tellin' 'em. I got my life to live and they got theirs. They try to tell me somethin', I tell 'em shit. I'm doin' fine."

"No trouble?"

"Trouble? Why for? You and me, we picked the wrong side. So what? Doesn't mean we gotta stop livin'."

"What have you been doing?"

43

Freddie looked irritated. "You asked before."

"Well?"

"Livin'. I been havin' a good time. I didn't rot two years without wantin' to catch up."

"What happens after you catch up?"

"Maybe I won't."

Ichiro walked over to the window and lit a cigarette. The alley was littered with rubbish and he saw a cat pawing through a trash can. Sitting on the sill, he turned again to Freddie. He wanted to talk to Freddie, who used to be a regular worrier. He wanted to get under the new protective shell of brave abandon and seek out the answers which he knew were never really to be buried. "Freddie."

The small, muscular shoulders sagged a little. "Okay, Itchy. It's eatin' my guts out too. Is that whatcha wanta hear? Is that why you come to see me? You miserable son of a bitch. Better you shoulda got a Kraut bullet in your balls."

"That bad, is it?"

Freddie looked at Ichiro and in the face of the little man were haggard creases attesting to his lonely struggle. "You know what I done the first week?"

"Tell me."

"Just what I'm doin' now. I sat here on my fanny for a whole week, thinkin'. And I come to a conclusion."

"Yes?"

"I figgered my brains are in my fanny. Same place yours are."

Looking out the window, he saw the cat still searching in the trash can. He chuckled, disappointed because Freddie offered no hope, but at the same time relieved to be assured that he was not the only one floundering in heavy seas.

"The second week," continued Freddie, "I went next door to borrow some smokes. I stayed there all day until the old man came home."

"2-A?"

"Huh?"

"She told me to tell you she'll fix breakfast."

Freddie blushed. "Funny, ain't it? I'm the guy what used to be so damn particular about dames. She's nothin' but a fat pig. Can't get enough of it. Bet she gave you the once over."

"How long do you expect to get away with it? Same house, same floor. Don't push your luck."

"Aw, can it. I know what you're thinkin'. Me, I don't give a damn. In the meanwhile, I got somethin' to hang on to."

Ichiro pictured little Freddie in bed with the fat woman in 2-A and couldn't resist a smile.

"Sure, funny as hell, but I'll lay you two bits you'll wish you had an anchor like her before the week's out. She don't care who I am or what I done or where I been. All she wants is me, the way I am, with no questions."

"Sure, I see your point."

"No, you don't. Me, I been out and around. I seen Kaz one day. Used to shoot megs together. That's how long I known him. He's goin' to school on the G.I. He was glad as hell to see me. Stuck his hand out, just like that, kinda nervous like. He said somethin' about bein' in a hurry and took off. That's how it is. Either they're in a big, fat rush or they don't know you no more. Great life, huh?"

"I saw Eto."

"That jerk. What'd he do? Spit on you?"

"Yeah, how did you know?"

"We got troubles, but that crud's got more and ain't got sense enough to know it. Six months he was in the army. You know that? Six lousy months and he wangled himself a medical discharge. I been hearin' about him. He ever try that on me, I'll stick a knife in him."

"Maybe he's got a right to."

"Nobody's got a right to spit on you."

Ichiro reached into his pocket and tossed the cigarettes to Freddie, who immediately lit another. "Keep them," he said. "I'll get some on the way home."

"You ain't goin' yet, are you? You just come."

"I'll see you again, Shorty. I want to look around by myself.

You know how it is. Maybe catch a bus and ride all over town. I feel like it."

"Sure, sure. Buzz me on the phone. It's in the book. We guys get together every Friday for poker. We can sure use a sixth hand."

"What guys?"

"Guys like you and me. Who else?"

"Oh." He couldn't hide his disappointment, and Freddie noticed it with a frown.

"Give me a little time, Shorty. I'll straighten out."

As he made his way out, Freddie shouted at his back: "You been stewin' about it for two years. How much time you need? Wise up, Itchy, wise up."

3

ICHIRO STARTED WALKING DOWN JACKSON STREET, PLUNG-
ing down the hill with quick strides which bore him away from
Freddie, who could be of no help to anyone else because he too
was alone against the world which he had denounced. He had
gone to seek assurance and not having found it had not increased
his despair. Freddie was waging a shallow struggle with a to-hell-
with-the-rest-of-the-world attitude, and he wasn't being very
successful. One could not fight an enemy who looked upon him as
much as to say: "This is America, which is for Americans. You have
spent two years in prison to prove that you are Japanese—go to
Japan!" These unspoken words were not to be denied.

Was it possible that he, striding freely down the street of an
American city, the city of his birth and schooling and the cradle of
his hopes and dreams, had waved it all aside beyond recall? Was
it possible that he and Freddie and the other four of the poker
crowd and all the other American-born, American-educated Japanese who had renounced their American-ness in a frightening
moment of madness had done so irretrievably? Was there no
hope of redemption? Surely there must be. He was still a citizen.
He could still vote. He was free to travel and work and study and
marry and drink and gamble. People forgot and, in forgetting,
forgave. Time would ease the rupture which now separated him
from the young Japanese who were Americans because they had

fought for America and believed in it. And time would destroy the old Japanese who, living in America and being denied a place as citizens, nevertheless had become inextricably a part of the country which by its vastness and goodness and fairness and plenitude drew them into its fold, or else they would not have understood why it was that their sons, who looked as Japanese as they themselves, were not Japanese at all but Americans of the country America. In time, he thought, in time there will again be a place for me. I will buy a home and love my family and I will walk down the street holding my son's hand and people will stop and talk with us about the weather and the ball games and the elections. I will take my family to visit the family of Freddie, whom I have just left as I did because time has not yet done its work, and our families together will visit still another family whose father was two years in the army of America instead of two years in prison and it will not matter about the past, for time will have erased it from our memories and there will be only joy and sorrow and sickness, which is the way things should be.

And, as his heart mercifully stacked the blocks of hope into the pattern of an America which would someday hold an unquestioned place for him, his mind said no, it is not to be, and the castle tumbled and was swallowed up by the darkness of his soul, for time might cloud the memories of others but the trouble was inside of him and time would not soften that.

He was at Fourteenth Street where Jackson leveled off for a block before it resumed its gradual descent toward the bay. A bus turned into the stop and he hurled himself into it. There were plenty of seats and he was glad for that because he could not have suffered a crowd. Sitting next to the window and glimpsing the people and houses and automobiles, he gradually felt more at ease. As the bus sped down Jackson Street and made a turn at Fourth to go through downtown, Ichiro visualized the blocks ahead, picturing in his mind the buildings he remembered and reciting the names of the streets lying ahead, and he was pleased that he remembered so much unerringly.

Not until the bus had traversed the business district and pointed itself toward the northeast did he realize that he was on the same bus which he used to take every morning as a university student. There had been such a time and he vividly brought to mind, with a hunger that he would never lose, the weighty volumes which he had carried against his side so that the cloth of his pants became thin and frayed, and the sandwiches in a brown grocery bag and the slide rule with the leather case which hung from his belt like the sword of learning which it was, for he was going to become an engineer and it had not mattered that Japan would soon be at war with America. To be a student in America was a wonderful thing. To be a student in America studying engineering was a beautiful life. That, in itself, was worth defending from anyone and anything which dared to threaten it with change or extinction. Where was the slide rule, he asked himself, where was the shaft of exacting and thrilling discovery when I needed it most? If only I had pictured it and felt it in my hands, I might well have made the right decision, for the seeing and feeling of it would have pushed out the bitterness with the greenness of the grass on the campus and the hardness of the chairs in the airy classrooms with the blackboards stretched wall-to-wall behind the professor, and the books and the sandwiches and the bus rides coming and going. I would have gone into the army for that and I would have shot and killed, and shot and killed some more, because I was happy when I was a student with the finely calculated white sword at my side. But I did not remember or I could not remember because, when one is born in America and learning to love it more and more every day without thinking it, it is not an easy thing to discover suddenly that being American is a terribly incomplete thing if one's face is not white and one's parents are Japanese of the country Japan which attacked America. It is like being pulled asunder by a whirling tornado and one does not think of a slide rule though that may be the thing which will save one. No, one does not remember, and so I am not really to blame, but—and still the answer is there unchanged and unchallenged—

I did not remember and Freddie did not remember. But Bob did, and his friend, who talks of Bob's dying because the father wishes it, did, and so did a lot of others who had no more or no less reason than I.

The bus stopped at the corner with the fountain lunch where he had had many a hamburger or coke or black coffee in cups that were solid and heavy but did not hold much coffee. From there he walked naturally toward the campus and on up the wide, curving streets which soon branched off into countless narrow walks and drives among countless buildings of Gothic structure which had flying buttresses and pointed arches and piers but failed as authentic Gothic because everyone called it bastard Gothic with laughing familiarity as though the buildings were imperfect children of their own.

As if he had come to the university expressly for the purpose, Ichiro went directly to the offices of the engineering school. He found the name Baxter Brown on the wall directory and proceeded up the stairs to the assistant professor's office in a remote corner of the building which was reached finally by climbing a steep flight of stairs no more than twenty inches wide. By their very narrowness, the stairs seemed to avoid discovery by the mass of students and thereby afforded the occupant of the office the seclusion to which the learned are entitled.

Mr. Brown, grayer and heavier, sat behind a desk impressively covered with books and journals and papers. He gaped at Ichiro in that vague, suddenly alert way that one instinctively manages when startled unexpectedly from a dozing mood.

"Professor Brown?" He knew it was Professor Brown and he hadn't meant to make it a question.

The professor wrenched himself out of his chair and came forth energetically with extended arm. "Yes, yes, have a chair."

He sat and waited until the professor got behind the desk. "I guess you don't remember me. It's been some time since I was one of your students."

"Of course I remember. I knew the moment you stepped inside. Let me think now. No, no, don't tell me." The professor studied him thoughtfully. "You're Su . . . Suzu . . . no . . . Tsuji . . ."

"It's Yamada. Ichiro Yamada."

"That's it. Another minute and I would have had it. How are you, Mr. Yamada?"

"Fine, sir."

"Good. Lot of you fellows coming back. Everything all right?"

"Yes."

"Excellent. Tough about the evacuation. I really hated to see it happen. I suppose you're disturbed about it."

"No, sir. Not too much, that is."

"Of course you are. Who wouldn't be? Families uprooted, businesses smashed, educations interrupted. You've got a right to be sore."

"Water under the bridge now."

Professor Brown smiled and leaned back in his chair, relaxing. "Admire you for saying that. You fellows are as American as I am. And you've proved it. That outfit in Italy. Greatest there ever was. You were there too, I suppose?"

"No, I—"

"Over in the Pacific then? Interrogating prisoners I bet."

"Well, no. You see—"

"Sure. We can't all get in. I was in the first one myself. Did some consulting work for the navy this last one, but as a civilian. Still, every bit helps. Good to see you're thinking about coming back to the university."

Relieved to get off the touchy matter of war and who was in it and who wasn't and, if not, why and so on until it was too late to turn and run, Ichiro spoke quickly: "Yes, sir, I'm thinking seriously about it. It'll probably take me a little time to adjust myself . . ."

"Everybody worries about that. No point to it. It'll come back in no time at all. You just pick up where you left off and you won't have any trouble. I've talked plenty of fellows out of repeating courses because they think they've forgotten so much and, you know, they all come back and thank me for it. You fellows are older and you've matured and you know what you want. Makes a whale of a difference, I'll tell you. You haven't forgotten a thing— not a thing. It'll be there when you need it. Take my word for it."

"If you say so, but—"

"I say so. What were you in? Double E? Mechanical? Civil?"

"Civil."

"Makes no difference, really. Big opportunities in any branch. Too bad you're late for this quarter."

"Yes."

"Well," Professor Brown stood up and extended his hand, "nice seeing you again. Drop in any time."

Ichiro took the hand and while being ushered to the door muttered something about the professor's being good enough to spend time with him. Outside the office and alone again, he went down the narrow stairs and hurried outside.

That wasn't the way I wanted it to happen, he thought. What happened? He was nice enough. Shook hands, talked, smiled. Still, it was all wrong. It was like meeting someone you knew in a revolving door, you going one way and the friend going the other. You smiled, maybe shouted "Hi" and then you were outside and he was swallowed up by the building. It was seeing without meeting, talking without hearing, smiling without feeling. We didn't talk about the weather at all only that's what it felt like all the way through. Was it him or was it me? Him or me? He or I? Brown or Itchy? It wasn't Brown, of course. Brown was heavier, his hair grayer, but he was still Brown of the engineering school of the university of the world of students and slide rules and he was Brown then and now of that tiny office with the books and papers which was cut off from the rest of the world by the narrow stairs which one would not think to climb unless he was six and curious and thought that the stairs led to the roof and the big blue sky. No, Brown is still Brown. It is I who reduces conversation to the inconsequential because Brown is of that life which I have forfeited and, forfeiting it, have lost the right to see and hear and become excited over things which are of that wonderful past.

And then he crossed the street and did not look back at the buildings and students and curved lanes and grass which was the garden in the forsaken land. He felt empty and quietly sad and hungry.

He was halfway through his second hamburger, sitting on the stool at the counter, when Kenji placed a hand on his shoulder

Ichiro turned and looked into the smiling face, the pleasant, thoughtful, old face of Kenji, who was also twenty-five.

"Ichiro, is it not?" It was said softly, much more softly than he had known the shy, unassuming Kenji to speak.

"Yes, and you're Ken."

"Same one. At least, what's left of me," said Kenji, shifting the cane from his right to his left hand and shaking with Ichiro.

So Kenji had gone too. Or had he? He hoped that it was an automobile accident or something else that had brought on the injury which necessitated the cane and inspired the remark. "Join me, Ken. We can talk," he said, displaying his hamburger.

"I've already had lunch, but I'll go for another coffee." The stools were high, and he had to hook his cane to the counter and lift himself up with both arms.

"Going to school?"

"Yes, I guess you could call it that." The waitress came and he ordered coffee, black.

"What does that mean?"

"I'm enrolled. I go when I feel like it and most of the time I don't. How about you?"

"No. Just looking around."

"Feel the same?"

"How's that?"

"Things. You've probably been walking around the campus, trying to catch the same smells and sounds and the other things which you've been thinking about all the time the government kept you away from Seattle. Is it still the same? Can you start back to school tomorrow and pick up just where you left off?"

"No, it's not the same and I'm not going back."

"Why?"

"Well, because it's not the same. Or rather, I'm not the same."

Kenji sipped his coffee gingerly. "So what are your plans?"

"Haven't got any."

"That makes it nice."

"Does it?"

"Sure."

"Why?"

"I haven't any either."

They left the café and walked slowly to Kenji's car, for Kenji could not hurry on his bad leg, which was stiff and awkward and not like his own at all. Ichiro felt he should ask about it but could not bring himself to do so.

The new Oldsmobile was parked by a meter with the flag up to indicate that the time had expired. There was a ticket on the windshield, which Kenji removed with the rubber tip of his cane. The pink ticket floated down and under the car.

"Is that the way to do it?"

"My way."

"Get away with it?"

"Sometimes."

They got in and started down the street. Ichiro sniffed the new upholstery and touched a finger to the shiny, spotless dash. "New?"

"Yes."

"These things must cost a fortune these days."

"It's a present."

"Must be a nice guy," he said, remembering Kenji's father, who had known only poverty and struggle after his wife died leaving six children.

"He is. Uncle Sam."

Ichiro turned so that he could see Kenji better and he saw the stiff leg extended uselessly where the gas pedal should have been but wasn't because it and the brake pedal had been rearranged to accommodate the good left leg.

"I was in, Ichiro, mostly in hospitals. I got this for being a good patient."

"I see."

"It wasn't worth it." He started to slow down for a red light and, seeing it turn green, pressed on the accelerator. The car responded beautifully, the power in the engine throwing the vehicle forward with smooth effort.

Ichiro looked out at the houses, the big, roomy houses of brick and glass which belonged in magazines and were of that world which was no longer his to dream about. Kenji could still hope. A leg more or less wasn't important when compared with himself, Ichiro, who was strong and perfect but only an empty shell. He would have given both legs to change places with Kenji.

"Am I a hero?"

"What?"

"They gave me a medal, too. Ever hear of the Silver Star?" Kenji was talking to him and, yet, he was talking to himself. Ichiro felt drawn to the soft-spoken veteran who voluntarily spoke of things that the battle-wise and battle-scarred were thought not to discuss because they had been through hell and hell was not a thing which a man kept alive in himself. If Eto had been a brave man, if Eto had been wounded and given a medal, he would have dramatized his bravery to any and all who could be cornered into listening, but he was not a brave man and so he would never have gone into battle and displayed the sort of courage of which one might proudly speak.

There was no trace of the braggart as Kenji continued: "A medal, a car, a pension, even an education. Just for packing a rifle. Is that good?"

"Yes, it's good."

Kenji turned and watched him long enough to make him feel nervous.

"Better watch the road," he warned.

"Sure." Kenji looked through the windshield and bit his lower lip thoughtfully.

"Ken."

"Yes?"

"Tell me about it."

The small man behind the wheel raised the leg which was not his own and let it fall with a thud to the floor board. "About this?"

"If you will. If it isn't too painful."

"No, it's not painful at all. Talking about it doesn't hurt. Not having it doesn't hurt. But it hurts where it ought to be. Sometimes I think about killing myself."

"Why?" There was anger in his voice.

"What makes you say why that way?"

"I didn't mean it to sound the way it did."

"Of course you did. I don't say that about killing myself to everybody. Sometimes it scares people. Sometimes it makes them think I'm crazy. You got angry right away and I want to know why."

"Tell me about it first."

"Sure." He turned the car into a park and drove slowly along a winding road, with trees and neat, green grass on both sides of them. "It's not important how I lost the leg. What's important are the eleven inches."

"I don't understand that about the eleven inches."

"That's what's left."

"I see."

"Do you? Do you really, Ichiro?"

"I think so."

A mother and a child strolled across the road ahead of them and Kenji slowed down more than necessary. "What I mean is, I've got eleven inches to go and you've got fifty years, maybe sixty. Which would you rather have?"

"I don't quite follow you, but I'll settle for eleven inches."

"Oh?" Kenji was surprised.

Ichiro regarded the thin, sensitive face carefully and said

bluntly: "I wasn't in the army, Ken. I was in jail. I'm a no-no boy."

There was a silence, but it wasn't uncomfortable. Ichiro could tell instantly that it did not matter to Kenji, who drove the new Oldsmobile aimlessly through the park because it was as good a place as any.

"Still," he said finally, "you've got your life ahead of you."

"Have I?"

"I should think so."

"Would you trade places with me? I said I would with you."

Kenji laughed softly. "I'll forget you said that."

"No, I meant it."

"Let me tell you about the eleven inches first."

"I'm listening."

Rolling down the window, Kenji let the cool air blow in on them. "Turned out to be a pretty nice day."

Ichiro waited without answering.

"The doctors didn't have to work too hard. The machine gun had done a pretty good job. They were pretty proud about having saved my knee. Makes things a lot easier with a sound knee, you know."

"Yes, that's not hard to see."

"They gave me a leg and it worked out pretty well, only, after a while, it started to hurt. I went back into the hospital and it turned out that there's something rotten in my leg that's eating it away. So they cut off a little more and gave me a new leg. As you've probably guessed by now, it wasn't long before I was back in and they whacked off another chunk. This time they took off more than they had to so as to make sure they got all the rottenness. That was five months ago. A couple of days ago I noticed the pains coming back."

"Bad?"

"No, but it's starting."

"Does that mean . . ."

"Yes. I'll go back and they'll chop again. Then, maybe, I'll only have eight inches to trade for your fifty or sixty years."

"Oh."

"Still want to trade?"

Ichiro shuddered and Kenji rolled up the window.

"How much time do they give you?"

"Depends, of course. Maybe the rottenness will go away and I'll live to a ripe old age."

"If not?"

"They say a fellow ought to trade in a car every third year to get the most out of it. My brother can take care of that."

"How long?"

"Two years at the most."

"You'll get well. They've got ways."

"Let's talk about something else," said Kenji and drove faster until they were out of the park and once again headed toward Jackson Street.

They didn't talk, because there was nothing to say. For a brief moment Ichiro felt a strange exhilaration. He had been envying Kenji with his new Oldsmobile, which was fixed to be driven with a right leg that wasn't there any more, because the leg that wasn't there had been amputated in a field hospital, which meant that Kenji was a veteran of the army of America and had every right to laugh and love and hope, because one could do that even if one of his legs was gone. But a leg that was eating itself away until it would consume the man himself in a matter of a few years was something else, for hobbling toward death on a cane and one good leg seemed far more disastrous than having both legs and an emptiness that might conceivably still be filled.

He gripped his knees with his hands, squeezing the hard soundness of the bony flesh and muscles, and fought off the sadness which seemed only to have deepened after the moment of relief. Kenji had two years, maybe a lifetime if the thing that was chewing away at him suddenly stopped. But he, Ichiro, had stopped living two years ago.

I'll change with you, Kenji, he thought. Give me the stump which gives you the right to hold your head high. Give me the eleven inches which are beginning to hurt again and bring ever closer the fear of approaching death, and give me with it the fullness of yourself which is also yours because you were man enough to wish the thing which destroyed your leg and, perhaps, you with it but, at the same time, made it so that you can put your one good foot in the dirt of America and know that the wet coolness of it is yours beyond a single doubt.

"I like you, Ichiro," said Kenji, breaking the silence.

Ichiro smiled, a little embarrassed. "I could say the same about you," he said.

"We've both got big problems, bigger than most people. That ought to mean something."

"Whose is bigger?"

"Huh?"

"I was thinking all the time we were silent and I decided that, were it possible, I might very well trade with you."

"For the eleven inches or for the seven or eight that'll be left after the next time?"

"Even for two inches."

"Oh." They were getting close to Ichiro's home and Kenji took his time as if reluctant to part with his friend.

Soon, however, they were in front of the grocery store.

"Well?" asked Ichiro, opening the door.

"Mine is bigger than yours in a way and, then again, yours is bigger than mine."

"Thanks for the lift," he said and climbed out onto the sidewalk.

"I'll pick you up tonight if you got nothing better to do," said Kenji.

"That'll be fine."

He watched the Oldsmobile pull away and then pushed open the door which jingled the bell of the grocery store with home in the back end.

His mother was at the counter ringing up a loaf of bread and a bag of Bull Durham for a white-haired pensioner. She glanced briefly at him, her eyes sharp and troubled. Feeling uneasy, he made his way past her into the kitchen.

Taro was playing solitaire at the kitchen table, his hands mechanically flipping and shifting the cards as if he found no enjoyment in the game. The father sat opposite his younger son and watched, not the cards, but the face of his son, with a kind of helpless sadness.

He sat on the end between them and watched for awhile.

"No school?" he said finally, noticing that it was still only a little after one o'clock.

"Keep out of it." His brother spit the words out angrily without taking his eyes off the cards.

Ichiro looked at his father with the unanswered question on his face and failed still to get an answer because the father did not remove his gaze from Taro.

"You will wait, ya? Please, Taro. It is not long."

He turned up the ace of spades and piled several cards in rapid succession upon it.

His mouth still open, the father forced more words out of it: "Mama does not understand, Taro, so you must understand her. Try. Try to understand. Until June. Then, if she still says no, you go. Anyway, finish high school."

"What's going on?" Ichiro looked from Taro to his father and back again and got no reply.

"That is all right, ya? June, you finish high school. Then, if you still feel the same, I will say nothing. Only a few months. Okay?"

The old man sighed, the weight of the problem noticeably too much for him. "Ahh," he groaned, then "Ahh" once more. He rose and got the bottle from the cupboard and wet his throat amply. After only a slight pause he took a second, shorter drink and returned the bottle to the shelf. Seconds later, he was back in the chair looking at Taro in the same lost fashion.

Ichiro tried again: "What's going on?"

"Birthday party," said Taro, looking up with a wry grin. "You gonna sing for me too?"

"I might."

"Sure, you can get your buddies from the pen and do it right. You can sing me happy birthday in Japanese. I'd go for that."

The blood rushed to his face and it was with considerable difficulty that he kept himself from swinging at his brother. "You hate me that much?"

"I don't know you." He shifted the diamond six to a club seven and put up the seven of spades.

"Ichiro," said the old man and he still did not take his eyes away from the other son.

"Yeah?"

"Taro is eighteen today. He came home at lunchtime, when he should be in school. Mama said: 'Why are you home?' 'It is my birthday,' he said. 'Why are you home?' said Mama, 'why are you not in school like you should be?' 'I am eighteen and I am going in the army,' he said. We were eating, Mama and me, and Taro stood here beside us and said: 'I am eighteen and I am going in the army.'"

"Are you?" he asked his brother.

"For crissake. You want me to write it down? You want me to send you a letter? I said I'm goin' in the army. You think the old man's just talkin'? Besides, it's none a your business." Extracting a red ten from the discard pile, he played it on a black jack, which enabled him to make several advantageous moves.

"You realize Ma won't get over it, don't you?"

"It doesn't matter."

The answer did not disturb him. If he were eighteen and in Taro's shoes he would probably do the same thing. And not having done it when it was his to do, there was really nothing for him to say. It was not Taro who was rejecting them, but it was he who had rejected Taro and, in turn, had made him a stranger to his own parents forever.

"Think it over," he said weakly, "give it time."

Taro threw the cards in his hand on the table and swept them onto the floor with an angry sweep of his arm. "It's been nice," he said and he might have been on the verge of tears. "I got things to do." He stood and looked down at Ichiro, wanting to speak but not finding the words in himself to tell his brother that he had to go in the army because of his brother whose weakness made it impossible for him to do otherwise and because he did not understand what it was about his mother that haunted him day and night and pulled his insides into meaningless bits and was slowly destroying him. And it was because of these things and because he was furiously mixed up that he had to cut himself free and spare himself the anguish of his brother which he knew must be there even if he was a stranger to him, and maybe that was still another reason why he was going.

In that brief moment when Taro looked at Ichiro and felt these things which he could not say, Ichiro felt them too and understood. So, when Taro stalked into the bedroom and banged the drawers and packed a small bag, he felt the heaviness lifting from his own shoulders. He did not even turn to look when Taro swept past him on the way out, for he saw in the fearful eyes of the father the departure of the son who was not a son but a stranger and, perhaps more rightly, an enemy leaving to join his friends. Then the bell tinkled to signal the opening of the door and it tinkled again as the door closed and shut them off from the world that Taro had entered.

The mother uttered a single, muffled cry which was the forgotten spark in a dark and vicious canyon and, the spark having escaped, there was only darkness, but a darkness which was now darker still, and the meaning of her life became a little bit meaningless.

Ichiro looked at his father, who did not look as would a father who had just lost a son, but as a man afraid. His face paled perceptibly as the mother came into the kitchen.

"Mama," said the father, and he might have been a boy the way he said it.

"We don't have enough nickels," she said, trying to sound the way she would have sounded if Taro had never been born, but it was not the same and Ichiro felt it.

"Ya, I get," the father almost shouted as he jumped up. "The bank will still be open." He threw on his overcoat and hastily departed.

Ichiro started to pick the cards off the floor and felt his mother's eyes on him. He took his time purposely, not wanting to look at her, for the strength that was the strength of Japan had failed and he had caught the realization of it in the cry and in the words which she had spoken. As if suddenly sensing what was in his mind, she quickly turned and left him alone.

4

THERE ARE STORES ON KING STREET, WHICH IS ONE BLOCK to the south of Jackson Street. Over the stores are hotels housed in ugly structures of brick more black than red with age and neglect. The stores are cafés and open-faced groceries and taverns and dry-goods shops, and then there are the stores with plate-glass windows painted green or covered with sun-faded drapes. Some bear names of exporting firms, others of laundries with a few bundles on dusty shelves. A few come closer to the truth by calling themselves society or club headquarters. The names of these latter are simple and unimaginative, for gambling against the house, whether it be with cards or dice or beans or dominoes, requires only a stout heart and a hunger for the impossible. And there are many of these, for this is Chinatown and, when the town is wide open, one simply walks into Wing's Hand Laundry, or Trans-Asia Exporting, Inc., or Canton Recreation Society with the stout heart and the hunger and there is not even a guard at the massive inner door with the small square of one-way glass.

Inside the second door are the tables and the stacks of silver dollars and the Chinese and Japanese and Filipinos and a few stray whites, and no one is smiling or laughing, for one does not do those things when the twenty has dwindled to a five or the twenty is up to a hundred and the hunger has been whetted into a mild frenzy by greed. The dealer behind the blackjack table is a sickly, handsome Chinese, a pokerfaced dignitary of the house, whose soft, nimble fingers automatically remove bunches of five and ten and fifteen from the silver stacks. He is master for the moment over the kingdom of green felt, but he neither jokes with the winners nor sympathizes with the losers, for when the day is over and the money for the day's labors is in his pocket he will set aside a dollar for his hotel room and give the rest back to the house because his is the hunger no longer accompanied by a stout heart, a sickness which drives him relentlessly toward the big kill which, when attained, drives him to the next bigger one and so on and on and on until he is again behind the table working toward his day's wages from which he will set aside a dollar for the hotel room and give the rest back to the house.

The dealer flipped up Kenji's cards and matched five dollars against the five that was bet, for the house had eighteen and the young Japanese with the cane held two face cards.

Ichiro watched Kenji ride the ten and hit twenty, then forty before he pulled it in and sat out several hands. Over at the dice table were half a dozen young Japanese who could not have been any older than Taro. A few were betting dimes and quarters, feeling their luck with the miserliness of the beginner who does not yet fully understand the game or the strained impulses within his young body. And there was one who held a fistful of bills and played with an intensity that was fearful to watch.

"Here," said Kenji to Ichiro, "play." He shoved a stack of ten silver dollars over to his friend.

"No," he said, wanting to play very much.

Kenji did not urge him. He played five as usual and again ran it up to forty. "For a change, I'm going to quit while I'm ahead." He traded the silver for four twenties, a ten, and a five.

They walked from game to game, watching the players for a little while.

"I feel like drinking it up," said Kenji, looking at Ichiro.

"Fine," said Ichiro, wanting to say that he did not want to go anyplace where too many would know him and of him, for he was afraid.

They walked down the ugly street with the ugly buildings among the ugly people which was a part of America and, at the same time, would never be wholly America. The night was cool and dark.

Halfway down an alley, among the forlorn stairways and innumerable trash cans, was the entrance to the Club Oriental. It was a bottle club, supposedly for members only, but its membership consisted of an ever growing clientele. Under the guise of a private, licensed club, it opened its door to almost everyone and rang up hefty profits nightly.

Up the corridor flanked on both sides by walls of glass brick, they approached the polished mahogany door. Kenji poked the buzzer and, momentarily, the electric catch buzzed in return. They stepped from the filthy alley and the cool night into the Club Oriental with its soft, dim lights, its long, curving bar, its deep carpets, its intimate tables, and its small dance floor.

There were a few people at the bar, a few more at the tables, and one couple on the dance floor, sliding around effortlessly to the Ralph Flanagan tune which was one of a hundred records offered by the massive, colorful juke box.

It wasn't until they had seated themselves at the bar and finished half their first bourbons on ice that their eyes became sufficiently accustomed to the darkness to enable them to distinguish the faces scattered around the club.

"I like it here," said Kenji contentedly.

"Yeah, I see what you mean."

Kenji sipped his drink appreciatively, knowing that the night was long and that there would be other days in spite of the hurting of his leg. "If I didn't have to sleep or eat, I'd stay right here. I'd work up to a nice, lazy feeling and keep it there by hoisting my arm every once in a while. That would be nice."

"Yeah, it would."

"For me, yes, but not for you."

"Oh?"

"I've been thinking about the things we said this afternoon."

"Have you?"

"Yes, and so have you." He looked at Ichiro with his face already flushed from the liquor.

"Sure," said Ichiro. "Seems like that's all I've been doing since the day I was born."

"Don't blame yourself."

"Then who's to blame?"

"Doesn't matter. Blame the world, the Japs, the Germans. But not yourself. You're killing yourself."

"Maybe I ought to."

"Now, you're talking like me." Kenji smiled and beckoned the bartender for refills.

"There used to be times, before the war," said Ichiro, "when I thought I had troubles. I remember the first time I laid a girl. She was a redhead in my history class. Knew her way around. I guess, actually, she laid me. I was scared, but I was more scared after it was done. Worried about it for weeks. I thought I really had troubles then."

"Sounds more like a good deal."

"Could have been. I think about that now and I feel good about it. If I had to do it over—" Leaving the rest unsaid, he played with the glass in his hands.

"I feel for you," said Kenji.

"I suppose that means you've decided not to change places with me."

"If it were possible to, no."

"If it were, Ken, if it were and there was just half an inch to trade for my fifty years, would you then?"

Kenji thought about that for a long while. "When it comes to the last half an inch and it starts to hurt, I'll sell the car and spend the rest of my life sitting here with a drink in my hand and feeling good."

"That means no, of course."

"That means no, yes."

"Thanks for being honest."

"I wish I could do something."

"You can't."

"But I wish I could."

"Nobody can."

"I want to anyway."

"Don't try."

"If you say so."

"I do."

So they sat silently through the next drink, one already dead but still alive and contemplating fifty or sixty years more of dead aliveness, and the other, living and dying slowly. They were two extremes, the Japanese who was more American than most Americans because he had crept to the brink of death for America, and the other who was neither Japanese nor American because he had failed to recognize the gift of his birthright when recognition meant everything.

The crowd was beginning to thicken now. The door seemed continually to be buzzing and, from their stools at the bar, they watched the laughing faces of the newcomers, who quickly settled down at the tables with a thirst for the drinks which would give them the relaxation and peace they sought.

A swarthy Japanese, dressed in a pale-blue suit that failed to conceal his short legs and awkward body, came in with a good-looking white girl. He spoke loudly and roughly, creating the commotion he intended so that, for a moment, all eyes were upon the couple. Seeing Kenji, he boomed out jovially: "For crissake, if it ain't Peg-leg. It's sure been a helluva long time since I seen you." He left the girl standing at the door and advanced upon Kenji with arms outstretched.

"Cut it out, Bull," said Kenji quietly. "I saw you last night."

Bull wedged himself between the stools with his back to Ichiro. "How'm I doin'?" he whispered slyly.

"She's all right," said Kenji examining the girl.

"C'mon, sit with us. I'll fix you up." Bull gave Kenji a hearty slap.

"I'm with a friend," said Kenji.

Bull turned around and looked at Ichiro with a meanness which was made darker by the heavy cheekbones and the rough stubble which defied a razor. He wiggled out into the open with exaggerated motions and began to brush himself furiously. "Goddammit," he said aloud, "brand-new suit. Damn near got it all cruddy."

There was a ripple of laughter and Ichiro turned and looked at the crowd without wanting to. Someone said something about "No-no boys don't look so good without the striped uniform" and that got a loud, boisterous laugh from the corner where a group of young Japanese who were too young to drink sat drinking. He scanned their faces quickly and saw, among them, the unsmiling, sick-looking face of Taro.

"Go on, Bull, your girl friend's waiting," said Kenji quietly.

"What's with you, nuts or somp'n?" said Bull wickedly.

"Go on."

Bull regarded the lean, solemn face stubbornly but only for a moment. "Sure, sure," he said lightly, "a friend of yours . . ." He paused and cast the meanness at Ichiro once more and added: ". . . is a friend of yours." Grinning at the crowd as though he were a performer who had just done his bit, he returned to his girl, who had been primping ostentatiously all the while.

Ichiro leaned over the bar, the fury inside of him seething uncontrollably, and shame, conceived of a great goodness momentarily corrupted by bitterness and the things he did not understand, deprived him of the strength to release the turbulence.

"Want to go?"

"No," he muttered savagely before he could stop himself.

"Bull didn't mean it. He might be a brute, but he's all right."

"He meant it. They all mean it. I can see it in their faces."

"You see too much."

"I feel it."

"Then you feel too much."

As if hoping to find escape in the whisky, he downed it quickly and motioned to the bartender to fill it. When the smiling Chinese behind the bar tipped the bottle over the glass, he held it down until the liquor spilled over the lip.

"Leave it, Al," said Kenji to the Chinese.

Al nodded his head and left the bottle in front of Ichiro.

They drank in silence, Kenji taking his leisurely and Ichiro gulping his purposefully.

"Take it slow," warned Kenji in a voice which was softer than usual because the whisky made him that way.

"Doesn't help," grumbled Ichiro thickly, "not a goddamned bit it doesn't help." He swung around on his stool and surveyed the crowd, which had long since forgotten about him. He noticed hazily that Taro and his friends were gone. "Son-of-bitches. That's what they are, all of them. Dirty, no-good son-of-bitches."

"I agree," said Kenji peacefully.

"You too."

Kenji nodded his head, "Sure, I'm a member too. World's full of us."

"I mean it. Everybody except me. Me, I'm not even a son of a bitch. I'm nobody, nothing. Just plain nothing."

"Let's get some air."

"No, no. After a while. Right now, I'm going to get stinko."

"You're drunk now."

"Hell, I'm just starting. I want to get so drunk I'll feel like a son of a bitch too." He lifted the glass to his mouth and emptied it, almost toppling off the stool.

Kenji grabbed his arm and straightened him out.

"Thanks. Thanks, Ken. You're okay and you've done plenty for me. Now, it's my turn. I'm going to do something for you."

"What's that?"

"You go over there and sit with your friend, the monkey in the blue suit, and I'll go out the door and I'll forget I ever saw

70

you. Fair enough, huh? Best thing I can do for you. Forget you, that's what."

"That's no good."

"It is. It is. You go get fixed up with that blond. Take her away from that monkey and I'll walk out the door and keep right on going all the way down Jackson Street and into the drink. I got no right to let you be my friend. I don't want you for a friend, friend. Please, huh?"

"We're going for a ride, remember?"

"Nope, you go, with blondie. That's for you. I don't want to go anyplace with you no more."

They stared at each other, Kenji smiling patiently at his friend, who spoke with drunken earnestness.

Someone said "Hey" softly and they both turned. It was Taro.

"Hay is for horses," he blurted out stiffly at his brother. "Don't you even know your own brother's own name? I'm I-chi-ro, remember?"

"I wanta talk to you."

"Talk then."

"C'mon outside."

"I like it here."

Taro fidgeted uncertainly and looked hostilely at Kenji.

"I have to hit the John anyway," said Kenji obligingly.

"No, stay. Piss on the floor. This ought to be good. He's finally got something to say to me and I want you to hear it. Well? What is it?" he demanded impatiently.

"If you'll come outside, I'll tell you."

Ichiro threw up his arms in disgust. "Come back when you feel like talking in here." He turned around to get his drink and did not see the two young Japanese step inside the doorway and look questioningly at Taro. Taro waved them away with a furtive motion of his hand, which Kenji noticed. The two youths hurried back out.

"You gonna come out?" asked Taro.

"Your brother is busy. Come back later," said Kenji.

"For crissake. Okay, okay, so I'll go." Ichiro tumbled off the stool.

"I'm coming too." Kenji reached for his cane.

Ichiro held back his friend's arm. "Nope. This is a family pow-wow. You keep my glass warm and I'll be right back. Right back."

"Watch yourself," cautioned Kenji.

"I'm not that drunk," laughed Ichiro. He lumbered after Taro, the weight of his body urging his legs unsteadily forward in quick, clumsy spurts.

Taro walked rapidly, turning down the alley away from King Street. Some thirty yards from the club entrance he angled off through a vacant lot which was gloomily illuminated by a distant street light.

Resolutely, Ichiro followed, his breath coming hard and the hot smell of the whisky swirling through his nostrils nauseatingly. He started across the lot and spied Taro far ahead. "Where in the hell you going? I'm tired." He stopped and fought for breath.

His brother had stopped too and faced him silently from the shadow of an old garage. Ichiro had to squint his eyes to barely see him.

There were sounds of feet shuffling in the gravelly earth. The sounds advanced from all sides. The darkness of the night and his own drunkenness made it difficult for him to realize immediately what was happening. Two youths stepped between him and Taro.

"That's a Jap, fellas," sneered one of them bravely.

A voice concurred from behind: "Yeah, this one's got a big, fat ass, fatter than its head."

"It's got legs," came a voice from the side, "and arms too. Just like us."

"Does it talk?"

"Talks Jap, I bet."

"Say something," egged the first youth. "Say no-no in Jap. You oughta be good at that."

"Yeah, I wanta hear."

"Me too. Say no-no."

Ichiro wove unsteadily, the humiliation and anger intensified by the dulling effect of the liquor into a heavy, brooding madness. He strove to keep his brother in sight, catching an occasional glimpse of the now fear-stricken face.

"It doesn't look very happy," said a voice, shaky but inspired by the knowledge of being on the stronger side.

"That's 'cause it's homesick."

"It's got a home?"

"Sure, on the other side of the pond."

"Comes from Japan, doesn't it?"

"Made in Japan. Says so right here."

A brutal kick on his behind sent Ichiro stumbling forward. His anger frothing over, he picked up momentum and lunged at the dim shape that was his brother. He swung his arms wildly at the two youths who stood between them. One of them threw himself athwart his legs and Ichiro sprawled heavily to the ground. He shook his head wearily and struggled to his knees.

"Pretty game," said one of the tormentors calmly.

"Wants to fight," said another.

"Just like a dog."

"Dogs don't wear pants."

"Right. We can't let it run around with pants on."

"No. People will think it's human."

Before he could struggle to his feet, his arms were pulled painfully behind him. Furiously, he attempted to kick himself loose. Immediately arms were clawing at his trouser legs and it was only a matter of moments before he was stretched out helplessly.

There was a sharp snap and a slender youth bent over him with a wide grin and started to slip the knife blade under the leather belt.

"That's enough. Let him go." Kenji limped across the lot and advanced upon the group. He poked his cane at one of the youths who hovered over Ichiro. Slowly, they backed away from their prey. Only the youth who held the knife did not move.

"You heard," said Kenji to him.

"Keep out of this. It's none of your business."

"It's certainly none of yours." The cane swished and smacked loudly against the wrist of the knife wielder.

Dropping the knife with a yelp of pain, the youth backed off, swearing menacingly at Kenji.

"Let's get out of here," said one of them urgently.

"Yeah, I heard about this guy. Kill-crazy, that's what. Even his buddies were afraid of him."

"Just like a madman. Couldn't kill enough krauts."

"I'm gonna beat it."

"Aw, he's just another Jap." The slender youth stooped over to retrieve his knife, mumbling "Jap-lover."

Kenji raised his cane and aimed a stiff blow at the youth's back.

"Ahh!" The youth fell across Ichiro, then picked himself up hastily and dashed into the shadows. The others followed in a mad rush.

"Your brother has nice friends," said Kenji, helping Ichiro to get up.

"No-good rotten bastard." Ichiro brushed himself with heavy, limp arms.

"Want to drink some more?"

They walked silently to the car and, a short while later, were driving swiftly along the highway leading southward out of the city. With both windows rolled down, the dulling effects of the whisky soon wore off.

Ichiro rested his head on the door, exposing his face to the stream of cold air. Hazily, he thought disgustedly of the recent happenings, of Bull and of Taro and his gang of weak hoodlums. He could understand Bull's subjecting him to the indignity in the Club Oriental. Bull's mind was about as thick and unpliable as a brick and the meanness which had prompted him to make a spectacle of him was less to blame than the dull, beastly desire to feel the approval of the crowd, which had laughed with him for a moment instead of at him. The blond was a compensation for his lack of acceptance also. Somehow, he had managed to date her

74

but, before the night was done, Bull would be looking stubbornly for her while someone else took her to bed. He could forgive Bull, but not Taro, who had baited him into the lot and was too cowardly to join in the game which he had made possible and too cowardly to come to his defense when the horror of what he had done dawned too late.

Taro, my brother who is not my brother, you are no better than I. You are only more fortunate that the war years found you too young to carry a gun. You are fortunate like the thousands of others who, for various reasons of age and poor health and money and influence, did not happen to be called to serve in the army, for their answers might have been the same as mine. And you are fortunate because the weakness which was mine made the same weakness in you the strength to turn your back on Ma and Pa and makes it so frighteningly urgent for you to get into uniform to prove that you are not a part of me. I was born not soon enough or not late enough and for that I have been punished. It is not just, but it is true. I am not one of those who wait for the ship from Japan with baggage ready, yet the hundreds who do are freer and happier and fuller than I. I am not to blame but you blame me and for that I hate you and I will hate you more when you go into the army and come out and walk the streets of America as if you owned them always and forever.

I have made a mistake and I know it with all the anguish in my soul. I have suffered for it and will suffer still more. Is it not just then that, for my suffering and repentance, I be given another chance? One steals and goes to prison and comes out a free man with his debt paid. Such a one can start over. He can tell himself that the mistake which he has made has been made right with the world. He can, without much difficulty, even convince himself that his wrong has been righted and that, with lesson learned, he can find acceptance among those of his kind. I, too, have made a mistake and I, too, have served time, two years all told, and I have been granted a full pardon. Why is it then that I am unable to convince myself that I am no different from any other American? Why is it that, in my freedom, I feel more imprisoned in the wrongness of myself and the thing I did than when I was in prison? Am I really never to know again what it is to be American? If there should be an answer, what is it? What penalty is it that I must pay to justify my living as I so fervently desire to?

There is, I am afraid, no answer. There is no retribution for one who is guilty of treason, and that is what I am guilty of. The fortunate get shot. I must live my punishment.

Overcome by the sense of futility which came back to him again and again, he moaned helplessly.

Kenji pointed the Oldsmobile down the broad stretch of concrete at an unwavering fifty-five. "Head starting to hurt?"

"Yeah."

"We can stop for a drink."

"No. That wouldn't help."

They sped past a drive-in movie, catching a glimpse of the silent drama on the part of the screen which was unobscured by the fence.

"Speed make you nervous?"

"No."

The Oldsmobile lunged up to seventy, then struggled more slowly to seventy-five and, soon, they were hurtling along at eighty. They rolled up the windows to stop the wicked rush of air.

"Where we headed?" asked Ichiro.

Kenji drove calmly, not tensing up the way some fellows do when they drive beyond their usual speeds, but he kept his eyes on the road. "I want you to meet a friend," he answered.

"Do we have to? Tonight, I mean."

"What's a better time?"

"I'm not exactly sober," said Ichiro, and he fought off a shudder. He wished he had a drink.

"She won't mind."

"She?"

"She."

He could have asked who she was, what she did, why he had to meet her tonight, and so on, but he'd find out soon enough. He leaned his head back against the seat and closed his eyes. He was sound asleep by the time they drove up to the small farmhouse situated in the middle of forty acres, partly wooded but mostly cleared.

Letting the motor idle, Kenji turned the car heater on low and walked the narrow curve of concrete leading to the front door. He brushed his hand alongside the door and found the button. The faint, muffled notes of the chime were barely audible. The pale, brownish glow visible through the window of the living room flicked twice into a warm brightness and, immediately after, the porch light snapped on.

Emi was several inches taller than Kenji. She was slender, with heavy breasts, had rich, black hair which fell on her shoulders and covered her neck, and her long legs were strong and shapely like a white woman's. She smiled and looked beyond him into the darkness.

"You left the car running." She questioned him with her round, dark eyes.

"A friend," he said, "sleeping it off."

"Oh." Leaving the porch light on, she followed Kenji into the living room. An old Zenith console, its round face with the zigzag needle glowing, hummed monotonously. She turned it off, saying: "Station just went off."

Slouching comfortably in an overstuffed chair beneath the lamp, Kenji grabbed a picture frame from the end-table and examined the several snapshots preserved under glass. There was one of a muscular-looking young Japanese sitting on a tractor. He looked from it to the fireplace mantel, where a large color portrait of the same fellow in uniform stood among an assortment of animals of glass and china. The other snapshots were of an elderly couple, pictures taken by a happy daughter on sunny days, with the mother and father posing stiffly as they would in a photographer's studio.

He set the frame back on the table asking: "Heard from anyone?"

"Dad wrote," she said.

"How is he?"

"Sick. Sick of Japan and Japanese and rotten food and sicker still of having to stay there."

"What can he do?"

"Nothing."

"No hope of getting back here?"

"No." She kicked her shoes off and rested her chin on her knees, not bothering to pull the skirt down over her legs.

Kenji stared at the legs and beyond, seeing but unresponsive. "Nothing from Ralph?"

Emi glanced briefly at the picture on the mantel. "No," she said, "Ralph is not the writing kind." It was said bravely, but her lips quivered.

He looked at her with a touch of sadness in his tired face. She met his gaze with the sadness all in her eyes, the deep, misty-looking eyes in the finely molded, lovely face.

"Still love him?"

"What's that?"

"You know what."

Dropping her feet to the rug, she squirmed uneasily for a moment. "Do I?" she said almost shrilly.

"That's what I'm asking."

"I think so. No, perhaps I should say I thought I did. Then again, there are times when I'm quite sure I do. Does it make sense to you, Ken?"

"Sounds mixed up."

"Yes."

From the end-table, Kenji helped himself to a cigarette. "If I were you and my husband signed up for another hitch in Germany without even coming home or asking me to go over and be with him, I'd stop loving him. I'd divorce him."

"That makes the twenty-ninth time you've said that and it's still none of your business."

"I didn't say it was."

She stood up abruptly, snatched the cigarette out of his hand, and turned her back on him, saying sharply: "Then stop saying it."

He reached out and squeezed her elbow tenderly.

Slowly, reluctantly she looked at him. "I'm sorry," she said.

She smiled, gazing fondly at him for a moment. "Coffee?" she asked sweetly.

"Sure. Make enough for the friend."

As soon as Emi had gone to the kitchen, Kenji decided to awaken Ichiro. Just as he was about to rise, Ichiro came into the house.

"Snap the light off," shouted Kenji.

Ichiro looked stupidly at him.

"The porch light. Switch is on the wall."

Looking around uncertainly, Ichiro located the switch and did as he was told. He examined the house, the pictures, the radio, the books, the lamps, the curtains, and the old upright near the fireplace but not flat against the wall. It was, rather, almost perpendicular to the wall so that the heavy, unpainted casing was in plain view. He caught Kenji's eye and tossed the car keys to him. Touching the piano keys hesitantly, he punched out several notes, then tried a series of chords with both hands.

"Sounds good. Play something," said Kenji.

Sliding onto the bench, Ichiro executed several runs before starting into a simple but smooth rendition of "Sentimental Journey." It sounded good, almost professional in spite of the monotony of the chording, and Kenji listened appreciatively.

Hearing the playing, Emi came out of the kitchen. As she turned toward the piano, the look of inquiry on her face suddenly changed to wide-eyed surprise. It wasn't horror exactly, but there might have been a trace of it. She let out a sharp utterance.

Ichiro stopped and twisted about until he was facing her.

"Forgive me. You looked—you reminded me of someone, sitting there like that." She turned toward Kenji.

"Hadn't thought about it," he said, "but, I guess you're right.

Ichiro is big and husky like Ralph. Emi, that's Ichiro. Ichiro, Emi."

Getting up from the bench self-consciously, Ichiro nodded to her.

"How are you at 'Chopsticks'?" she asked, recovered from her initial shock.

"So-so," he replied.

Emi pulled him back onto the bench and sat beside him. They fumbled the beginning several times, laughing at their own ineptitude and quickly losing the sense of strangeness in their mutual endeavor. Finally, getting off to an even start, they played loudly and not always together to the finish.

"You play much better than I do," she commented gaily.

"I try," he said modestly.

They walked together to the sofa and sat down facing Kenji.

"Never knew you could play at all," said Kenji.

"I learned from an old German named Burk," replied Ichiro. "He was a good guy, a real musician. Played one time with some symphony outfit—San Francisco, I think it was. He was fifty years old and looked sixty-five with flabby creases on his face and his shoulders stooped over. His hands were big, with thick, stubby fingers more like a bricklayer's than a pianist's. He made music with those ugly hands and he also used them to choke his wife to death. He taught me while I was in prison."

"Prison," echoed Emi. "You were in prison?"

"Yeah, I guess Ken doesn't talk enough. I was in for not wanting to go in the army."

"I'm sorry, frightfully sorry," she said sincerely.

"So am I."

She studied him quizzically, then rose to get the coffee.

"Where are we?" he asked Kenji.

"You've sobered up," he replied.

"Thanks for keeping me warm."

"Didn't want you to catch cold."

"Drunks don't catch cold."

"You're out of practice. You weren't really drunk."

"I was."

"Okay. You were."

"Where are we?" he repeated.

"Out in the country. Away from it all. You'll see what it's like in the morning."

Ichiro jerked his head up and waited for an explanation.

"We can sleep here. Emi doesn't mind." Kenji reached out and pulled the coffee table in front of them as Emi returned from the kitchen.

The coffee was black and hot. Emi sat beside Ichiro, looking at him with wondering eyes. It was as if she yearned to reach out and touch him. Ichiro felt uncomfortable, yet drawn to her, for she was young and lovely and attractive.

Kenji sat smiling, so much so that Ichiro commented upon it.

"Just feeling good and satisfied," said Kenji, leaning back and lifting the stiff limb with both hands onto the coffee table.

They sipped their coffee, saying little and occasionally looking at one another. Kenji kept grinning, apparently with meaning to Emi, for she began to fidget nervously. Suddenly, she stood up and said not unpleasantly that she was going to bed.

"I'll sack down on the sofa out here," said Kenji, watching Emi intently.

Her face flushed. She started to say something, then merely nodded her head and, without looking at Ichiro, left them.

"What goes on?" inquired Ichiro.

"I didn't notice anything. Why do you ask?"

"I must be getting sleepy. Forget it." He stood up and studied the sofa. "We might as well fix up the bed. How does this thing work?"

"It doesn't."

"Aren't we sleeping here?"

"I am."

"And me?"

"In the bedroom, of course."

"Which one?"

Kenji said steadily, "There's only one—that is, only one with a bed in it."

Appalled by the realization of the fantastic situation, Ichiro sank down upon the sofa. "Where," he said pointedly, "does she sleep?"

"In the bedroom."

"What the hell is this?" he boomed out indignantly.

"She likes you."

"Sure, that's great. I like her too, but this is crazy. I hardly know her."

"Does it make a difference?"

"Yes, it does."

"She needs you," said Kenji. "No, I should say she needs someone. Just like you need someone. Just like I need someone sometimes. I won't apologize for her because then I'd have to apologize for myself. She waited four years for Ralph to come back. We were in the same outfit. Ralph signed up for another hitch. Don't ask me why. He did. He asked me to look her up and tell her he wasn't coming back for a while. No explanations. Just tell her he wasn't coming back just yet. Would you wait?"

"No."

"I'm only half a man, Ichiro, and when my leg starts aching, even that half is no good."

The hot color rose to his face as he lashed out at Kenji angrily: "So you're sending in a substitute, is that it?"

Kenji sighed. "The conversation is getting vulgar, but the facts aren't vulgar because I don't feel that they are wrong or loose or dirty or vulgar. You can sleep on the floor or take the car and go back to town." He threw the keys on the sofa beside Ichiro.

Ichiro sat and fumed, struggling to do the right thing and not knowing what it was. If Kenji had said another word or allowed even a tiny smile to rise to his lips, he would have snatched the keys and rushed out.

His face an unchanging mask of serious patience, Kenji sat quietly.

"I'll see you in the morning," said Ichiro placidly.

Kenji grasped the leg and lowered it from the table, wincing as he did so. With his cane, he pointed beyond the kitchen.

Walking up to the partly open door, Ichiro paused and glanced back at Kenji. Slowly, he pushed it open and shut it silently behind him. There were two windows in the back, shining dimly against the darkness of the unlighted room. As his eyes became accustomed to the dark, he was able to make out the shape of the bed and the slender hump that was Emi. Moving cautiously forward, he glimpsed the fine trail of chain hanging from the ceiling. He raised his arm toward it gropingly.

"Don't," she whispered.

He untied his shoes by kneeling down and then let his shirt and trousers drop to the floor. Debating whether or not to strip all the way down, he pondered the matter for a long while. Then, like a swimmer plunging decisively into the cold water, he removed his underclothes and crawled into the bed.

His body taut and uncomfortable, he lay stiffly and stared at the ceiling. He fought for something to say, some remark to start bridging the gap of starched sheet that stretched between them. He listened to her soft, even breathing and tried to control the heaving of his own breast. At length, she stirred and her hand found his under the covers. It was warm and friendly and relaxing.

"This house," he said.

"Yes?"

"You live here all alone?"

"Very much so."

"No brothers or sisters."

"No. No brothers or sisters."

"Folks. How about them?"

"Mother died in thirty-nine."

"That's tough."

"It was just as well," she said. "The war would have made her suffer and she didn't have that. She had a wonderful funeral. It seemed as if everyone in the valley came with little white envelopes bearing quarters and dollars and some with even five and ten dollars and a few with much, much more. Paid for the funeral, they did. If father were here, he'd still be talking about it. It made him proud to tell people how he actually made money on the funeral. He didn't really mean it that way, of course. It was just his way of saying that he had a lot of good friends."

He lay there thinking about his own mother, thinking what might have been if she had died mercifully before Pearl Harbor also.

"Dad is in Japan," she continued. "He asked to be repatriated and he's been there five months."

"My ma thinks Japan won the war," he said.

"So did Dad. But he doesn't any more. He wants to come back."

"What makes them that way?"

"I don't know. It's like a sickness."

He turned to face her, his leg touching hers. "I want to know," he said loudly and distinctly. "I've ruined my life and I want to know what it is that made me do it. I'm not sick like them. I'm not crazy like Ma is or your father was. But I must have been."

"It's because we're American and because we're Japanese and sometimes the two don't mix. It's all right to be German and American or Italian and American or Russian and American but, as things turned out, it wasn't all right to be Japanese and American. You had to be one or the other."

"So?"

"I don't know," she answered, "I don't know."

"I've got to know," he sobbed out, holding desperately to her hand with both of his.

Emi reached out her free hand and drew his face against her naked breast. Lost and bewildered like a child frightened, he sobbed quietly.

It was hardly seven o'clock when Ichiro stirred wearily and dug his chin deeper into the covers to ward off the sharp coolness of the morning country air. He rolled half a turn, expecting to encounter the soft warmth of the girl who was a woman and could not wait for her husband but waited, and she was not there. He lay there for a moment, wanting to sleep some more and finding it difficult because Emi was gone. Slowly, he eased out from under the covers and sat shivering on the edge of the bed.

On a chair near the bed were neatly laid out a fresh shirt, a clean pair of slacks, even underwear and socks. His own clothes were not in sight. He dressed hurriedly, his body tingling from the brisk, unheated air and his head heavy and dull.

In the kitchen he let the cold water run over his head and neck, shocking himself into a wide-eyed yet somewhat drowsy state of wakefulness. The table bore signs of someone's having break-fasted. There was a cup with a film of coffee in the bottom and a small plate with toast crumbs and a butter-stained knife. When he put his hand to the coffeepot, it was still warm. He poured a cupful and drank it down.

Kenji was still sleeping soundly and, while he stood over his friend, wondering whether or not to awaken him, he heard the water spraying in the yard. He walked softly to the door and stepped outside.

It was a glorious morning. The sun, barely starting to peek over the eastern rim, was forcing its crown of vivid yellows and oranges and reds against the great expanse of hazy blue. The utter stillness of the countryside seemed even more still against the occasional distant crowing of a rooster and the chirping of the birds.

Through the misty, swirling pattern from the revolving sprinkler on the neat, green lawn he saw Emi kneeling over the flower bed.

"Morning," he said and, when she didn't respond, he said more loudly: "Hey."

She turned and, smiling, waved. Taking time to pull a few more weeds, she rose finally and made her way around the flying water. She wore a pair of man's overall pants, encircled with dampness at the knees, and a heavy athletic sweater with two gold stripes on the arm and an over-sized F on the front. It hung on her like an old potato sack, limp and faded from repeated use. She paused a short distance in front of him and examined him skeptically.

"Pants are a little snug around the waist, but they fit good," he said.

"I thought they would. You're about the same size as him."

Watching her standing there, he felt the need to say something about the previous night. "I want you to know—" he started hesitantly.

The color rose faintly to her cheeks. "You mustn't," she said quickly. "Talking will make it sound bad and unclean and it was not so."

He fidgeted uneasily, then saw the truth in her words. "No, it wasn't."

"There's a jacket in the hall closet," she said as she bent down to grab the hose and pull the sprinkler closer to the concrete walk.

It wasn't any longer than a minute or so before he had come back out with the snug-fitting leather jacket. Emi was sitting on the bottom step and he dropped down beside her. She sat with her wrists on her knees, her soiled hands carefully arched away from the soiled overalls as if she were wearing a clean skirt.

"There's someone out there," he said, peering into the distance across the level field and catching the movement of a tiny, dark shape stooped over in earnest industry.

"That's Mr. Maeno," she replied. "He leases my land."

"Looks like he's all alone."

"Oh, no. There's Mrs. Maeno, of course, and they have two young daughters who help after school and they hire help when necessary."

"And work from daylight till sundown, seven days a week, three hundred and sixty-five days a year. I can tell he's that kind of a man without ever having met him but by just watching him from here."

"Is that bad?"

"Bad?" He thought about it for a while before answering. "It's good. I used to think farmers were crazy working the way they do. I don't any more. I envy him."

"Why?"

"Because he's got a purpose in life. He's got something to do. He's got a goal of some kind and it gives meaning to his life and he's probably pretty satisfied."

"And me?"

He turned and looked at her. She was smiling, half seriously, half teasingly.

"I envy you too," he said without hesitation.

"And Ken? Poor Ken."

"Him also."

"You're bitter and you've no right to be." She brushed her palm against her eye irritatedly.

He stood up, digging his fists angrily into his pockets because she was nice and he had no right to make her partner to his gloom. "What kind of flowers did you plant?" he said cheerfully.

"Sit down, Ichiro."

Obeying her, he said: "I want to talk about something else."

"I don't. I want to talk about you, about how you feel and why you feel as you do."

"It's a lousy way to spend a fine morning," he protested.

She put a hand on his arm until he turned and looked at her. "I think I know how you feel."

He shook his head. "You can't. No one can."

"I thought about it while you were sleeping. I put myself in your place and I know how you feel. It's a very hopeless sort of feeling."

There was nothing he could say to that and he didn't.

"A hopeless feeling, however, doesn't mean that there is no hope."

"Are you saying there is?"

"There must be." She rubbed her hands together, flaking the dry dirt onto the walk.

"Thanks for trying," he said, "thanks for trying to help."

Emi faced him with a look of surprise and hurt anger: "Do you really think it's so hopeless? What do you propose to do during the rest of your life? Drown yourself in your selfish bitterness?"

Ichiro opened his mouth to mollify her.

"Are you blind?" she continued without waiting for an answer. "Deaf? Dumb? Helpless? You're young, healthy, and supposedly intelligent. Then *be* intelligent. Admit your mistake and do something about it."

"What?"

"Anything. It doesn't matter what you do. This is a big country with a big heart. There's room here for all kinds of people. Maybe what you've done doesn't make you one of the better ones but you're not among the worst either."

"If I were Ralph, if Ralph had done what I did, would you still feel the same way?"

"Yes, I would."

"Ralph's a lucky guy," he said.

"And you are too. In any other country they would have shot you for what you did. But this country is different. They made a mistake when they doubted you. They made a mistake when they made you do what you did and they admit it by letting you run around loose. Try, if you can, to be equally big and forgive them and be grateful to them and prove to them that you can be an American worthy of the frailties of the country as well as its strengths."

"The way you say that, it seems to make sense, but I don't know."

"You do know," she said quickly, for she was spurred by the effect her words were having on him. "It's hard to talk like this without sounding pompous and empty, but I can remember how full I used to get with pride and patriotism when we sang 'The Star-Spangled Banner' and pledged allegiance to the flag at school assemblies, and that's the feeling you've got to have."

"It was different then."

"Only because you think so. Next time you're alone, pretend you're back in school. Make believe you're singing 'The Star-Spangled Banner' and see the color guard march out on the stage and say the pledge of allegiance with all the other boys and girls. You'll get that feeling flooding into your chest and making you want to shout with glory. It might even make you feel like crying. That's how you've got to feel, so big that the bigness seems to want to bust out, and then you'll understand why it is that your mistake was no bigger than the mistake your country made."

Ichiro pushed himself off the step and walked slowly to the end of the yard. Turning, he looked at Emi, who stared back at him with an intentness which made him uncomfortable. Keeping his eyes on her, he made his way back until he was looking down upon her.

"It's nice out here," he said, "nice house, nice yard, nice you. No cars whizzing by, no people making noise. It's quiet and peaceful and clean and fresh and nice. It feels good just being here and even what you've just been saying sounds all right. But I don't live here. I don't belong here. It's not the same out there." He motioned toward the highway and beyond, where the city lay.

For a moment she looked as if she might scream to relieve herself of the agony in her soul for him. Fighting to regain her composure, she beckoned him to sit down.

He did so wearily, not wanting to pursue the subject but sensing that she was not yet ready to abandon it.

"How old are you?" she asked.

"Twenty-five," he answered, skeptical.

"I'm twenty-seven. So is Ralph, and Mike is fifty."

"Mike?"

"Yes, Mike, a good American name for a good American—at least, he was. Mike is Ralph's brother."

"I see."

"No, you don't. Not yet, anyway. I want to tell you about him."

"Sure."

"Do you want to go to Japan and live there?"

He furrowed his brow, not understanding. "You were going to tell me about Mike."

"I am," she said impatiently. "Do you?"

"No, of course not."

"Mike did."

"He did?"

"Yes, not because he wanted to, but because he had to."

"I still don't get it."

"You will. I'll start from the beginning."

"Fine."

As if preparing the story in her mind, she gazed silently over the fields before she began. "Mike was born in California and went to college there. He knocked around for a while and was doing graduate work in Louisiana when the war, the first world war, started. He'd left California because he didn't like the way the white people treated the Japanese and he was happy in Louisiana because they treated him like a white man there. So, when the war came, he wanted to get into it and did. He spent a year in France, came back, joined the VFW, returned to California, and got into the produce business. He did well, got married, and had two children. Then the second war started. When talk about the evacuation started, he wouldn't believe it. He was an American and a veteran of the first war. He thought there might be justification in interning some of the outspokenly pro-Japanese aliens, but he scoffed at the idea of the government doing such a thing to him. When it became apparent that the government proposed to do just that, he burst into a fury of anger and bitterness and swore that if they treated him like a Japanese, he would act like one. Well, you know what happened and he stuck to his words. Along with the other rabidly pro-Japanese, he ended up at the Tule Lake Center, and became a leader in the troublemaking, the strikes and the riots. His wife and children remained in this country, but he elected to go to Japan, a country he didn't know or love, and I'm sure he's extremely unhappy."

"I can't say I blame him."

"I'm sure he wishes he were back here."

"He's got more right than I have."

She swung around to face him, her eyes wide with anger. "You don't understand. Mike doesn't have any more right than you have to be here. He has no right at all any more. It was as if he joined the enemy by antagonizing the people against the government, and you certainly never did that. All you did was to refuse to go in the army and you did so for a reason no worse than that held by a conscientious objector who wasn't a conscientious objector."

"I don't follow you."

"No?" She looked at him pleadingly, her mouth quivering uncontrollably. "I want so much to help," she cried softly, "but nothing seems to make any sense."

He patted her back awkwardly, trying to think of what to say to soothe her.

"Ralph won't come back because of Mike. He's ashamed," she whimpered. "How am I to tell him that it makes no difference what Mike has done? Why is it that Ralph feels he must punish himself for Mike's mistake? Why?"

"He'll come back. Takes time to work these things out."

"I'm sorry," she said, wiping her eyes on the sleeve of the sweater.

"So am I. Hungry too."

They rose together and entered the house.

Inside, they found Kenji getting breakfast ready. He looked up from the frying eggs and bacon and grinned sheepishly. His face was drawn and pale. The cane was hooked to his belt, for he held the spatula in one hand and a water glass half full of whisky in the other.

"We were talking outside," said Ichiro.

"Yeah, nice morning. You should have stayed out a while longer. Breakfast isn't quite ready."

Emi washed her hands and took over at the stove. Sadly, she watched as Kenji limped carefully to the table. "How did you sleep?"

"Not very well." He sipped the whisky appreciatively.

"It—it— She bit her lips for control and managed to utter: "Did it—does it . . .?"

"It does, Emi."

"Oh." She flipped the eggs over unthinkingly. "I—I hope you weren't expecting sunny side up."

Shrugging his shoulders, Ichiro said assuringly: "Makes no difference to me."

Moving about quietly as if fearing to jar the floor, Emi fixed the plates and set them on the table. Ichiro poured the coffee and loaded the toaster.

Kenji leaned back in his chair and gazed through the window above the sink. "Swell day for a picnic," he said. "How about it, Emi? Pack a lunch."

Ichiro retrieved the toast, saying: "Sounds good to me."

"Go home and see your father and your brothers and sisters," she answered. "They'll want to see you before you go. We can have our picnic after you come back. Please."

"I suppose you're right. You always are." He turned to Ichiro: "Feel like going to Portland tomorrow?"

"What's there?"

Emi's fork clattered against the plate. "The VA hospital," she said curtly.

"Sure," he said, looking at Emi, who was avoiding his eyes, "I'd be happy to."

While Ichiro ate and Kenji drank, Emi got up and left them. She returned a few minutes later, shed of the baggy work clothes and wearing a trim, blue-Shantung dress and high heels. He eyed her approvingly, but Kenji seemed to take no notice until it was time for them to leave.

At the door Kenji said fondly to her: "Thanks for not choosing black. You look wonderful."

"I'll wait for you," she said softly, fighting to hold back the tears. She slipped out of her shoes and, when Kenji kissed her lightly on the cheek, grasped him about the neck and put her lips to his.

As he backed the car down the driveway to the road, Ichiro saw her standing very still on the porch, neither waving nor shouting. He had a feeling that she was crying.

5

AN HOUR LATER ICHIRO WAS AT HOME WITH A PROMISE
from Kenji to pick him up early the next morning. As he walked
into the store, his mother looked up from a sheaf of bills and
receipts. If there was any indication of relief, he didn't notice it.

"Where have you been?" she said accusingly.

"Out." On the way home he had felt a twinge of guilt for having spent the night away without telling his folks, but whatever
regrets he might have had were quickly dispelled by the tone of
her voice.

"Where have you been?" she repeated harshly.

"With Kenji, Kanno-san's boy." He approached the counter
and faced her. "You know him."

"Ahh," she said shrilly and distastefully, "that one who lost a
leg. How can you be friends with such a one? He is no good."

He gripped the counter for fear of having his hands free.
"Why?" he rasped.

His discomfort seemed strangely to please her. She raised her
chin perceptibly and answered: "He is not Japanese. He fought
against us. He brought shame to his father and grief to himself. It
is unfortunate he was not killed."

"What's so good about being Japanese?" He felt the pressure
of the wood against his nails.

She seemed not to hear him. Quite calmly, she continued,

talking in the tone of mother to son: "You can be a good boy, a fine son. For my sake and yours do not see him again. It is just as well."

Pushing himself away from the counter, he let his arms drop to his sides. "I'm going to Portland with him tomorrow."

Her face, which had dropped to regard a column of figures on an invoice from the wholesale grocer, jerked up. For a moment, it glared at him, the twisted mouth contorting the slender, austere face into a hard mass of dark hatred. "Do as you will," she cried out. Then the tension drained just as quickly from her face and she was putting her mind to the figures once more.

Through his anger crept up a sudden feeling of remorse and pity. It was an uneasy, guilty sort of sensation which made him want almost to take her into his arms and comfort her, for he saw that the sickness of the soul that was Japanese once and forever was beginning to destroy her mind. Right or wrong, she, in her way, had tried harder than most mothers to be a good mother to him. Did it matter so much that events had ruined the plans which she cherished and turned the once very possible dreams into a madness which was madness only in view of the changed status of the Japanese in America? Was it she who was wrong and crazy not to have found in herself the capacity to accept a country which repeatedly refused to accept her or her sons unquestioningly, or was it the others who were being deluded, the ones, like Kenji, who believed and fought and even gave their lives to protect this country where they could still not rate as first-class citizens because of the unseen walls?

How is one to talk to a woman, a mother who is also a stranger because the son does not know who or what she is? Tell me, Mother, who are you? What is it to be a Japanese? There must have been a time when you were a little girl. You never told me about those things. Tell me now so that I can begin to understand. Tell me about the house in which you lived and of your father and mother, who were my grandparents, whom I have never seen or known because I do not remember your ever speaking of them except to say that they died a long time ago. Tell me everything and just a little bit and a little bit more until their lives and yours and mine are fitted together, for they surely must be. There is time now while there are no customers and you and I are all alone. Begin from the beginning when your hair was straight and black and everyone was Japanese because that was where you were born and America was not yet a country beyond the ocean where fortunes were to be made or an enemy to hate. Quick, now, quick, Mother, what was the name of your favorite school teacher?

While he wrestled with the words which cried to be spoken, the mother glanced up and looked surprised as if to say: Oh, I thought you had gone. She riffled through the papers and dug out an envelope arrayed with an assortment of expensive-looking stamps. It was similar to the other ones from Japan which he had seen in his father's hands two nights previously.

"For Papa," she sneered, flipping it across the counter at him.

He snatched it as it was about to slide over the edge. If he had been about to say something, the moment was gone. Wretchedly, he turned and stumbled into the kitchen.

The father turned from the cutting board, where he was chopping up a head of cabbage for pickling. Around his waist was a bright plastic apron and his wide, stubby, stockinged feet were crammed into a pair of shapeless reed slippers.

"Ichiro, my son," he chuckled, "you are home." He gazed fondly at him and added: "Had a nice time, yes?"

He looked up at his father, not immediately understanding what the old man meant. "Sure," he said, interpreting the sly, friendly smile, "not enough to make up for two years, but I had a big time."

"Ya," the father said gleefully and brought his hands together as might a child in a brief moment of ecstasy, "I was young once too. I know. I know." He picked up the broad, steel blade and sank it energetically into the cabbage.

Whatever the old man thought he knew was probably wilder and lewder and more reckless than the comparatively gentle night that he had spent with Emi. It bothered him to have his

96

father thinking that he had spent the night carousing when such was not the case. He could imagine what it must have been like for the young Japanese new to America and slaving at a killing job on the railroad in Montana under the scorching sun and in the choking dust. Once a month, or even less, the gang of immigrants would manage to make it to town for a weekend. There would be gambling and brawling and hard drinking and sleeping with bought women, and then the money would be gone. Monday would find them swinging their sledge hammers and straining mercilessly against the bars to straighten the hot, gleaming strips of railing while the foul smell of cheap liquor oozed out of their listless bodies. Occasionally, one of them would groan aloud with guilty resolve that he would henceforth stay in camp and save his money and hoard and cherish it into a respectable sum, for was that not what he had come to America for? And there would be murmurs of approbation from those who harbored the same thoughts and were thinking what foolishness it is to work like an animal and have nothing but a sick faintness in the head to show for it. If it is not work and save and go back to Japan a rich man, which is why one comes to America, it is better never to have left Japan. The will is there and, in this moment when the shame and futility is greatest, the vow is renewed once and for always. No more gambling. No more drinking. No more whoring. And the ones who had long since stopped repeating the vow snickered and guffawed and rested their bodies by only seeming to heave when the gang boss commanded but by not really heaving at all so that the younger ones had to exert themselves just that much more and thereby became more fervent in their resolution to walk a straight path.

"I got pretty drunk," he said vaguely.

"Ya, I drink pretty good too." He bent over the cabbage, mumbling: "Pretty good—pretty good."

Ichiro laid the letter on the table and pressed it flat with his hands. "Another letter, Pa. Just came."

Laying down the knife and wiping his hands on a dish towel,

the old man sat at the table and took the letter. Holding it at arm's length, he examined the envelope curiously. "So much money to send such a tiny piece of paper. Still, they write. For Mama, this one. From her sister. They would die with happiness if they saw our little store so full of cans and bottles and boxes of things to eat."

He inserted a pudgy finger under the flap and ran it through from end to end. The thin sheets of rice paper crackled softly as he removed them. He read the letter slowly and deliberately, his eyes barely moving and his mouth silently forming words. After he had finished, he sat staring at the last page for a long time without moving, looking extremely thoughtful. Slowly, he shook his head several times.

"Mama!" he shouted suddenly in a loud voice.

The mother stuck her head through the curtain, looking unhappy about being disturbed.

"Sit down, Mama."

"Who will watch the store?"

"Please. I say sit down."

She did so but not without making it obvious that she disapproved. "What is it?"

The old man shoved the letter before her. "It is from your sister for you. Read."

"I do not have to read it," she said flippantly. "Is this why you ask me to leave the store unattended and sit in the kitchen?" She started to rise.

"No," he said and pushed her roughly back into the chair. "Then I will read."

She glared stubbornly at him, but was momentarily too surprised to defy him.

Ichiro was watching his father, who continued to speak: "It is from your sister who calls you Kin-chan. She has not written before."

"Kin-chan?" voiced the mother stupidly, hardly believing the sound of her own diminutive, which she had almost forgotten.

"Many, many pardons, dear Kin-chan," the father read, "for not having written to you long before this, but I have found it difficult to write of unpleasant things and all has been unpleasant since the disastrous outcome of the war which proved too vast an undertaking even for Japan. You were always such a proud one that I am sure you have suffered more than we who still live at home. I, too, have tried to be proud but it is not an easy thing to do when one's children are always cold and hungry. Perhaps it is punishment for the war. How much better things might have been had there been no war. For myself, I ask nothing, but for the children, if it is possible, a little sugar, perhaps, or the meat which you have in cans or the white powder which can be made into milk with water. And, while I know that I am already asking too much, it would be such a comfort to me and a joy to the children if you could somehow manage to include a few pieces of candy. It has been so long since they have had any. I am begging and feel no shame, for that is the way things are. And I am writing after many long years and immediately asking you to give assistance, which is something that one should not do in a letter until all the niceties have been covered, but, again, that is the way things are. Forgive me, Kin-chan, but the suffering of my children is the reason I must write in this shameless manner. Please, if you can, and I know not that you can, for there have been no answers to the many letters which brother and uncle and cousin have written, but, if you can, just a little will be of such great comfort to us—"

"Not true. I won't listen." She did not, however, move. Nervously, she rubbed her palms against her lap.

"One more place I will read," said the father and, casting aside the first sheet, searched along the second until he found the place he wanted. "Here she writes: 'Remember the river and the secret it holds? You almost drowned that day for the water was deeper and swifter than it looked because of the heavy rains. We were frightened, weren't we? Still, they were wonderful, happy times and, children that we were, we vowed never to tell anyone how close to dying you came. Had it not been for the log on the bank,

I could only have watched you being swallowed up by the river. It is still your secret and mine for I have never told anyone about it. It no longer seems important, but I do think about such things if only to tell myself that there were other and better times."

He laid the sheets on the table and looked firmly at his wife as he had not done for a long, long time. Then, as if sensing the enormity of the thing he had been trying to prove, his mouth trembled weakly and he retreated timidly to the cabbage, which he began industriously to stuff into a stone tub partly filled with salt water. On the cabbage he placed a board, and on the board, a large, heavy stone weight. Not until then did he fearfully cock his head and look askance at the woman who was his wife and the mother of his sons.

She sat stonily with hands in lap, her mouth slightly ajar in the dumb confusion that raged through her mind fighting off the truth which threatened no longer to be untrue. Taking the letter in her hands finally, she perused it with sad eyes which still occasionally sparked with suspicious contempt.

Ichiro watched wordlessly, having understood enough of the letter to realize what was taking place. The passive reaction of his mother surprised him, even caused him to worry uncomfortably.

"Oh, they are so clever," she suddenly said very clearly in a voice slightly nasal, "even to the secret which I had long forgotten. How they must have tortured her to make her reveal it. Poor, poor sister." With letter in hand, she rose and disappeared into the bedroom.

The father glanced nervously at Ichiro and shoved the cabbage-filled stone tub under the sink. "It is happening, ya? She is beginning to see how things are?"

"I don't know, Pa. I think so."

"What is it you think?"

"She didn't look too happy. Maybe it means she's not so sure any more about Japan winning the war."

Muttering under his breath, the father hastened to get the bottle from the cupboard and tilted it hungrily to his mouth. Taking more than he had intended, he gagged noisily and stamped his foot on the floor until the agony passed. Tears streaming down his beet-red face, he stumbled to the table and flopped down hard on the chair. "Aagh," he grunted hoarsely, "good stuff, good stuff."

Ichiro fetched a glass of water, which the old man downed promptly. He nodded gratefully to his son. When his discomfort had passed, he uttered with obvious embarrassment: "I do not mean to hurt her, Ichiro. I do not mean to do any wrong. It is not right for her to go on hugging like a crazy woman to her dreams of madness when they are not so, is it? Is it, Ichiro?"

"No, it's not right."

"I am not wrong, no?"

"No, you're not wrong. She should know."

"Ya," he said, greatly relieved, "I do only what is right. A woman does not have the strength of a man, so it is I who must make her see the truth. She will be all right."

When Ichiro did not answer, the old man, looking concerned again, repeated: "She will be all right, ya, Ichiro?"

"Sure, Pa, sure. Give her time."

"Ya, time. We have plenty time. She will be all right, but look anyway."

"What?"

"Look. Look in the bedroom. See that she is all right now."

His disgust mounting rapidly, Ichiro peeked into the bedroom doorway. In the semi-darkness of the room, the mother sat on the edge of the bed, staring blankly at the sheets of paper in her hand. Her expression was neither that of sadness nor anger. It was a look which meant nothing, for the meaning was gone.

"How is it?" asked the father anxiously. "What is she doing, Ichiro?"

"Sitting," he replied.

"Only sitting?"

"Maybe thinking too. How should I know?"

"I make lunch. After she eat, she be fine. You watch the store, ya?"

"Sure." Ichiro settled himself on a stool behind the cash register and lighted a cigarette. He thought of the trip to Portland the following day and wished that he were already on his way. Then it occurred to him that he might look for work down there without returning home.

I haven't got a home, he said to himself, smiling ironically. Why should I come back? Too many people know me here. Best I can do around Seattle is knock my head against the wall. The sensible thing to do would be to find work in Portland, mind my own business, keep away from the Japs, and there's no reason why things couldn't work out. It's the only chance I've got. I've got to start clean. I've got to get away from Pa and Ma and forget the past. To forget completely would be impossible, but I don't have to stay here where I'll be reminded of it every moment of the day. I don't owe them a thing. They loused up my life for me and loused up their own in the process. Why can't they be like other people, other Japs, and take things as they are? . . . They? Ma's the one. Pa, he's just around. Still, his weakness is just as bad as Ma's strength. He might have prevented all this. He saw what was going on. He could have taken her in hand and straightened her out long ago. Or could he? No, I guess not. Pa's okay, what there is of him, but he missed out someplace. He should have been a woman. He should have been Ma and Ma should have been Pa. Things would have worked out differently then. How, I don't know. I just know they would have.

I won't be running away. I'll be getting away from them and here, but I won't really be running away because the thing that's inside of me is going along and always will be where it is. It's just that I've got to do things right and, in order for things to be right, I've got to be in a new place with new people. I'll talk to Pa about it. Somebody ought to know and I certainly can't tell Ma. She wouldn't understand. She never has and never will. Pa won't really understand either, but he'll agree. Maybe it'll make him happy. He should have been a woman, dammit. Poor Ma. Wonder what kind of hell she's going through now.

The door latch clicked, the bell tinkled, and a small boy walked in. He gaped at Ichiro with the doorknob still in his hand and said: "Who are you?"

"I work here," he said.

"Oh." The boy closed the door and proceeded to the bread rack, where he methodically squeezed each loaf of bread. "Day-old stuff," he grimaced and reluctantly selected a small loaf. He placed it on the counter and examined the coins in his hand. "Gimme two black-whips too," he said.

"Black-whips? What are they?"

"If you work here, how come you don't know? I know more'n you."

"Yeah, you're smart. What are black-whips?"

"Lik-rish. Them over there." He pointed behind Ichiro at the assortment of candy, indicating the long strips of red and black licorice. "I want the black ones."

Without further comment, Ichiro took two strips from the box and handed them to the boy, who put his coins on the counter and departed after again eyeing him skeptically.

He was telling himself that he'd better pack his suitcase, when his father called to say that lunch was ready.

Somehow, he knew that his mother wouldn't be in the kitchen, and she wasn't. After they had been eating for a while, the father got up and looked into the bedroom. "Mama," he said, trying to sound cheerful, "Mama, come and eat. I made fresh rice and it is good and hot. You must eat, Mama."

Rocking hesitantly from one slippered foot to the other, he suddenly made as if to go in but quickly stepped back and continued to watch, the sad concern making the puffiness of his cheeks droop. "Mama," he said more quietly and hopelessly, "one has to eat. It gives strength."

And still he stood and watched, knowing that no amount of urging would move the beaten lump on the edge of the bed and vainly searching for the words to bring her alive. He brushed an arm to his eye and pressed his lips into a near pout. "The letter," he continued, "the letter, Mama. It could be nothing." Hope and encouragement caused his voice to rise in volume: "Your own sister would never write such a letter. You have said so yourself. It is not to be believed. Eat now and forget this foolishness."

Enraged by his father's retreat, Ichiro swore at him: "Goddammit, Pa, leave her alone. Feed your own stupid mouth."

"Ya, ya," he mumbled and returned to the table. He picked distractedly at the food, jabbing the faded chopsticks repeatedly into the plate only to pinch a tiny bit of food, which he placed unappetizingly on his tongue.

"I'm sorry, Pa."

"Ya, but you are right. I do not know what I am doing."

"She'll work it out okay."

"What is she thinking? She is like a baby dog who has lost its mother."

"It'll be all right, Pa," he said impatiently. "It isn't anything she won't live through."

The father weighed his words carefully before answering: "You can say that, but, when I see her sitting and not moving but only sitting like that, I am afraid."

"Can it, Pa," he lashed out angrily. "Nothing's going to happen. Things like this take lots of time. Look at me. Two years, Pa, two years I've thought about it and I'm not through yet. Maybe I'll spend the rest of my life thinking about it."

The old man looked at him, not understanding how it was that his problem could be compared to the mother's. "You are young," he said. "Old minds are not so easily changed. Besides, if it was wrong that you went to prison, it is over, all done. With Mama, it is deeper, much harder."

Hardly believing what his father had said, Ichiro reared back in his chair, then leaned far forward, at the same time bringing his fists down on the table so viciously that the dishes bounced crazily. "You really think that?"

"What is that?"

"About me. About what I've done. I've ruined my life for you, for Ma, for Japan. Can't you see that?"

"You are young, Ichiro. It does not matter so much. I understand, but it is not the same."

"You don't understand."

"Ya, I do. I was young once."

"You're a Jap. How can you understand? No. I'm wrong. You're nothing. You don't understand a damn thing. You don't understand about me and about Ma and you'll never know why it is that Taro had to go in the army. Goddamn fool, that's what you are, Pa, a goddamn fool."

The color crept into the father's face. For a moment it looked as if he would fight back. Lips compressed and breathing hastened, he glared at his son who called him a fool.

Ichiro waited and, in the tense moment, almost found himself hoping that the father would strike back with fists or words or both.

The anger drained away with the color as quickly as it had appeared. "Poor Mama," he mumbled, "poor Mama," and he had to slap his hand to his mouth for he was that close to crying out.

At the tinkle of the doorbell, the father hastily dabbed his eyes with a dishcloth and rose heavily from his chair.

"I'll go," said Ichiro to the man who was neither husband nor father nor Japanese nor American but a diluted mixture of all, and he went to wait on the customer.

6

HOME FOR KENJI WAS AN OLD FRAME, TWO-STORY, SEVEN-room house which the family rented for fifty dollars a month from a Japanese owner who had resettled in Chicago after the war and would probably never return to Seattle. It sat on the top of a steep, unpaved hill and commanded an uninspiring view of clean, gray concrete that was six lanes wide and an assortment of boxy, flat store buildings and spacious super gas-stations.

Kenji eased the car over into the left-turn lane and followed the blinking green arrow toward the hill. At its foot, he braked the car almost to a full stop before carefully starting up, for the sharp angle of the hill and the loose dirt necessitated skill and caution.

As he labored to the top, he saw his father sitting on the porch reading a newspaper. Before he could depress the horn ring, the man looked up and waved casually. He waved back and steered the Oldsmobile into the driveway.

When he walked around the side of the house and came up front, the father said "Hello, Ken" as matter-of-factly as if he had seen his son a few hours previously, and returned his attention to the newspaper to finish the article he had been reading.

"Who's home, Pop?" he asked, holding out the bag.

"Nobody," said the father, taking the present and looking into the bag. It held two fifths of good blended whisky. He was a big man, almost six feet tall and strong. As a painter and paper hanger he had no equal, but he found it sufficient to work only a few days a week and held himself to it, for his children were all grown and he no longer saw the need to drive himself. He smiled warmly and gratefully: "Thank you."

"Sure, Pop. One of these days, I'll bring home a case."

"Last me two days. Better bring a truckful," he said, feigning seriousness.

They laughed together comfortably, the father because he loved his son and the son because he both loved and respected his father, who was a moderate and good man. They walked into the house, the father making the son precede him.

In the dining room the father deposited the two new bottles with a dozen others in the china cabinet. "I'm fixed for a long time," he said. "That's a good feeling."

"You're really getting stocked up," said Kenji.

"The trust and faith and love of my children," he said proudly. "You know I don't need clothes or shaving lotion in fancy jars or suitcases or pajamas, but whisky I can use. I'm happy."

"Are you, Pop?"

The father sat down opposite his son at the polished mahogany table and took in at a glance the new rugs and furniture and lamps and the big television set with the radio and phonograph all built into one impressive, blond console. "All I did was feed you and clothe you and spank you once in a while. All of a sudden, you're all grown up. The government gives you money, Hisa and Toyo are married to fine boys, Hana and Tom have splendid jobs, and Eddie is in college and making more money in a part-time job than I did for all of us when your mother died. No longer do I have to work all the time, but only two or three days a week and I have more money than I can spend. Yes, Ken, I am happy and I wish your mother were here to see all this."

"I'm happy too, Pop." He shifted his legs to make himself comfortable and winced unwillingly.

Noticing, the father screwed his face as if the pain were in himself, for it was. Before the pain turned to sorrow, before the suffering for his son made his lips quiver as he held back the tears, he hastened into the kitchen and came back with two jigger-glasses.

"I am anxious to sample your present," he said jovially, but his movements were hurried as he got the bottle from the cabinet and fumbled impatiently with the seal.

Kenji downed his thankfully and watched his father take the other glass and sniff the whisky appreciatively before sipping it leisurely. He lifted the bottle toward his son.

"No more, Pop," refused Kenji. "That did it fine."

The father capped the bottle and put it back. He closed the cabinet door and let his hand linger on the knob as if ashamed of himself for having tried to be cheerful when he knew that the pain was again in his son and the thought of death hovered over them.

"Pop."

"Yes?" He turned slowly to face his son.

"Come on. Sit down. It'll be all right."

Sitting down, the father shook his head, saying: "I came to America to become a rich man so that I could go back to the village in Japan and be somebody. I was greedy and ambitious and proud. I was not a good man or an intelligent one, but a young fool. And you have paid for it."

"What kind of talk is that?" replied Kenji, genuinely grieved. "That's not true at all."

"That is what I think nevertheless. I am to blame."

"It'll be okay, Pop. Maybe they won't even operate."

"When do you go?"

"Tomorrow morning."

"I will go with you."

"No." He looked straight at his father.

In answer, the father merely nodded, acceding to his son's wish because his son was a man who had gone to war to fight for the abundance and happiness that pervaded a Japanese household in America and that was a thing he himself could never fully comprehend except to know that it was very dear. He had long forgotten when it was that he had discarded the notion of a return to Japan but remembered only that it was the time when this country which he had no intention of loving had suddenly begun to become a part of him because it was a part of his children and he saw and felt it in their speech and joys and sorrows and hopes and he was a part of them. And in the dying of the foolish dreams which he had brought to America, the richness of the life that was possible in this foreign country destroyed the longing for a past that really must not have been as precious as he imagined or else he would surely not have left it. Where else could a man, left alone with six small children, have found it possible to have had so much with so little? He had not begged or borrowed or gone to the city for welfare assistance. There had been times of hunger and despair and seeming hopelessness, but did it not mean something now that he could look around and feel the love of the men and women who were once only children?

And there was the one who sat before him, the one who had come to him and said calmly that he was going into the army. It could not be said then that it mattered not that he was a Japanese son of Japanese parents. It had mattered. It was because he was Japanese that the son had to come to his Japanese father and simply state that he had decided to volunteer for the army instead of being able to wait until such time as the army called him. It was because he was Japanese and, at the same time, had to prove to the world that he was not Japanese that the turmoil was in his soul and urged him to enlist. There was confusion, but, underneath it, a conviction that he loved America and would fight and die for it because he did not wish to live anyplace else. And the father, also confused, understood what the son had not said and gave his consent. It was not a time for clear thinking because the sense of loyalty had become dispersed and the shaken faith of an American interned in an American concentration camp was indeed a flimsy thing. So, on this steadfast bit of conviction that remained, and knowing not what the future held, this son had gone to war to prove that he deserved to enjoy those rights which should rightfully have been his.

And he remembered that a week after Kenji had gone to a camp in Mississippi, the neighbor's son, an American soldier since before Pearl Harbor, had come to see his family which was in a camp enclosed by wire fencing and had guards who were American soldiers like himself. And he had been present when the soldier bitterly spoke of how all he did was dump garbage and wash dishes and take care of the latrines. And the soldier swore and ranted and could hardly make himself speak of the time when the president named Roosevelt had come to the camp in Kansas and all the American soldiers in the camp who were Japanese had been herded into a warehouse and guarded by other American soldiers with machine guns until the president named Roosevelt had departed. And he had gone to his own cubicle with the seven steel cots and the potbellied stove and the canvas picnic-chairs from Sears Roebuck and cried for Kenji, who was now a soldier and would not merely turn bitter and swear if the army let him do only such things as the soldier had spoken of, but would be driven to protest more violently because he was the quiet one with the deep feelings whose anger was a terrible thing. But, with training over, Kenji had written that he was going to Europe, and the next letter was from Italy, where the Americans were fighting the Germans, and he found relief in the knowledge, partly because Kenji was fighting and he knew that was what his son wished and partly because the enemy was German and not Japanese.

He thought he remembered that he had not wanted Kenji to go into the army. But when he was asked, he had said yes. And so this son had come back after long months in a hospital with one good leg and another that was only a stick where the other good one had been. Had he done right? Should he not have forbidden him? Should he not have explained how it was not sensible for Japanese to fight a war against Japanese? If what he had done was wrong, how was it so and why?

"Would you," he said to his son, "have stayed out of the army if I had forbidden it?"

Kenji did not answer immediately, for the question came as

a surprise to disturb the long, thought-filled silence. "I don't think so, Pop," he started out hesitantly. He paused, delving into his mind for an explanation, then said with great finality: "No, I would have gone anyway."

"Of course," said the father, finding some assurance in the answer.

Kenji pushed himself to a standing position and spoke gently: "You're not to blame, Pop. Every time we get to talking like this, I know you're blaming yourself. Don't do it. Nobody's to blame, nobody."

"To lose a leg is not the worst thing, but, to lose a part of it and then a little more and a little more again until . . . Well, I don't understand. You don't deserve it." He shrugged his shoulders wearily against the weight of his terrible anguish.

"I'm going up to take a nap." He walked a few steps and turned back to his father. "I'll go upstairs and lie down on the bed and I won't sleep right away because the leg will hurt a little and I'll be thinking. And I'll think that if things had been different, if you had been different, it might have been that I would also not have been the same and maybe you would have kept me from going into the war and I would have stayed out and had both my legs. But, you know, every time I think about it that way, I also have to think that, had such been the case, you and I would probably not be sitting down and having a drink together and talking or not talking as we wished. If my leg hurts, so what? We're buddies, aren't we? That counts. I don't worry about anything else."

Up in his room, he stretched out on his back on the bed and thought about what he had said to his father. It made a lot of sense. If, in the course of things, the pattern called for a stump of a leg that wouldn't stay healed, he wasn't going to decry the fact, for that would mean another pattern with attendant changes which might not be as perfectly desirable as the one he cherished. Things are as they should be, he assured himself, and, feeling greatly at peace, sleep came with surprising ease.

After Kenji had left him, the father walked down the hill to the neighborhood Safeway and bought a large roasting chicken. It was a fat bird with bulging drumsticks and, as he headed back to the house with both arms supporting the ingredients of an ample family feast, he thought of the lean years and the six small ones and the pinched, hungry faces that had been taught not to ask for more but could not be taught how not to look hungry when they were in fact quite hungry. And it was during those years that it seemed as if they would never have enough.

But such a time had come. It had come with the war and the growing of the children and it had come with the return of the thoughtful son whose terrible wound paid no heed to the cessation of hostilities. Yet, the son had said he was happy and the father was happy also for, while one might grieve for the limb that was lost and the pain that endured, he chose to feel gratitude for the fact that the son had come back alive even if only for a brief while.

And he remembered what the young sociologist had said in halting, pained Japanese at one of the family-relations meetings he had attended while interned in the relocation center because it was someplace to go. The instructor was a recent college graduate who had later left the camp to do graduate work at a famous Eastern school. He, short fellow that he was, had stood on an orange crate so that he might be better heard and seen by the sea of elderly men and women who had been attracted to the mess hall because they too had nothing else to do and nowhere else to go. There had been many meetings, although it had early become evident that lecturer and audience were poles apart, and if anything had been accomplished it was that the meetings helped to pass the time, and so the instructor continued to blast away at the unyielding wall of indifference and the old people came to pass an hour or two. But it was on this particular night that the small sociologist, struggling for the words painstakingly and not always correctly selected from his meager knowledge of the Japanese language, had managed to impart a message of great truth. And this message was that the old Japanese, the fathers and mothers, who sat courteously attentive, did not know their own sons and daughters.

"How many of you are able to sit down with your own sons and own daughters and enjoy the companionship of conversation? How many, I ask? If I were to say none of you, I would not be far from the truth." He paused, for the grumbling was swollen with anger and indignation, and continued in a loud, shouting voice before it could engulf him: "You are not displeased because of what I said but because I have hit upon the truth. And I know it to be true because I am a Nisei and you old ones are like my own father and mother. If we are children of America and not the sons and daughters of our parents, it is because you have failed. It is because you have been stupid enough to think that growing rice in muddy fields is the same as growing a giant fir tree. Change, now, if you can, even if it may be too late, and become companions to your children. This is America, where you have lived and worked and suffered for thirty and forty years. This is not Japan. I will tell you what it is like to be an American boy or girl. I will tell you what the relationship between parents and children is in an American family. As I speak, compare what I say with your own families." And so he had spoken and the old people had listened and, when the meeting was over, they got up and scattered over the camp toward their assigned cubicles. Some said they would attend no more lectures; others heaped hateful abuse upon the young fool who dared to have spoken with such disrespect; and then there was the elderly couple, the woman silently following the man, who stopped at another mess hall, where a dance was in progress, and peered into the dimly lit room and watched the young boys and girls gliding effortlessly around to the blaring music from a phonograph. Always before, they had found something to say about the decadent ways of an amoral nation, but, on this evening, they watched longer than usual and searched longingly to recognize their own daughter, whom they knew to be at the dance but who was only an unrecognizable shadow among the other shadows . . .

Halting for a moment to shift the bag, Kenji's father started up the hill with a smile on his lips. He was glad that the market had had such a fine roasting chicken. There was nothing as satisfying as sitting at a well-laden table with one's family whether the occasion was a holiday or a birthday or a home-coming of some member or, yes, even if it meant somone was going away.

Please come back, Ken, he said to himself, please come back and I will have for you the biggest, fattest chicken that ever graced a table, American or otherwise.

Hanako, who was chubby and pleasant and kept books for three doctors and a dentist in a downtown office, came home before Tom, who was big and husky like his father and had gone straight from high school into a drafting job at an aircraft plant. She had seen the car in the driveway and smelled the chicken in the oven and, smiling sympathetically with the father, put a clean cloth on the table and took out the little chest of Wm. & Rogers Silverplate.

While she was making the salad, Tom came home bearing a bakery pie in a flat, white box. "Hello, Pop, Sis," he said, putting the box on the table. "Where's Ken?"

"Taking a nap," said Hanako.

"Dinner about ready?" He sniffed appreciatively and rubbed his stomach in approval.

"Just about," smiled his sister.

"Psychic, that's what I am."

"What?"

"I say I'm psychic. I brought home a lemon meringue. Chicken and lemon meringue. Boy! Don't you think so?"

"What's that?"

"About my being psychic."

"You're always bringing home lemon meringue. Coincidence, that's all."

"How soon do we eat?"

"I just got through telling you—in a little while," she replied a bit impatiently.

"Good. I'm starved. I'll wash up and rouse the boy." He started to head for the stairs but turned back thoughtfully. "What's the occasion?" he asked.

"Ken has to go to the hospital again," said the father kindly. "Wash yourself at the sink and let him sleep a while longer. We will eat when he wakes up."

"Sure," said Tom, now sharing the unspoken sadness and terror which abided in the hearts of his father and sister. He went to the sink and, clearing it carefully of the pots and dishes, washed himself as quietly as possible.

It was a whole hour before Kenji came thumping down the stairs. It was the right leg, the good one, that made the thumps which followed the empty pauses when the false leg was gently lowered a step. When he saw the family sitting lazily around the table, he knew that they had waited for him.

"You shouldn't have waited," he said, a little embarrassed. "I slept longer than I intended."

"We're waiting for the chicken," lied the father. "Takes time to roast a big one."

Hanako agreed too hastily: "Oh, yes, I've never known a chicken to take so long. Ought to be just about ready now." She trotted into the kitchen and, a moment later, shouted back: "It's ready. Mmmm, can you smell it?"

"That's all I've been doing," Tom said with a famished grin. "Let's get it out here."

"Sorry I made you wait," smiled Kenji at his brother.

Tom, regretting his impatience, shook his head vigorously. "No, it's the bird, like Pop said. You know how he is. Always gets 'em big and tough. This one's made of cast iron." He followed Hanako to help bring the food from the kitchen.

No one said much during the first part of the dinner. Tom ate ravenously. Hanako seemed about to say something several times but couldn't bring herself to speak. The father kept looking at Kenji without having to say what it was that he felt for his son. Surprisingly, it was Tom who broached the subject which was on all their minds.

"What the hell's the matter with those damn doctors?" He slammed his fork angrily against the table.

"Tom, please," said Hanako, looking deeply concerned.

"No, no, no," he said, gesturing freely with his hands, "I won't please shut up. If they can't fix you up, why don't they get somebody who can? They're killing you. What do they do when you go down there? Give you aspirins?" Slumped in his chair, he glared furiously at the table.

The father grasped Tom's arm firmly. "If you can't talk sense, don't."

"It's okay, Tom. This'll be a short trip. I think it's just that the brace doesn't fit right."

"You mean that?" He looked hopefully at Kenji.

"Sure. That's probably what it is. I'll only be gone a few days. Doesn't really hurt so much, but I don't want to take any chances."

"Gee, I hope you're right."

"I ought to know. A few more trips and they'll make me head surgeon down there."

"Yeah," Tom smiled, not because of the joke, but because he was grateful for having a brother like Kenji.

"Eat," reminded the father, "baseball on television tonight, you know."

"I'll get the pie," Hanako said and hastened to the kitchen.

"Lemon meringue," said Tom hungrily, as he proceeded to clean up his plate.

The game was in its second inning when they turned the set on, and they had hardly gotten settled down when Hisa and Toyo came with their husbands and children.

Tom grumbled good naturedly and, giving the newcomers a hasty nod, pulled up closer to the set, preparing to watch the game under what would obviously be difficult conditions.

Hats and coats were shed and piled in the corner and everyone talked loudly and excitedly, as if they had not seen each other for a long time. Chairs were brought in from the dining room and, suddenly, the place was full and noisy and crowded and comfortable.

The father gave up trying to follow the game and bounced a year-old granddaughter on his knee while two young grandsons fought to conquer the other knee. The remaining three grandchildren were all girls, older, more well-behaved, and they huddled on the floor around Tom to watch the baseball game.

Hisa's husband sat beside Kenji and engaged him in conversation, mostly about fishing and about how he'd like to win a car in the Salmon Derby because his was getting old and a coupe wasn't too practical for a big family. He had the four girls and probably wouldn't stop until he hit a boy and things weren't so bad, but he couldn't see his way to acquiring a near-new used car for a while. And then he got up and went to tell the same thing to his father-in-law, who was something of a fisherman himself. No sooner had he moved across the room than Toyo's husband, who was soft-spoken and mild but had been a captain in the army and sold enough insurance to keep two cars in the double garage behind a large brick house in a pretty good neighborhood, slid into the empty space beside Kenji and asked him how he'd been and so on and talked about a lot of other things when he really wanted to talk to Kenji about the leg and didn't know how.

Then came the first lull when talk died down and the younger children were showing signs of drowsiness and everyone smiled thoughtfully and contentedly at one another. Hanako suggested refreshments, and when the coffee and milk and pop and cookies and ice cream were distributed, everyone got his second wind and immediately discovered a number of things which they had forgotten to discuss.

Kenji, for the moment alone, looked at all of them and said to himself: Now's as good a time as any to go. I won't wait until tomorrow. In another thirty minutes Hana and Toyo and the kids and their fathers will start stretching and heading for their hats and coats. Then someone will say "Well, Ken" in a kind of hesitant way and, immediately, they will all be struggling for something to say about my going to Portland because Hana called them and told them to come over because I'm going down there again and that's why they'll have to say something about it. If I had said to Pop that I was going the day after tomorrow, we would have had a big feast with everyone here for it tomorrow night. I don't want that. There's no need for it. I don't want Toyo to cry and Hana to dab at her eyes and I don't want everyone standing around trying to say goodbye and not being able to make themselves leave because maybe they won't see me again.

He started to get up and saw Hanako looking at him. "I'm just going to get a drink," he said.

"Stay, I'll get it," she replied.

"No. It'll give me a chance to stretch." He caught his father's eye and held it for a moment.

Without getting his drink, he slipped quietly out to the back porch and stood and waited and listened to the voices inside.

He heard Hisa's husband yell something to one of his girls and, the next minute, everyone was laughing amusedly. While he was wondering what cute deviltry the guilty one had done, his father came through the kitchen and out to stand beside him.

"You are going."

Kenji looked up and saw the big shoulders sagging wearily. "I got a good rest, Pop. This way, I'll be there in the morning and it's easier driving at night. Not so many cars, you know."

"It's pretty bad this time, isn't it?"

"Yes," he said truthfully, because he could not lie to his father, "it's not like before, Pop. It's different this time. The pain is heavier, deeper. Not sharp and raw like the other times. I don't know why. I'm scared."

"If . . . if . . ." Throwing his arm around his son's neck impulsively, the father hugged him close. "You call me every day. Every day, you understand?"

"Sure, Pop. Explain to everyone, will you?" He pulled himself free and looked at his father nodding, unable to speak.

Pausing halfway down the stairs, he listened once more for the voices in the house.

Hoarsely, in choked syllables, his father spoke to him: "Every day, Ken, don't forget. I will be home."

"Bye, Pop." Feeling his way along the dark drive with his cane, he limped to the car. Behind the wheel, he had to sit and wait until the heaviness had lifted from his chest and relieved the mistiness of his eyes. He started the motor and turned on the headlights and their brilliant glare caught fully the father standing ahead. Urged by an overwhelming desire to rush back to him and be with him for a few minutes longer, Kenji's hand fumbled for the door handle. At that moment, the father raised his arm once slowly in farewell. Quickly, he pulled back out of the driveway and was soon out of sight of father and home and family.

He fully intended to drive directly to the grocery store to get Ichiro, but found himself drawn to the Club Oriental. Parking in the vacant lot where only the previous night Ichiro had experienced his humiliation, he limped through the dark alley to the club.

It was only a little after ten, but the bar and tables were crowded. Ignoring several invitations to sit at tables of acquaintances, he threaded his way to the end of the bar and had only to wait a moment before Al saw him and brought the usual bourbon and water.

Not until he was on his third leisurely drink did he manage to secure a stool. It was between strangers, and for that he was grateful. He didn't want to talk or be talked to. Through the vast mirror ahead, he studied the faces alongside and behind him. By craning a bit, he could even catch an occasional glimpse of couples on the dance floor.

It's a nice place, he thought. When a fellow goes away, he likes to take something along to remember and this is what I'm taking. It's not like having a million bucks and sitting in the Waldorf with a long-stemmed beauty, but I'm a small guy with small wants and this is my Waldorf. Here, as long as I've got the price of a drink, I can sit all night and be among friends. I can relax and drink and feel sad or happy or high and nobody much gives a damn, since they feel the same way. It's a good feeling, a fine feeling.

He followed Al around with his eyes until the bartender looked back at him and returned the smile.

The help knows me and likes me.

Swinging around on the stool, he surveyed the crowd and acknowledged a number of greetings and nods.

I've got a lot of friends here and they know and like me.

Jim Eng, the slender, dapper Chinese who ran the place, came out of the office with a bagful of change and brought it behind the bar to check the register. As he did so, he grinned at Kenji and inquired about his leg.

Even the management's on my side. It's like a home away from home only more precious because one expects home to be like that. Not many places a Jap can go to and feel so completely at ease. It must be nice to be white and American and to be able to feel like this no matter where one goes to, but I won't cry about that. There's been a war and, suddenly, things are better for the Japs and the Chinks and—

There was a commotion at the entrance and Jim Eng slammed the cash drawer shut and raced toward the loud voices. He spoke briefly to someone in the office, probably to find out the cause of the disturbance, and then stepped outside. As he did so, Kenji caught sight of three youths, a Japanese and two Negroes.

After what sounded like considerable loud and excited shouting, Jim Eng stormed back in and resumed his task at the register though with hands shaking.

When he had calmed down a little, someone inquired: "What's the trouble?"

"No trouble," he said in a high-pitched voice which he was

endeavoring to keep steady. "That crazy Jap boy Floyd tried to get in with two niggers. That's the second time he tried that. What's the matter with him?"

A Japanese beside Kenji shouted out sneeringly: "Them ignorant cotton pickers make me sick. You let one in and before you know it, the place will be black as night."

"Sure," said Jim Eng, "sure. I got no use for them. Nothing but trouble they make and I run a clean place."

"Hail Columbia," said a small, drunken voice.

"Oh, you Japs and Chinks, I love you all," rasped out a brash redhead who looked as if she had come directly from one of the burlesque houses without changing her make-up. She struggled to her feet, obviously intending to launch into further oratory.

Her escort, a pale, lanky Japanese screamed "Shut up!" and, at the same time, pulled viciously at her arm, causing her to tumble comically into the chair.

Everyone laughed, or so it seemed, and quiet and decency and cleanliness and honesty returned to the Club Oriental.

Leaving his drink unfinished, Kenji left the club without returning any of the farewells which were directed at him.

He drove aimlessly, torturing himself repeatedly with the question which plagued his mind and confused it to the point of madness. Was there no answer to the bigotry and meanness and smallness and ugliness of people? One hears the voice of the Negro or Japanese or Chinese or Jew, a clear and bell-like intonation of the common struggle for recognition as a complete human being and there is a sense of unity and purpose which inspires one to hope and optimism. One encounters obstacles, but the wedge of the persecuted is not without patience and intelligence and humility, and the opposition weakens and wavers and disperses. And the one who is the Negro or Japanese or Chinese or Jew is further fortified and gladdened with the knowledge that the democracy is a democracy in fact for all of them. One has hope, for he has reason to hope, and the quest for completeness seems to be a thing near at hand, and then . . .

the woman with the dark hair and large nose who has barely learned to speak English makes a big show of vacating her bus seat when a Negro occupies the other half. She stamps indignantly down the aisle, hastening away from the contamination which is only in her contaminated mind. The Negro stares silently out of the window, a proud calmness on his face, which hides the boiling fury that is capable of murder.

and then . . .

a sweet-looking Chinese girl is at a high-school prom with a white boy. She has risen in the world, or so she thinks, for it is evident in her expression and manner. She does not entirely ignore the other Chinese and Japanese at the dance, which would at least be honest, but worse, she flaunts her newly found status in their faces with haughty smiles and overly polite phrases.

and then . . .

there is the small Italian restaurant underneath a pool parlor, where the spaghetti and chicken is hard to beat. The Japanese, who feels he is better than the Chinese because his parents made him so, comes into the restaurant with a Jewish companion, who is a good Jew and young and American and not like the kike bastards from the countries from which they've been kicked out, and waits patiently for the waiter. None of the waiters come, although the place is quite empty and two of them are talking not ten feet away. All his efforts to attract them failing, he stalks toward them. The two, who are supposed to wait on the tables but do not, scurry into the kitchen. In a moment they return with the cook, who is also the owner, and he tells the Japanese that the place is not for Japs and to get out and go back to Tokyo.

and then . . .

the Negro who was always being mistaken for a white man becomes a white man and he becomes hated by the Negroes with whom he once hated on the same side. And the young Japanese hates the not-so-young Japanese who is more Japanese than himself, and the not-so-young, in turn, hates the old Japanese who is all Japanese and, therefore, even more Japanese than he . . .

And Kenji thought about these things and tried to organize them in his mind so that the pattern could be seen and studied and the answers deduced therefrom. And there was no answer because there was no pattern and all he could feel was that the world was full of hatred. And he drove on and on and it was almost two o'clock when he parked in front of the grocery store.

The street was quiet, deathly so after he had cut the ignition. Down a block or so, he saw the floodlighted sign painted on the side of a large brick building. It said: "444 Rooms. Clean. Running Water. Reasonable Rates." He had been in there once a long time ago and he knew that it was just a big flophouse full of drunks and vagrant souls. Only a few tiny squares of yellowish light punctuated the softly shimmering rows of windowpanes. Still, the grocery store was brightly lit.

Wondering why, he slid out of the car and peered through the upper half of the door, which was of glass. He was immediately impressed with the neatness of the shelves and the cleanness of the paint on the walls and woodwork. Inevitably, he saw Ichiro's mother and it gave him an odd sensation as he watched her methodically empty a case of evaporated milk and line the cans with painful precision on the shelf. He tried the door and found it locked and decided not to disturb her until she finished the case. It was a long wait, for she grasped only a single can with both hands each time she stooped to reach into the box. Finally, she finished and stood as if examining her handiwork.

Kenji rapped briskly on the door but she took no notice. Instead, she reached out suddenly with her arms and swept the cans to the floor. Then she just stood with arms hanging limply at her sides, a small girl of a woman who might have been pouting from the way her head drooped and her back humped.

So intent was he upon watching her that he jumped when the door opened. It was Ichiro, dressed only in a pair of slacks.

"You're early," he said, blinking his eyes sleepily.

"Yes. Is it okay?"

"Sure. Be ready in a minute. Can't get any sleep anyway." He shut the door without asking Kenji inside and disappeared into the back.

Looking back to where the woman had been, he was astonished not to see her. He searched about and eventually spied her on hands and knees retrieving a can which had rolled under one of the display islands. He followed her as she crawled around in pursuit of more cans, which she was now packing back into the case. Ichiro came out with a suitcase and went directly to the car.

Kenji looked once more before driving off and noticed that she, having gathered all the cans, was once more lining them on the same shelf.

"We'll make good time driving at night. Won't be so many cars on the road." Out of the corner of his eye he watched Ichiro light a cigarette.

"Snapped," he said harshly.

"What?"

"Snapped. Flipped. Messed up her gears." Drawing deeply on the cigarette, he exhaled a stream of smoke noisily. He twisted about on the seat as if in great anguish.

"Is it all right for you to be going?"

"Sure, sure, nothing I can do. It's been coming for a long time."

"You knew?"

Ichiro rolled down the window and flung the lighted butt into the wind. As it whisked back, spraying specks of red into the dark, he craned his neck to watch it until it disappeared from sight. "Something had to happen," he said, cranking the window shut. "Still, I guess you could say she's been crazy a long time."

"How long?"

"I don't know. Maybe ever since the day she was born." He turned abruptly to face Kenji and said appealingly: "Tell me, what's your father like?"

"My dad is one swell guy. We get along."

"Why?"

"I don't know why. We just do."

Ichiro laughed.

124

"What's funny?"

"Things, everything's funny because nothing makes sense. There was an Italian fellow in prison I used to talk to. Sometimes I'd confide in him because he once wanted to be a priest and so he was the kind of guy you could talk to. He got sent up for taking money from old ladies. You can see what I mean. I used to tell him about how tough it was for kids of immigrants because parents and kids were so different and they never really got to know each other. He knew what I meant because his folks were born in Italy and raised there. And he used to tell me not to worry because there would come a time when I'd feel as if I really knew my folks. He said the time would come when I grew up. Just how or when was hard to say because it's different with everyone. With him, it was when he was thirty-five and went home on parole after four years in prison. Then it happened. He sat at the kitchen table like he'd been doing all his life and he looked at his mother and then at his father and he no longer had the urge to eat and run. He wanted to talk to them and they talked all through that night and he was so happy he cried."

Slowing down a little, Kenji pointed through the windshield. "That road goes to Emi's place. Go see her when you get a chance."

Ichiro didn't answer, but he seemed to be studying the landmarks. "It won't ever happen to me," he said.

"What won't happen?"

"The thing that happened to the Italian."

"You never can tell."

"She's really crazy now. You saw her with those milk cans. Ever since eight o'clock tonight. Puts them on the shelf, knocks them down, and puts them back up again. What's she trying to prove?"

"Aren't you worried?"

"No. I've been more worried about you."

After that, they didn't talk very much. Some eighty miles out of Seattle, they stopped for coffee and sandwiches at the roadside café and then Ichiro took over the wheel. There were few cars on the road and he drove swiftly, not bothering to slow down from sixty-five or seventy to twenty-five or thirty as specified on the signs leading into small towns where nothing was open or no one was up at about five o'clock in the morning. As the needle of the speedometer hovered just under seventy for almost an hour without any letdown except for forced caution at curves, monotony slowly set in and it began to feel as if all that separated them from Portland was an interminable stretch of asphalt and concrete cutting through the darkness. Occasionally, Ichiro would feel his foot easing down even harder on the accelerator pedal, but he restrained himself from tempting danger. Rounding a curve and shooting down a long hill, he saw a bunch of houses sitting darkly and quietly at the bottom in the filmy haze of earliest morning. The trees and foliage along the highway thinned out visibly as the car sped closer to the village and, as always, the signs began to appear. "Approaching Midvale, Lower Speed to 40. Speed Laws Strictly Enforced." "You Are Now Entering Midvale. Population 367." "20 MPH. Street Patrolled." He had almost traversed the eight or ten blocks which comprised the village and was looking for the sign which would tell him that he was leaving Midvale and thank you for observing the law and come back again, when he became aware of the siren building up to an awful scream in the night.

"Damn," he uttered, "lousy bastards."

"Slow down," said Kenji, suddenly coming alive. He moved to the middle of the seat. "When he pulls up ahead, switch places."

The plain, black Ford sedan with the blinking red light on its roof passed and cut in ahead of them. Just before they came to a halt, Ichiro rose and let Kenji slide in behind him.

They saw the big, uniformed cop get out of the Ford and lumber toward them. Pointing a long flashlight into the car, he played it mercilessly on their faces. "Going pretty fast," he said.

They didn't answer, knowing that whatever they said would be wrongly construed.

"What were you doing?" the cop demanded.

"Forty-five, maybe fifty," said Kenji, blinking into the light.

"Seventy," said the cop. "You were doing seventy." He walked around the car and got in beside Ichiro. "Drive back through town."

Kenji made a U-turn and drove slowly to the sign which said "20 MPH. Street Patrolled."

"You Japs can read, can't you?"

"Sure," said Kenji.

"Read what it says there," he ordered as he shined his light on the sign.

"Twenty M-P-H. Street Patrolled," read Kenji in a flat, low voice.

Then they drove back to where the Ford was parked.

Even sitting down, the cop towered over them, his broad, heavy features set into an uncompromising grimace. "Well?" he said.

"We're guilty. Put us in jail," answered Kenji. "We're in no hurry."

The cop laughed. "Funny. You got a sense of humor." He reared back and, when he settled down, his manner was obviously more friendly. "Tell you what. Next court won't be until the day after tomorrow. Now, you don't want to come all the way back here and get fined fifty bucks. That's what it's going to be, you know. You haven't got a chance."

"No, I guess we haven't." Kenji was not going to accept the cordiality of the cop.

"You might just happen to go over to my car and accidentally drop ten bucks on the seat. Simple?"

"We haven't got ten bucks between us."

"Five? I'm not hard to please." He was grinning openly now.

"Give me the ticket. I'll show up for court." There was no mistaking the enmity in his voice.

"All right, smart guy, let's have your license." The cop pulled out his pad furiously and began scribbling out a ticket.

Hurtling over the road again, with Kenji driving intently as if trying to flee as quickly as possible from the infuriating incident,

Ichiro picked up the ticket and studied it under the illumination from the dash. "Son of a bitch," he groaned, "he's got us down for eighty, drunk driving, and attempting to bribe."

Before he could say more of what was seething through his mind, Kenji grabbed the piece of paper out of his hand and, crumpling it hatefully, flung it out of the window.

Not until they got into Portland two hours later and were having breakfast did they feel the necessity to talk. Ichiro was watching an individual in overalls, with a lunch box under one arm, pounding determinedly on a pinball machine.

"What will you do?" he asked Ichiro.

Waiting until the waitress had set their plates down, Ichiro replied: "I'm not sure. I'll be all right."

"When you get ready to go, take the car."

Sensing something in the way Kenji had spoken, Ichiro looked up uncomfortably. "I'll wait for you. I might even look for a job down here."

"Fine. You ought to do something."

"When will you know about the leg?"

"A day or two."

"What do you think?"

"I'm worried. I get a feeling that this is it."

Shocked for a moment by the implication of his friend's words, Ichiro fiddled uneasily with his fork. When he spoke it was with too much eagerness. "That's no way to talk," he said confidently, but feeling inside his own terror. "They'll fix you up. I know they will. Hell, in a few days, we'll go back to Seattle together."

"Just before I left last night, I told my pop about it. I told him it was different this time. I told him I was scared. I've never lied to him."

"But you can be wrong. You've got to be wrong. A fellow just doesn't say this is it, I'm going to die. Things never turn out the way you think. You're going to be okay."

"Sure, maybe I will. Maybe I am wrong," he said, but, in the way he said it, he might just as well have said this is one time when I know that, no matter how much I wish I were wrong, I don't think I am.

The waitress came back with a silex pot and poured coffee into their cups. The overalled man at the pinball machine sighted his bus coming down the street and, shooting three balls in quick succession, dashed out of the café.

Ichiro buttered a half-slice of toast and chewed off a piece almost reluctantly. When they had finished he picked up the bill for a dollar-eighty and noticed that Kenji left a half dollar on the table.

Driving through town to the hospital, they ran into the morning traffic and it was nearly nine o'clock or almost an hour after leaving the café when they reached their destination. It was a big, new hospital with plenty of glass and neat, green lawns on all sides.

They walked up the steps together and halted in front of the doorway. Kenji was smiling.

Ichiro gazed at him wonderingly. "You seem to be all right."

"I was thinking about that cop. I bet he can't wait to see me in court and get the book thrown at me. He'll have to come a long ways to catch up with this Jap." He stuck out his hand stiffly.

Grabbing it but not shaking, Ichiro managed with some distinctness: "I'll be in to see you."

"Don't wait too long." Avoiding the revolving door, he stepped to the side and entered the hospital through a swinging glass door.

7

ALONE AND FEELING VERY MUCH HIS ALONENESS, ICHIRO drove the Oldsmobile back into the city proper and found a room in a small, clean hotel where the rates seemed reasonable. Having picked up a newspaper in the lobby, he turned to the classified section and studied the job ads. Most of them were for skilled or technical help, and only after considerable searching was he finally able to encircle with pencil three jobs which he felt he might be able to investigate with some degree of hope. Putting the paper aside, he washed, shaved, and put on a clean shirt.

I mustn't hesitate, he told himself. If I don't start right now and make myself look for work, I'll lose my nerve. There's no one to help me or give me courage now. All I know is that I've just got to find work.

With the folded paper under his arm, he walked the six blocks to the hotel which was advertising for porters. It was a big hotel with a fancy marquee that extended out to the street and, as he walked past it, he noticed a doorman stationed at the entrance. He went down to the end of the block and approached the hotel once more. He paused to light a cigarette. Then, when he saw the doorman watching, he started toward him.

"If it's a job you want, son, take the employee's entrance in the alley," said the doorman before he could speak.

He muttered his thanks a bit unsteadily and proceeded around and through the alley. There was a sign over the door for which he was looking, and he went through it and followed other signs down the corridor to the employment office. Inside, two men and a woman, obviously other job seekers, sat at a long table filling out forms. A white-haired man in a dark suit, sitting behind a desk, looked at him and pointed to the wall. On it was another sign, a large one, instructing applicants to fill out one of the forms stacked on the long table, with pen and ink. He sat opposite the woman and studied the questions on the form. With some relief, he noted that there was nothing on the front that he couldn't adequately answer. As he turned it over, he saw the questions he couldn't answer. How was he to account for the past two years of the five for which they wanted such information as name of employer and work experience? What was he to put down as an alternative for military duty? There was no lie big enough to cover the enormity of his mistake. He put the form back on the stack and left without satisfying the questioning look on the face of the white-haired, dark-suited employment manager, because there really was nothing to be said.

Over a cup of coffee at a lunch counter, he examined the other two ads which he had selected for investigation. One was for a draftsman in a small, growing engineering office and the other for a helper in a bakery, the name of which he recognized as being among the larger ones. He figured that the bakery would give him a form to fill out just as the hotel had. As for the engineering office, if it wasn't a form, there would be questions. No matter how much or how long he thought about it, it seemed hopeless. Still, he could not stop. He had to keep searching until he found work. Somewhere, there was someone who would hire him without probing too deeply into his past. Wherever that someone was, it was essential that he find him.

Before further thought could reduce his determination to bitterness or despair or cowardice or utter discouragement, he boarded a trolley for fear that, if he took the time to walk back to the car, he would find a reason to postpone his efforts. The trolley, a trackless affair which drew its motive power from overhead wires, surged smoothly through the late morning traffic with its handful of riders.

It was a short ride to the new, brick structure which had recently been constructed in an area, once residential, but now giving way to the demands of a growing city. Low, flat, modern clinics and store buildings intermingled with rambling, ugly apartment houses of wood and dirt-ridden brick.

Striding up a path which curved between newly installed landscaping, Ichiro entered the offices of Carrick and Sons. A middle-aged woman was beating furiously upon a typewriter.

He waited until she finished the page and flipped it out expertly. "Mam, I . . ."

"Yes?" She looked up, meanwhile working a new sheet into the machine.

"I'm looking for a job. The one in the paper. I came about the ad."

"Oh, of course." Making final adjustments, she typed a couple of lines before she rose and peeked into an inner office. "Mr. Carrick seems to be out just now. He'll be back shortly. Sit down." That said, she resumed her typing.

He spotted some magazines on a table and started to leaf through a not-too-old issue of *Look*. He saw the pictures and read the words and turned the pages methodically without digesting any of it.

A muffled pounding resounded distantly through the building and he glanced at the woman, who met his gaze and smiled sheepishly. He returned to the flipping of the pages, wondering why she had smiled in that funny way, and she bent her head over the typewriter as soon as the pounding stopped and went back to work.

When the pounding noise came again, she muttered impatiently under her breath and went out of the room.

She was gone several minutes, long enough for him to get

through the magazine. He was hunting through the pile of magazines in search of another when she stuck her head into the room and beckoned him to follow.

There was a big office beyond the door with a pile of rolled-up blueprints on a corner table and big photographs of buildings on the walls. They went through that and farther into the back, past a small kitchen and a utility room and, finally, came to stop by a stairway leading down into the basement.

"I told Mr. Carrick you were here. He's down there," the woman said, slightly exasperated.

As he started down, the same pounding began, only it was clearer now and he thought it sounded like a hammer being struck against a metal object of some kind. The object turned out to be what looked like a small hand-tractor with a dozer blade in front, and a small man with unkempt gray hair was whacking away at it with a claw hammer.

"Mr. Carrick?" It was no use. There was too much noise, so he waited until the man threw the hammer down in disgust and straightened up with a groan.

"Cockeyed," the man said, rubbing both his hands vigorously over the top of his buttocks. "I guess I'll have to take her apart and do it over right." He smiled graciously. "Doesn't pay to be impatient, but seems I'll never learn. That there blade isn't quite level and I thought I could force her. I learned. Yup, I sure did. How does she look to you?"

"What is it?"

Mr. Carrick laughed, naturally and loudly, his small, round stomach shaking convulsively. "I'm Carrick and you're . . . ?" He extended a soiled hand.

"Yamada, sir. Ichiro Yamada."

"Know anything about snowplows?"

"No, sir."

"Name's Yamada, is it?" The man pronounced the name easily.

"Yes, sir."

"*Nihongo wakarimasu ka?*"

"Not too well."

"How did I say that?"

"You're pretty good. You speak Japanese?"

"No. I used to have some very good Japanese friends. They taught me a little. You know the Tanakas?"

He shook his head. "Probably not the ones you mean. It's a pretty common name."

"They used to rent from me. Fine people. Best tenants I ever had. Shame about the evacuation. You too, I suppose."

"Yes, sir."

"The Tanakas didn't come back. Settled out East someplace. Well, can't say as I blame them. What brought you back?"

"Folks came back."

"Of course. Portland's changed, hasn't it?"

"I'm from Seattle."

"That so?" He leaned over the snowplow and tinkered with the bolts holding the blade in place.

Thinking that spring was not far away, Ichiro ventured to ask: "Does it snow that much down here?"

"How much is that?"

"Enough for a plow."

"No, it doesn't. I just felt I wanted to make one."

"Oh."

Adjusting a crescent wrench to fit the bolts, he grunted them loose and kicked the blade off. "Let's have some coffee." He rinsed off his hands at the sink and led the way up the stairs to the kitchen, where he added water to an old pot of coffee and turned on the burner.

"The Tanakas were fine people," he said, sitting down on a stool. In spite of his protruding belly and gray hair, he seemed a strong and energetic man. As he talked, his face had a way of displaying great feeling and exuberance. "The government made a big mistake when they shoved you people around. There was no reason for it. A big black mark in the annals of American history. I mean that. I've always been a big-mouthed, loud-talking, back-slapping American but, when that happened, I lost a little of my wind. I don't feel as proud as I used to, but, if the mistake has been made, maybe we've learned something from it. Let's hope so. We can still be the best damn nation in the world. I'm sorry things worked out the way they did."

It was an apology, a sincere apology from a man who had money and position and respectability, made to the Japanese who had been wronged. But it was not an apology to Ichiro and he did not know how to answer this man who might have been a friend and employer, a man who made a snowplow in a place where one had no need for a snowplow because he simply wanted one.

Mr. Carrick set cups on the table and poured the coffee, which was hot but weak. "When do you want to start?" he asked.

The question caught him unprepared. Was that all there was to it? Were there to be no questions? No inquiry about qualifications or salary or experience? He fumbled with his cup and spilled some coffee on the table.

"It pays two-sixty a month. Three hundred after a year."

"I've had two years of college engineering," he said, trying frantically to adjust himself to the unexpected turn of events.

"Of course. The ad was clear enough. You wouldn't have followed it up unless you thought you could qualify and, if you did, we'll soon find out. Don't worry. You'll work out. I got a feeling." He pursed his lips gingerly and sipped his coffee.

All he had to say was "I'll take it," and the matter would be settled. It was a stroke of good fortune such as he would never have expected. The pay was good, the employer was surely not to be equaled, and the work would be exactly what he wanted.

He looked at Mr. Carrick and said: "I'd like to think about it."

Was it disbelief or surprise that clouded the face of the man who, in his heartfelt desire to atone for the error of a big country which hadn't been quite big enough, had matter-of-factly said two-sixty a month and three hundred after a year when two hundred a month was what he had in mind when he composed the ad since a lot of draftsmen were getting less but because the one who came for the job was a Japanese and it made a difference to him? "Certainly, Ichiro. Take all the time you need."

And when he said that, Ichiro knew that the job did not belong to him, but to another Japanese who was equally as American as this man who was attempting in a small way to rectify the wrong he felt to be his own because he was a part of the country which, somehow, had erred in a moment of panic.

"I'm not a veteran," he said.

Mr. Carrick creased his brow, not understanding what he meant.

"Thanks for the coffee. I'm sorry I bothered you." He pushed himself back off the stool.

"Wait." His face thoughtfully grave, Mr. Carrick absently drew a clean handkerchief from his trousers pocket and ran it over the coffee which Ichiro had spilled. He straightened up quickly, saying simultaneously: "It's something I've said. God knows I wouldn't intentionally do anything to hurt you or anyone. I'm sorry. Can we try again, please?"

"You've no apology to make, sir. You've been very good. I want the job. The pay is tops. I might say I need the job, but it's not for me. You see, I'm not a veteran."

"Hell, son. What's that got to do with it? Did I ask you? Why do you keep saying that?"

How was he to explain? Surely he couldn't leave now without some sort of explanation. The man had it coming to him if anyone ever did. He was, above all, an honest and sincere man and he deserved an honest reply.

"Mr. Carrick, I'm not a veteran because I spent two years in jail for refusing the draft."

The man did not react with surprise or anger or incredulity. His shoulders sagged a bit and he suddenly seemed a very old man whose life's dream had been to own a snowplow and, when he had finally secured one, it was out of kilter. "I am sorry, Ichiro," he said, "sorry for you and for the causes behind the reasons which made you do what you did. It wasn't your fault, really. You know that, don't you?"

136

"I don't know, sir. I just don't know. I just know I did it."

"You mustn't blame yourself."

"I haven't much choice. Sometimes I think my mother is to blame. Sometimes I think it's bigger than her, more than her refusal to understand that I'm not like her. It didn't make sense. Not at all. First they jerked us off the Coast and put us in camps to prove to us that we weren't American enough to be trusted. Then they wanted to draft us into the army. I was bitter—mad and bitter. Still, a lot of them went in, and I didn't. You figure it out. Thanks again, sir."

He was in the front room and almost past the woman when Mr. Carrick caught up with him.

"Miss Henry," he said to the woman at the typewriter, and there was something about his manner that was calm and reassuring, "this is Mr. Yamada. He's considering the drafting job."

She nodded, smiling pleasantly. "You'll like it here," she said. "It's crazy, but you'll like it."

He walked with Ichiro to the door and drew it open. "Let me know when you decide."

They shook hands and Ichiro took the bus back to the hotel. He had every reason to be enormously elated and, yet, his thoughts were solemn to the point of brooding. Then, as he thought about Mr. Carrick and their conversation time and time again, its meaning for him evolved into a singularly comforting thought. There was someone who cared. Surely there were others too who understood the suffering of the small and the weak and, yes, even the seemingly treasonous, and offered a way back into the great compassionate stream of life that is America. Under the hard, tough cloak of the struggle for existence in which money and enormous white refrigerators and shining, massive, brutally-fast cars and fine, expensive clothing had ostensibly overwhelmed the qualities of men that were good and gentle and just, there still beat a heart of kindness and patience and forgiveness. And in this moment when he thought of Mr. Carrick, the engineer with a yen for a snowplow that would probably never get used, and of what he had said, and, still more, of what he offered to do, he glimpsed the real nature of the country against which he had almost fully turned his back, and saw that its mistake was no less unforgivable than his own.

He blew a stream of smoke into the shaft of sunlight that slanted through the window and watched it lazily curl upward along the brightened path. Stepping to the window, he looked down for a moment upon a parking lot with its multi-colored rows of auto-mobile hoods and tops. And beyond was the city, streets and buildings and vehicles and people for as far as the eye could reach.

Then he drew the shade and found himself alone in the dark-ness, feeling very tired and sleepy because he had been a long time without rest. It was all he could do to remove his clothes before he fell on the bed and let himself succumb to the weariness which was making him dizzy and clumsy.

He slept soundly, hardly stirring until he awoke in the quiet which was the quiet of the night, disturbed only by the infrequent hum of an automobile in the streets below. As the drowsiness faded reluctantly, he waited for the sense of calm elation which he rather expected. It did not come. He found that his thoughts were of his family. They were not to be ignored, to be cast out of mind and life and rendered eternally nothing. It was well that Kenji wished him to take the Oldsmobile back to Seattle. A man does not start totally anew because he is already old by virtue of having lived and laughed and cried for twenty or thirty or fifty years and there is no way to destroy them without destroying life itself. That he understood. He also understood that the past had been shared with a mother and father and, whatever they were, he too was a part of them and they a part of him and one did not say this is as far as we go together, I am stepping out of your lives, without ren-dering himself only part of a man. If he was to find his way back to that point of wholeness and belonging, he must do so in the place where he had begun to lose it. Mr. Carrick had shown him that there was a chance and, for that, he would be ever grateful.

Crawling out of the bed, he switched on the light and started to search through the drawers of the dresser. In the third one he found a Gideon Bible, a drinking glass in a cellophane bag, and two picture postcards. Lacking a desk, he stood at the dresser and penned a few lines to Mr. Carrick informing him that, grateful as he was, he found it necessary to turn down the job. He paused with pen in hand, wanting to add words which would adequately express the warmth and depth of gratitude he felt. What could he say to this man whom he had met but once and probably would never see again? What words would transmit the bigness of his feelings to match the bigness of the heart of this American who, in the manner of his living, was continually nursing and worrying the infant America into the greatness of its inheritance? Knowing, finally, that the unsaid would be understood, he merely affixed his signature to the postcard and dressed so that he could go out to mail it and get something to eat.

Outside, he walked along the almost deserted streets. It was only a little after ten o'clock but there were few pedestrians and traffic was extremely light. He came to a corner with a mailbox and paused to drop the card. Lifting his eyes upward along the lamppost, he saw that he was on Burnside Street. In a small way, Burnside was to Portland what Jackson Street was to Seattle or, at least, he remembered that it used to be so before the war when the Japanese did little traveling and Portland seemed a long way off instead of just two hundred miles and the fellows who had been to Portland used to rave about the waitresses they had in the café on Burnside. He could almost hear them: "Burnside Café. Remember that. Boy, what sweet babes! Nothing like them in Seattle. Sharp. Sharp. Sharp."

He ambled up the walk past a tavern, a drugstore, a café, a vacant store space, a cigar stand, a laundromat, a secondhand store, another tavern, and there it was. Just as they said it would be, Burnside Café in huge, shameless letters plastered across two big windows with the door in between.

A young fellow in a white apron with one leg propped up on the inside ledge smoked his cigarette and looked out on the world, waiting for business to walk in. When he saw Ichiro, his eyes widened perceptibly. He followed the stranger through the door and said familiarly: "Hi."

Ichiro nodded and walked to the rear end of the counter where a middle-aged woman was standing on a milk box and pouring hot water into the top of a large coffee urn.

The young fellow pursued him from the other side of the counter and greeted him with a too-friendly grin: "Hungry, I bet." He plucked a menu wedged between the napkin holder and sugar dispenser and held it forth.

"Ham and eggs. Coffee now," he said, ignoring the menu.

"Turn the eggs over?"

"No."

"Ma, ham and eggs sunny side up." He got the coffee himself and set it in front of Ichiro. He didn't go away.

Thick as flies, thought Ichiro to himself with disgust. A Jap can spot another Jap a mile away. Pouring the sugar, he solemnly regarded the still-grinning face of the waiter and saw the clean white shirt with the collar open and the bronze discharge pin obtrusively displayed where the ribbons might have been if the fellow had been wearing a uniform.

"You're Japanese, huh? Where you from?"

He could have said yes and they would have been friends. The Chinese were like that too, only more so. He had heard how a Chinese from China by the name of Eng could go to Jacksonville, Florida, or any other place, and look up another Chinese family by the same name of Eng and be taken in like one of the family with no questions asked. There was nothing wrong with it. On the contrary, it was a fine thing in some ways. Still, how much finer it would be if Smith would do the same for Eng and Sato would do the same for Wotynski and Laverghetti would do likewise for whoever happened by. Eng for Eng, Jap for Jap, Pole for Pole, and like for like meant classes and distinctions and hatred and prejudice and wars and misery, and that wasn't what Mr. Carrick would want at all, and he was on the right track.

"I've got two Purple Hearts and five Battle Stars," Ichiro said. "What does that make me?"

The young Japanese with the clean white shirt and the ruptured duck to prove he wasn't Japanese flinched, then flushed and stammered: "Yeah—you know what I meant—that is, I didn't mean what you think. Hell, I'm a vet, too . . ."

"I'm glad you told me."

"Jeezuz, all I said was are you Japanese. Is that wrong?"

"Does it matter?"

"No, of course not."

"Why'd you ask?"

"Just to be asking. Make conversation and so on. You know."

"I don't. My name happens to be Wong. I'm Chinese."

Frustrated and panicky, the waiter leaned forward earnestly and blurted out: "Good. It makes no difference to me what you are. I like Chinese."

"Any reason why you shouldn't?"

"I didn't say that. I didn't mean that. I was just trying to . . ." He did a harried right face and fled back toward the window grumbling: "Crissake, crissake . . ."

A moment later, the woman emerged from the kitchen with his plate and inquired in Japanese if he would like some toast and jam. She did it very naturally, seeing that he was obviously Japanese and gracefully using the tongue which came more easily to her lips.

He said that would be fine and noticed that the son was glaring out of the window at a world which probably seemed less friendly and more complicated than it had been a few minutes previously. The woman brought the toast and jam and left him alone, and he cleaned the plate swiftly. He would have liked another cup of coffee but the greater need was to get out and away from the place and the young Japanese who had to wear a discharge button on his shirt to prove to everyone who came in that he was a top-flight American. Having the proper change in his pocket, he laid it and the slip on the little rubber mat by the cash register and hurried out without seeing the relief-mixed-with-shame look on the waiter's face.

From the café he walked the few steps to the tavern next door and ordered a double shot of whisky with a beer chaser. He downed both, standing up, by the time the bartender came back with his change, and then he was out on the street once more. On top of the ham and eggs and toast with jam, the liquor didn't hit him hard, but he felt woozy by the time he got back to the hotel. He had to wait in the elevator for a while because the old fellow who ran it also watched the desk and was presently on the telephone.

On the way up, the old man regarded his slightly flushed face and smiled knowingly. "Want a girl?" he asked.

"I want six," he said, hating the man.

"All at one time?" the old man questioned unbelievingly.

"The sixth floor, pop." The hotness in his face was hotter still with the anger inside of him.

"Sure," he said, bringing the elevator to an abrupt halt, "that's good. I thought you meant you wanted six of them. That is good."

The old man was chuckling as Ichiro stepped out of the elevator and headed toward his room.

"Filthy-minded old bastard," he muttered viciously under his breath. No wonder the world's such a rotten place, rotten and filthy and cheap and smelly. Where is that place they talk of and paint nice pictures of and describe in all the homey magazines? Where is that place with the clean, white cottages surrounding the new, red-brick church with the clean, white steeple, where the families all have two children, one boy and one girl, and a shiny new car in the garage and a dog and a cat and life is like living in the land of the happily-ever-after? Surely it must be around here someplace, someplace in America. Or is it just that it's not for me? Maybe I dealt myself out, but what about that young kid on Burnside who was in the army and found it wasn't enough so that he has to keep proving to everyone who comes in for a cup of coffee that he was fighting for his country like the button on his shirt says he did because the army didn't do anything about his face to make him look more American? And what about the poor niggers on Jackson Street who can't find anything better to do than spit on the sidewalk and show me the way to Tokyo? They're on the outside looking in, just like that kid and just like me and just like everybody else I've ever seen or known. Even Mr. Carrick. Why isn't he in? Why is he on the outside squandering his goodness on outcasts like me? Maybe the answer is that there is no in. Maybe the whole damned country is pushing and shoving and screaming to get into someplace that doesn't exist, because they don't know that the outside could be the inside if only they would stop all this pushing and shoving and screaming, and they haven't got enough sense to realize that. That makes sense. I've got the answer all figured out, simple and neat and sensible.

And then he thought about Kenji in the hospital and of Emi in bed with a stranger who reminded her of her husband and of his mother waiting for the ship from Japan, and there was no more answer. If he were in the tavern, he would drink another double with a beer for a chaser and another and still another but he wasn't in the tavern because he didn't have the courage to step out of his room and be seen by people who would know him for what he was. There was nothing for him to do but roll over and try to sleep. Somewhere, sometime, he had even forgotten how to cry.

In the morning he checked out of the hotel and drove to the hospital. Visiting hours were plainly indicated on a sign at the entrance as being in the afternoons and evenings. Feeling he had nothing to lose by trying, he walked in and stood by the registration desk until the girl working the switchboard got a chance to help him.

"What can I do for you?" she asked sweetly enough and then, prodded into action by the buzzing of the board, pulled and inserted a number of brass plugs which were attached to extend-

143

ible wire cords. Tiny lights bristled actively as if to give evidence to the urgency of the calls being carried by the board.

"I've got a friend here. I'd like to find out what room he's in."

"Sure. His name?"

"Kanno."

"Kanno what?"

"Kenji. Kanno is the last name."

"How do you spell it?" She consulted the K's on the cardex.

"K-A-N-"

"Never mind. I've got it." Looking up, she continued: "He's in four-ten but you'll have to come back this afternoon. Visiting hours are posted at the entrance. Sorry."

"I'm on my way out of town. I won't be here this afternoon."

"Hospital rules, sir."

"Sure," he said, noticing the stairway off toward the right, "I understand."

The board buzzed busily and the operator turned her attention to the plugs and cords once more. Ichiro walked to the stairs and started up. Between the second and third floors he encountered two nurses coming down. When they saw him they cut short their chattering and one of them seemed on the point of questioning him. Quickening his pace, he rushed past them purposefully and was relieved when he heard them resume their talking.

Up on the fourth floor, no one bothered him as he set out to locate Kenji's room. Four-ten wasn't far from the stairway. A screen was placed inside the doorway so that he couldn't look directly in. He went around it and saw the slight figure of his friend up on the high bed with the handle of the crank poking out at the foot.

"Ken," he said in almost a whisper though he hadn't deliberately intended to speak so.

"Ichiro?" His head lay on the pillow with its top toward the door and Ichiro noted with a vague sense of alarm that his hair was beginning to thin.

He waited for Kenji to face him and was disappointed when he did not move. "How's it been with you?"

"Fine. Sit down." He kept looking toward the window.

Ichiro walked past the bed, noticing where the sheet fell over the stump beneath. It seemed to be frighteningly close to the torso. His own legs felt stiff and awkward as he approached the chair and settled into it.

Kenji was looking at him, a smile, weak yet warm, on his mouth.

"How's it going?" he asked, and he hardly heard his own voice, for Kenji had aged a lifetime during the two days they had been apart. Exactly what it was he couldn't say, but it was all there, the fear, the pain, the madness, and the exhaustion of mind and body.

"About as I expected, Ichiro. I should have been a doctor."

Kenji had said he was going to die.

"You could be wrong. Have they said so?"

"Not in so many words, but they know it and I know it and they know that I do."

"Why don't they do something?"

"Nothing to be done."

"I shouldn't be here," he said, not knowing why except that it suddenly seemed important to explain. "They told me to come back this afternoon but I came up anyway. Maybe I shouldn't have. Maybe you're supposed to rest."

"Hell with them," said Kenji. "You're here, stay."

It was quiet in the hospital. He'd heard someplace a long time ago that visitors were not allowed in the morning in hospitals because that's when all the cleaning and changing of beds and mopping of floors were done. There wasn't a sound to be heard. "Quiet here," he said.

"Good for thinking," said Kenji.

"Sure, I guess it is." He wished Kenji would move, roll his head a little or wiggle his arm, but he lay there just as he was.

"Go back to Seattle."

"What?"

145

"Go back. Later on you might want to come to Portland to stay, but go back for now. It'll turn out for the best in the long run. The kind of trouble you've got, you can't run from it. Stick it through. Let them call you names. They don't mean it. What I mean is, they don't know what they're doing. The way I see it, they pick on you because they're vulnerable. They think just because they went and packed a rifle they're different but they aren't and they know it. They're still Japs. You weren't here when they first started to move back to the Coast. There was a great deal of opposition—name-calling, busted windows, dirty words painted on houses. People haven't changed a helluva lot. The guys who make it tough on you probably do so out of a misbegotten idea that maybe you're to blame because the good that they thought they were doing by getting killed and shot up doesn't amount to a pot of beans. They just need a little time to get cut down to their own size. Then they'll be the same as you, a bunch of Japs."

He paused for a long time, just looking and smiling at Ichiro, his face wan and tired. "There were a lot of them pouring into Seattle about the time I got back there. It made me sick. I'd heard about some of them scattering out all over the country. I read about a girl who's doing pretty good in the fashion business in New York and a guy that's principal of a school in Arkansas, and a lot of others in different places making out pretty good. I got to thinking that the Japs were wising up, that they had learned that living in big bunches and talking Jap and feeling Jap and doing Jap was just inviting trouble. But my dad came back. There was really no reason why he should have. I asked him about it once and he gave me some kind of an answer. Whatever it was, a lot of others did the same thing. I hear there's almost as many in Seattle now as there were before the war. It's a shame, a dirty rotten shame. Pretty soon it'll be just like it was before the war. A bunch of Japs with a fence around them, not the kind you can see, but it'll hurt them just as much. They bitched and hollered when the government put them in camps and put real fences around them, but now they're doing the same damn thing to themselves. They screamed because the government said they were Japs and, when they finally got out, they couldn't wait to rush together and prove that they were."

"They're not alone, Ken. The Jews, the Italians, the Poles, the Armenians, they've all got their communities."

"Sure, but that doesn't make it right. It's wrong. I don't blame the old ones so much. They don't know any better. They don't want any better. It's me I'm talking about and all the rest of the young ones who know and want better."

"You just got through telling me to go back to Seattle."

"I still say it. Go back and stay there until they have enough sense to leave you alone. Then get out. It may take a year or two or even five, but the time will come when they'll be feeling too sorry for themselves to pick on you. After that, head out. Go someplace where there isn't another Jap within a thousand miles. Marry a white girl or a Negro or an Italian or even a Chinese. Anything but a Japanese. After a few generations of that, you've got the thing beat. Am I making sense?"

"It's a fine dream, but you're not the first."

"No," he uttered and it seemed as if he might cry, "it's just a dream, a big balloon. I wonder if there's a Jackson Street wherever it is I'm going to. That would make dying tough."

Ichiro stood and, walking to his friend, placed his hand on the little shoulder and held it firmly.

"I'm going to write to Ralph," said Kenji.

"Ralph?"

"Emi's husband. I'm going to write him about how you and Emi are hitting it off."

"Why? It's not true." He felt the heat of indignation warm around his collar.

"No, it isn't true, but what they're doing to each other is not right. They should be together or split up. If I tell him about you and how you're hot for her, it might make him mad enough to come back."

Understanding what Kenji meant, Ichiro worked up a smile. "Seems like I'm not so useless after all."

"Tell her I've been thinking about her."

"Sure."

"And I'm thinking about you. All the time."

"Sure."

"Have a drink for me. Drink to wherever it is I'm headed, and don't let there be any Japs or Chinks or Jews or Poles or Niggers or Frenchies, but only people. I think about that too. I think about that most of all. You know why?"

He shook his head and Kenji seemed to know he would even though he was still staring out the window. "He was up on the roof of the barn and I shot him, killed him. He wasn't the only German I killed, but I remember him. I see him rolling down the roof. I see him all the time now and that's why I want this other place to have only people because if I'm still a Jap there and this guy's still a German, I'll have to shoot him again and I don't want to have to do that. Then maybe there is no someplace else. Maybe dying is it. The finish. The end. Nothing. I'd like that too. Better an absolute nothing than half a meaning. The living have it tough. It's like a coat rack without pegs, only you think there are. Hang it up, drop, pick it up, hang it again, drop again . . . Tell my dad I'll miss him like mad."

"I will."

"Crazy talk?"

"No, it makes a lot of sense."

"Goodbye, Ichiro."

His hand slipped off his friend's shoulder and brushed along the white sheet and dropped to his side. The things he wanted to say would not be said. He said "Bye" and no sound came out because the word got caught far down inside his throat and he felt his mouth open and shut against the empty silence. At the door he turned and looked back and, as Kenji had still not moved, he saw again the spot on the head where the hair was thinning out so that the sickly white of the scalp filtered between the strands of black. A few more years and he'll be bald, he thought, and then he started to smile inwardly because there wouldn't be a few more years and as quickly the smile vanished because the towering, choking grief was suddenly upon him.

It was almost seven hours later when Ichiro, nearing the outskirts of Seattle, turned off the highway and drove to Emi's house.

He pressed the doorbell and waited and pressed it again. When no one appeared, he pounded on the door. Thinking, hoping that she must be nearby, he walked around to the back. With a sense of relief, he noted that the shed which served as a garage housed a pre-war Ford that looked fairly new. It probably meant that she hadn't driven to town. He tried the back door without any luck and made his way around to the front once more.

Tired and hungry, he sat on the step and lit a cigarette. It was then that he saw her, walking toward the house from out in the fields about where the man had been stooped over his labors a few mornings previously. Looking carefully, he saw that he was still there, still stooped over, still working.

Emi covered the ground with long, sure strides. Occasionally she broke into a run, picking her way agilely over the loose dirt and leaping over mounds and the carefully tended rows of vegetables. He stood and waved and got no response, so he waited until she was closer before he raised his arm again. Still she did not wave back. Seeming deliberately to avoid looking at him, she approached the gate. Once there, she jerked her head up, her face alive and expectantly tense.

"Hello, Emi."

"I saw the Oldsmobile. I thought . . ." She didn't hide her disappointment.

He felt embarrassed and unwanted. "I'm sorry," he said quietly.

She grasped the gate, which he had left open, and slammed it fiercely. With chin lowered, she pouted, her face swollen and defiant. Then she came up the walk, moving her legs reluctantly, and dropped on the step.

Unnerved by her reaction, Ichiro fidgeted uneasily, thinking of something to say. At length, he too sat down beside her and remained silent. Without looking at her, he could sense that she was struggling to keep the tears from starting. There was a streak of brown dirt clinging across the toe of her shoe and he restrained the urge to brush it off.

"It's just that I wanted so much for him to come back." She started speaking, almost in a whisper. "It somehow seemed more important for him to come back this time than the other times he went down there. He's not coming back, is he?"

"No, I think not. He told me to tell you that he's thinking about you."

"I'm sorry," she blurted out.

"Sorry?"

"I'm sorry I made you feel bad just now."

"You didn't."

"I did and I'm sorry."

"Sure."

"I'll make you something to eat," she said and before he could refuse, rose and went into the house.

In the kitchen, he watched as she moved from the refrigerator to the sink to the stove, fussing longer than necessary with each little thing that had to be done.

He got the dishes and utensils from the cupboard and set them on the table. "Were you in love with him?" he asked.

She turned and, apparently neither startled nor hurt, softly smiled. "In a way. Not the way I love Ralph. Not the way I might love you, but I loved him—no, he's not gone yet—I love him too much but not enough."

"Any other time I might not understand the way you put that, but I do."

"It doesn't matter. I'm glad if you do, but it really doesn't matter. Love is not something you save and hoard. You're born with it and you spend it when you have to and there's always more because you're a woman and there's always suffering and

150

pain and gentleness and sadness to make it grow."

"He said he was thinking about you."

"You already said that. Besides, it doesn't need to be said." She put the meat and potatoes in his plate and urged him to eat. For herself she poured a cup of coffee and stirred it absent-mindedly without adding cream or sugar.

Hungry as he had thought himself to be, he found himself chewing lengthily on each little mouthful.

"And you?"

He looked at her, not quite understanding the intention of her words.

"What will you do now?"

"I haven't decided," he said honestly. "Strangely enough, I had a wonderful job offer in Portland, but I turned it down."

"Tell me about it."

He did so, dwelling at great length on his admiration for Mr. Carrick and the reasons for his final decision to refuse the job. Somehow, he had expected her to be impatient with what he had done, but when he finished she merely said: "It's good."

"That I turned down the job?"

"No, it's good that you found out things aren't as hopeless as you thought."

"Just like you said."

"I did say that, didn't I?" She looked pleased. "This Mr. Carrick you speak of sounds like the kind of American that Americans always profess themselves to be."

"One in a million," he added.

"Less than that," she said quickly. "If a lot more people were like him, there wouldn't have been an evacuation."

"No, and one might even go farther and say there might not have been a war."

"And no problems for you and me and everybody else."

"Nothing for God to do either," he said, without knowing why and, as soon as he had, he knew that they had just been talking. What it amounted to was that there was a Mr. Carrick in Portland, which did not necessarily mean that there were others like him. The world was pretty much the same except, perhaps, that Emi and he were both sadder.

"Mr. Maeno will give you work, if you wish. I was speaking to him about you just before you came."

Rising, he went to the stove to get the coffeepot and did not answer until he sat down again. "That would be nice, but I can't. Thanks, anyway."

"Why?"

"It won't do any good. It'll be like hiding. He's Japanese. Probably admires me for what I did, I suppose. Maybe it doesn't make any difference to him what I've done, but it does to me."

"What will you do then?"

"Find a girl that's not Japanese that'll marry me." Seeing the incredulous look in her face, he rapidly explained what Kenji had said to him.

"He didn't really mean it," she replied. "He only meant that things ought to be that way, but I think he knew he was only dreaming."

"He did. It's probably what makes him so unhappy and kind of brooding underneath."

"Is he really going to die?" She looked at him pleadingly, as if beseeching him to say that it was not true.

All he could do was nod his head.

Emi pushed her cup away abruptly, splashing some of the coffee onto the table. Then she cupped her face with her hands and began to sob, scarcely making a sound.

"I have to go now," he said. "I may not come to see you again and, then, I might. I like you a lot already and, in time, I'll surely love you very deeply. That mustn't happen because Ralph will probably come back."

"He won't," she cried, without taking her hands away.

"I think he will. Ken said he was writing to Ralph. He's got something in mind that'll jolt him hard enough to make him see what he's doing. He'll come back. Soon."

He stood beside her a moment, wanting to comfort her. Slowly, he raised his arms, only to let them drop without touching her. Quickly he brushed his lips against her head and ran out of the house.

8

ICHIRO'S FATHER CRADLED THE BROWN PAPER BAG PRE-
ciously in the soft crook of his arm and, with the other hand,
pressed it firmly against his breast. In his hurry to get to the
liquor store before it closed at eight o'clock, he had left home
without a coat or hat. Now, his legs moved quickly, sweeping
him along the walk, which he felt hazily underneath him. It was
still March and cool enough for a topcoat. He shivered a little
and felt fuzzy all over because it had been a while since the last
drink and that's how he felt when the effect of the liquor was
beginning to wear off. It scared him to think that he might be
sobering up. He ran, squeezing the bag tighter when its contents began to jiggle. The bag would have made a snug fit for
four bottles, but he had only bought three and that meant they
were fairly loose.

"Next time I'll be sure to buy four," he muttered to himself.
"Ya, four is best; a whole case, better. Sonagabitch, I'm thirsty.
Sonagabitch, cold too. Plenty cold."

A block from the store he attempted to leap over the curb-
ing and didn't quite make it. Clutching the bag desperately, he
managed to twist himself sufficiently in mid-air so that he hit the
sidewalk with his shoulder. The impact cut his breath off momentarily and, as he lay gasping for air, he saw several people running
toward him.

When his breathing became regular, he ran his fingers over the bag, inspecting it for any wetness or jagged pieces of glass. Nothing seemed to be broken.

"Okay," he said in halting English to the inquiring faces above him, "everything okay. Just fall."

He let the people help him to his feet and resumed his journey home. Not until he was at the door and had to shift the bag to reach for the key did he notice the soreness in his shoulder and back. Wincing a bit, he got himself inside and into the kitchen, where he'd left the bulb burning. With clumsy skill and haste, he tore the celluloid collar off one of the bottles and tilted it to his mouth. He had to grit his teeth and shake his head until the liquor settled inside of him. It was good—horrible, but good. Craning his neck, he peered at the sore shoulder and he could see where the fall had shredded his shirt and bruised the flesh. He poured some of the whisky into his palm and rubbed it vigorously against the injury. It burned painfully, so much so that he had to take another big gulp from the bottle. Finally, he felt reasonably relaxed. Then he sat down and sadly regarded the untouched plate of food and the bowl of cold rice which he had set out a few hours before. It was not the first time, nor the second. Mama had not eaten for two days, not since Ichiro had gone to Portland. He swigged at the bottle and forced himself to the bedroom door.

"Mama," and he said it plaintively, "Mama, eat a little bit."

She was lying on the bed, silent and unmoving, and it made him afraid. It was not the thought of death, but the thought of madness which reduced him to a frightened child in the darkness. When she was not lying or sitting almost as if dead in her open-eyed immobility, she was doing crazy things. It had started with the cans, the lining of them on the shelves, hurling them on the floor, brooding, fussing, repacking them in the boxes, and then the whole thing over and over again until hours after Ichiro had gone. Then silence, and he forgot now whether the silence was of her lying or sitting on the bed, the silence which was of the water quietly heating to boil. Following that silence had come the rain, the soft rain as always, drizzling and miserable and deceivingly cold. And he had not heard a sound, but when he had gone to the bedroom to see about throwing another blanket on her, she was out in back hanging things on the line. How long she had been out in the rain, he couldn't say. Her hair was drenched and hanging straight down, reaching almost to the tiny hump of her buttocks against which the wet cotton dress had adhered so that he could see the crease. He called her from the doorway and was not disappointed when she hadn't heeded him, for that was how he knew it would be. So he had watched until he could stand it no longer and this time he had run right up to her and shouted for her to stop the foolishness and come in out of the rain, and it still had done no good. He had come in then and waited and drunk some whisky, and the bottle which had been half-full was almost gone when the back door slammed. And then, once again, the awful silence. She was sitting that time. He remembered because when he went out to take the rain-soaked things off the line, he had to turn sideways to get past her.

After that? He gazed sorrowfully at the bed on which his wife lay. It didn't matter what had happened after that. It only mattered what would happen now or tonight or tomorrow. Where and how would all this end? What was happening to her?

"Mama," he wailed, "eat or you will take sick. Eat or you will die."

As if in response to his voice, she stirred and rose and looked at him.

"Ya, Mama, eat."

She walked a few steps toward him hesitantly.

Backing excitedly away from the door, he quickly made room for her to pass.

Stopping short of the kitchen, she stood undecidedly for a moment, shaking her head slowly as though to reshuffle her senses. Resolutely then she leaped onto the foot of the bed and began to pull down the several suitcases which had been piled atop the cardboard wardrobe.

"Mama!" It was an utterance filled with despair. He watched wretchedly as she pulled open drawers and proceeded to cram the cases full of whatever came into her grasping hands. How long this time, he thought gently rubbing the ache in his shoulder with an unsteady hand, let himself drop heavily into a chair. He gripped the bottle with both hands and his body shook tremulously. Biting his lip to imprison the swollen sob which would release a torrent of anguish, he crumpled forward until he felt the coolness of the table spreading across his forehead. It helped to relax him. Suddenly the scuffling and banging and scurrying in the bedroom stopped. Slowly, he looked up and, just as his gaze encompassed the door to the bedroom, he glimpsed her striding out and into the bathroom. She shut the door firmly behind her and, a moment later, he heard the bolt being slid into place. Then the water sounded its way into the tub, not splashing or gurgling heavily, but merely trickling, almost reluctantly so it seemed.

He gulped from the bottle and listened to the trickling of the water against the bottom of the white tub as it slowly changed into a gentle splashing of water against water as the tub began to fill.

Why doesn't she turn the faucets on full he thought impatiently. Turn it on like you always do. Be quick and efficient and impatient, which is the way you have always been. Start the water in the tub and scrub the kitchen floor while it is filling up. When the floor is done and the mop wrung out and hung in back to dry, the water is good, just the right depth. Like a clock you are. Not a second wasted.

He gulped again and the progress of the water was so painfully slow that he could hardly discern any change in the pattern of its splashing.

At length, irritated, he retreated into the store, holding the bottle in one hand and groping his way through the darkness almost to the front door, where the sounds from the bathroom couldn't reach him. Upending an apple box which contained a few discolored Jonathans, he sat himself down as the apples tumbled across the floor.

Straightening up to tilt the bottle to his mouth, he was suddenly overcome by the worry and strain of the past several days.

"Tired, so very much tired," he groaned aloud as he doubled over his knees and set the whisky on the floor. Remaining thus, stretching the pain in his bruised shoulder so that it felt like a row of needles clawing into the heaviness which weighted him down, he bemoaned his fate:

Kin-chan, that is what your sister calls you now. Now that life has become too hard for her to bear, she once again calls you Kin-chan, for then she thinks of the days when we were all young and strong and brave and crazy. Not crazy like today or yesterday, but crazy in the nice, happy way of young people. No, not crazy like you, old woman. Once, I too called you Kin-chan. Kin-chan. Kin-chan. Kin-chan. You were good then. Small and proud and firm and maybe a little bit huffy, but good and soft inside. Ya, ya, I was smart too. I found out how good and soft before we married. Right under their eyes almost. Your papa was there and you beside him and your mama was already dead. Then there was myself and my mama and papa and the man who was the village mayor's brother, whose name I forget but who was making the match. How he could talk, that man, talk and drink and talk, talk, talk. But he was only talking then because it was time for business and he was talking about how fine a wife you would make for the son of my father and mother, and your head was down low but I could see you smiling. How sweet it was then. How wonderful! Then he was talking about me and I sat up straight and full and puffed my chest and I could see you stealing a look once or twice and you were pleased. I was pleased too. Everybody was pleased and the thing was settled quickly, for that time was only for making the matter final. And when one is feeling gay and full of joy, the saké must be brought out to lift the spirits higher. And they drank, your papa and mine and the mayor's brother, and I only a little because I was even happier than they and needed no false joy. Then the moment was at hand when Mama was telling Papa not to drink so much and you were in the kitchen heating more saké and your papa and that man were singing songs not to be heard by such as you. It was to the toilet I was going when you saw me and I, you. There was nothing to be said. It was not a time for words but only deep feeling. And there, in the darkness of the narrow corridor between the house and the smelly toilet, I made you my wife, standing up. It was wonderful, more wonderful I think than even the night of the day when we really were married. Do you know it was never that good for me again? Ya, Kin-chan, that was the mistake. We should have waited and then everything would have been proper. We were not proper and so we suffer. Your papa, my papa, my mama, and that man did not know, but the gods knew. It was dark and we were standing, but they were watching and nodding their heads and saying: "Shame, black shame."

"Aaagh," he moaned. Then, peering into the darkness, he called softly: "Taro? Ichiro?"

There was no answer, only the darkness and the little bit of light that slanted into the other end under the curtains that blocked off the kitchen.

He leaned forward intently, smiling pleasantly as if the boys were in front of him. He knew they were not there, but the desire to voice their names could not be resisted and so again he called: "Taro? Ichiro?"

As if to catch their eager responses, he cocked his head, playing the game for all the pleasure that he could derive from it in momentary escape from the soul-crippling truth. There was a gurgle, faint and muffled. Curious, he listened. The gurgling continued for a while longer and ceased the moment he realized it was the bath water, and, abruptly, the present was crammed back into his tired being.

Snatching the bottle off the floor with a swoop of his arm, he reared back against the staggering weight of his depression and poured the whisky into his gaping mouth. All, he resolved silently to himself, I will drink all like the man that I am. Holding his breath so as not to taste the cheap liquor, he gulped greedily. He endeavored stubbornly, his stomach now extended to the point of bursting and his mouth jerking in labored gasps as his whole being clawed for air. Then he became frightened and wanted to stop, but the dizziness set in and all he could think was that his mouth was off at a distance by itself and mechanically jawing like a spasmodic reflex. Soon his mouth was filled to overflowing. His fingers no longer seemed to respond to his will and he instinctively averted his face as he sensed the bottle slipping free. Spewing whisky out of his mouth with a noisy roar, he toppled off the box and onto the floor, where he lay utterly exhausted.

Dimly, he heard a car scraping its tires against the curb beyond the thin outer wall. The illumination from its headlights filtered into the store and he found himself trying to focus upon the Lucky Strike poster which was stapled above the shelves of canned goods. The colors kept running together and the big red circle he knew was there refused to stay still or single. It kept doubling and tripling and constantly distorting itself into fuzzy-edged, lopsided circles. Sick and tired and drunk, he closed his eyes and listened to the steady purr of the idling motor and quickly succumbed to sleep.

Outside in the car, Ichiro sat undecided. He felt very much alone. He knew he would not see Kenji or Emi again. They had been good to him. Kenji and Emi and Mr. Carrick, three people who had given a little of themselves to him because they liked him. It had not mattered to any of them about the thing that he had done. True, he was alone again, but not quite as nakedly alone as he had been the first day out of prison and walking up Jackson Street on the way home. The motor still idling, he squinted a bit and peered into the store. Cracks of light were visible far inside. They were home, of course. Where could they go? He wondered how his mother was doing and he thought distastefully about the business of the cans.

Where the headlights sprayed into the store, he saw the red top of the Coca-Cola freezer and, beyond it, the wall full of canned goods. He looked at the Lucky Strike sign and felt somewhat bothered when he couldn't quite make out what he knew were the words "It's toasted." Settling back against the seat, he peered in the opposite direction at the clock tower of the depot under which Eto had made him crawl. It was still only a few minutes after nine. Making up his mind impulsively, he pressed the accelerator pedal and, without another glance at home, drove to Kenji's house.

When he rang the bell at the top of the steep hill, the father came to the door.

"Hello, Mr. Kanno," he said, recognizing the man who seemed not to have changed a great deal in appearance since he had last seen him years ago in the camp in Idaho.

"I brought the car back," he said.

"The car?"

"Yes, Ken's car. I went to Portland with him."

"Come in," the man said earnestly, "please come in."

"No, I should get on home." He held out the keys.

"Just for a minute, please." Kenji's father motioned him inside.

He stepped into the house and watched as the big man strode across the living room and turned off the television set. Then Mr. Kanno came back to where he stood waiting, and regarded him thoughtfully. "I seem to recall your face, but . . ."

"I'm Ichiro Yamada. I guess I've changed."

"Of course. I remember. How's your family?"

"Fine, sir."

"Sit down. I'm all alone tonight. Been watching the ball game."

"I'm sorry I interrupted."

"Doesn't matter. Seattle's got a rotten team this year." He pulled his chair closer to Ichiro and it was apparent that his mind was not on baseball.

"The keys," said Ichiro and placed them in the other's palm.

"Thank you."

It was quiet in the house, quiet and warm and comfortable.

"Would you care for a drink?"

"No."

"When did you see him?"

"This morning."

"How was he?"

"Seemed pretty fair." He knew he should have remained still, but he found himself clumsily shifting on the sofa.

Mr. Kanno waited until he had settled down once more before saying: "Still alert was he? Able to talk and see and feel?"

Alarmed, he suddenly began to ramble with too much fervor: "Of course. He's fine. He was in excellent spirits when I left him this morning. A week, ten days, before you know it, he'll—" and he stopped as suddenly upon seeing the look in the father's eyes which said: My son and I had no secrets and if death is the truth about which you wish not to speak to me, do not speak at all.

"You mean well, but this is not the time for kindness," said the father gently.

"I'm sorry."

"We're all sorry. Now, tell me."

"We drove down two nights ago and, on the way, got a ticket for speeding in some hick town. I was driving but Ken switched places with me because he knew I didn't have a driver's license. The cop tried to make us pay off but Ken said no and got a ticket, which he tore up. Then, just before he went into the hospital, he said something about the cop having to come a long ways to get him. He was implying that he was going to die and . . ."

"Yes, that sounds like him." The father looked pleased.

"In the hospital I just saw him the one time this morning. He knows he's going to die. He said as much. He looked bad, physically that is, and he sounded a little bitter. I wish he were wrong, but I don't think there's any doubt. It's a matter of time, I guess."

"But his mind, it was all right? He talked sensibly?"

"Yes. He seemed a little weak, but otherwise he was just as usual."

"Good. If he had to go, I wanted it to be quick and so it has been."

Not grasping what the father meant, Ichiro regarded the man questioningly.

"Ken is dead. Three o'clock this afternoon."

At three o'clock he had been in a roadside café, eating pie and drinking coffee while Kenji's Oldsmobile was being gassed up. There were no words to describe the numbness of feeling in himself and he made no attempt to seek them.

"Let me drive you home now before the others start returning," said the father softly. "I did not tell them at dinner because they had planned to see a movie tonight and I could see no reason for denying them the fulfillment of the day's pleasures. Tomorrow, I will go to Portland and make arrangements for the funeral."

"You will be bringing him back here?"

"No. We were talking once, Ken and I, one of the several times when we talked about his dying . . ." He shut the door without locking it and they walked slowly to the car. "'Don't bother about me when I die, Pop,' he said, 'no fuss, no big funeral. If I'm in Portland when it happens, let them take care of it. Let them dig the hole.' And then he said: 'I'll come back and haunt you if you stick me in Washelli with the rest of the Japs. I've got ideas about the next place and I want to get started right.'"

Starting the car, the man swung the Oldsmobile in a tight semicircle and eased down the hill. "I thought it was pretty nice when the community got together and secured permission to bury their dead in Washelli. For a long time it was only for white people, you know. True, they keep the Japanese dead off in a section by themselves, but, still, I thought it was pretty nice. Ken, well, he was upset. 'Put my ashes in an orange crate and dump them in the Sound off Connecticut Street Dock where the sewer runs out,' he used to say. He knew I wouldn't do that, but I'll see he's not put in Washelli. We'll have a small service, just the family, and maybe they'll find a place for him down there where he'll be happy."

Ichiro listened to the quiet voice of the father and, when he turned to say something, he saw the glistening of the tears on the sorrow-stricken face. Turning away, he replied: "He deserved to live."

"And to be happy," added the father. "He was a good boy, pleasant, thoughtful, well-liked, but never really happy. The others, they seem not to mind so much. They say to themselves this is the way things are, and they are quite happy. He was not that way. He was always asking why things had to be the way they were. For him, I often think I should have never come to America. For him, I think I should have stayed in Japan, where he would have been a Japanese with only other Japanese, and then, maybe, he would not now be dead. It is too late now for such thoughts."

They did not speak again until the car was beside the grocery store. It was Ken's father who said: "Thank you for all you've done for us."

"I did nothing. Ken did much for me. I can't tell you how sorry I am."

"The family must know," said the man. "I must go home and tell them that Ken is dead. It will be very difficult."

"Yes."

"Goodbye, Ichiro."

He waved in return and watched until the car turned out of sight at the end of the block.

Finding the door unlocked, he entered the store and stood for a moment in the dark. He wondered at the complete stillness and frowned slightly at the stench of whisky. Slowly, he started toward the living quarters of the building. His foot struck a bottle and, when he peered over the floor to locate it, he noticed the several winding rivulets of water working their way across the boards and making shallow pools in the low spots. Perplexed, he traced the water into the kitchen and there, underneath the bathroom door, the flow was wide and strong and steady. His hand already reaching, for the doorknob, he suddenly felt the necessity of looking into the bedroom. He did so, seeing the pile of suitcases stacked neatly on his parents' bed but no sign of his mother or father.

Frightened now, sensing the tragedy inherent in the stillness, he rushed to the bathroom door and found it locked. Angrily, he drove his shoulder repeatedly against the door, feeling it give grudgingly a tiny bit each time until the final assault threw him into the bathroom.

She was half out of the tub and half in, her hair of dirty gray and white floating up to the surface of the water like a tangled mass of seaweed and obscuring her neck and face. On one side, the hair had pulled away and lodged against the overflow drain, damming up the outlet and causing the flooding, just as her mind, long shut off from reality, had sought and found its erratic release.

Feeling only disgust and irritation, Ichiro forced his hand into the tub to shut off the flow of water. He looked at her again and felt a mild shiver working up his back and into his shoulders. Momentarily unnerved, he found himself thinking frantically that she ought to be pulled out of the water. With movements made awkward by an odd sense of numbness, he bent over to grasp her about the waist. At the touch of her body against his hands, it occurred to him that all he need do was to pull the plug. Calm now, he reached for the chain and pulled it out and over the side. He watched for a while as the water level fell, drawing her tangled hair with it until the sickly white of her neck stood revealed.

Dead, he thought to himself, all dead. For me, you have been dead a long time, as long as I can remember. You, who gave life to me and to Taro and tried to make us conform to a mold which never existed for us because we never knew of it, were never alive to us in the way that other sons and daughters know and feel and see their parents. But you made so many mistakes. It was a mistake to have ever left Japan. It was a mistake to leave Japan and to come to America and to have two sons and it was a mistake to think that you could keep us completely Japanese in a country such as America. With me, you almost succeeded, or so it seemed.

Sometimes I think it would have been better had you fully succeeded. You would have been happy and so might I have known a sense of completeness. But the mistakes you made were numerous enough and big enough so that they, in turn, made inevitable my mistake. I have had much time to feel sorry for myself. Suddenly I feel sorry for you. Not sorry that you are dead, but sorry for the happiness you have not known. So, now you are free. Go back quickly. Go to the Japan that you so long remembered and loved, and be happy. It is only right. If it is only after you've gone that I am able to feel these things, it is because that is the way things are. Too late I see your unhappiness, which enables me to understand a little and, perhaps, even to love you a little, but it could not be otherwise. Had you lived another ten years or even twenty, it would still have been too late. If anything, my hatred for you would have grown. You are dead and I feel a little peace and I want very much for you to know the happiness that you tried so hard to give me . . .

Stooping over, he lifted her easily and carried her to the bedroom, where he laid her beside the pile of suitcases. Lingering a while longer, he brushed the damp hair away from her face and pushed it carefully behind her head. Then he made his way through the kitchen and into the store behind the counter to the telephone. He wasn't quite sure whom he intended to call, but he realized that there were people to be informed. He thought of the Kumasakas and the Ashidas and he recalled having heard mention of a young Japanese whom he had known slightly at one time and who now was a mortician, cashing in on the old Japanese who were dropping off like flies. He tried to think of the fellow's name and could only vaguely remember what the fellow looked like years ago in a faded pair of wide-ribbed corduroy trousers that stopped about three inches above ugly, thin ankles. Then he thought of the coroner and decided that he was the one to call. Having to look up the number, he reached overhead and turned on the light. He blinked his eyes at the sudden illumination and, as he did so, sighted the whisky bottle on the floor over against the vegetable stand, where he had kicked it. Wondering why the bottle had been so carelessly placed, he glanced about the store and saw the overturned apple box and, alongside of it, his father's stockinged feet. Hurrying out from behind the counter, he examined the prostrate figure on the floor.

"Pa!" he shouted with alarm.

The father lay on his back with his face turned sideways, and a thin streak of spittle oozed out of the corner of his partly open mouth. He was asleep and snoring softly.

Grabbing the old man by the shoulders, Ichiro shook him vigorously. He stopped when he saw the eyes open lazily and regard him with drunken indifference. The mouth curved into a silly grin and, immediately, the eyes shut and the heavy breathing was resumed.

Furiously, he shook him again, pulling as he did so and bringing the body to a sitting position. The eyes opened once more and the mouth emitted several unintelligible grunts of protest.

"Pa, are you all right?" he shouted.

His father grinned and shook his head.

"Ma is dead. You hear me? Dead. Killed herself. Ma killed herself."

He continued to grin, giving no sign of understanding. "Sick," he mouthed thickly, "Mama sick. Papa sick. Ichiro good boy. Everybody sick."

"Goddamn you, Pa. I'm telling you Ma's dead."

"Tell Taro he should come home. Mama needs him." With that, he shut his eyes and let himself collapse.

Ichiro hung on for a moment and then let him drop. Angrily, he returned to the telephone and leafed through the book in search of the coroner's number.

9

THE FUNERAL WAS HELD SEVERAL DAYS LATER AT THE BUD-
dhist church up on the hill next to a playground. Ichiro sat uncomfortably in a small waiting room and listened impatiently to the
talking of the men gathered around the table in the center of the
room. His father sat with the men and, while appearing ill at ease
in a navy-blue suit obviously new and purchased for the occasion,
seemed nonetheless to be enjoying himself. When he spoke, he did
so eagerly, striving to maintain an air of solemnity, but too often
unable to suppress a pleased grin.

"Ya, ya, a good wife," he was saying, "but she is gone and we
talk no more about her. There is no use for tears."

His protestations went unheeded, for they were gathered to
attend a funeral and one was expected to say the right things.

"How many years, Yamada-san?" questioned respectfully
a tall, thin individual who, playing his part to the full, had not
smiled at all.

"Twenty-eight years, Noji-san," replied the father.

"Such a long time. My wife and I have been together thirty-two
years, but twenty-eight years is also a long time. How lonely you
must be." Mr. Noji sniffed loudly and poked at his eye with a
soiled handkerchief.

"It is very sad indeed," added Mr. Ashida, who sat by the window in a crumpled, gray suit, "but she has given you two fine boys. Two fine boys, indeed."

Everyone turned and looked for a moment at Ichiro, who sat alone on a sofa against the wall. He squirmed uneasily and wondered if Taro would acknowledge the telegram which he had sent the day before after finally having hunted down the information that he was taking basic training in a California camp. When it finally came time to fill out the yellow form, all he had been able to write was: "Ma dead. Suicide." Was there something more he should have written?

"Almost time," said Mr. Kumasaka softly. As a close friend of the family, he was graciously handling all the details of the funeral.

Several of the men took out pocket watches or regarded their wrists and mumbled and nodded.

"Has everything been seen to?" queried a large man whose name Ichiro could not remember.

"I believe so," answered Mr. Kumasaka, whose thoughtful look indicated that he was hurriedly running a mental check.

"The telegrams. You have someone to read the telegrams?" The large man, having suddenly recalled that no mention had been made of telegrams, was quite excited.

Mr. Kumasaka tried staring him down.

"Ah, I felt something had been overlooked. There is so much to do, so many details." Equal to the occasion, the large man rose to his feet and beckoned to Mr. Ashida. "Please, Ashida-san, be so kind as to find someone. One of the younger people who are here. There is little time, hurry."

Mr. Ashida started hastily out of the room, but got no farther than Mr. Kumasaka, who had stretched out a restraining arm. "There is no need, Ashida-san. There are no telegrams." He looked up at the large man and repeated with a softness which was weighted with disapproval: "There are no telegrams."

Flustered, the man dropped back into his chair. "Of course, of course. I was only trying to be of assistance."

"It is just as well," said the tall, thin one. "They are always the same. Someone reads telegrams at all the funerals and I do not understand them but I know they are the same. You pick them from a card at the telegraph office. I know because I have sent them. They have cards for any occasion—funerals, weddings, holidays. I have sent them myself. You go to the telegraph office and say I want to send a funeral wire and the woman gives you a card and there are maybe ten different ones on it and you simply pick the one you want. If it is a good friend, you pick the longest. If not so good a friend, you pick one of the shorter ones. Years ago, when my cousin's youngest boy was killed by a train in Oregon, I went to the telegraph office and—"

"It is time, gentlemen, please." The church attendant addressed them from the doorway.

The men filed out solemnly down the hall after the attendant. The father and Ichiro walked a few steps in the opposite direction and entered the auditorium from a side door which led them directly to the first row of seats, which had been reserved for them. As they took their places and glumly regarded the open casket only a few feet away, the priest sauntered across the stage with its lavish, gold-bedecked shrine and seated himself beside an urn-like gong. Without acknowledging the people present, he struck the gong several times and promptly proceeded to recite the unintelligible mumbo-jumbo revered by all the old ones present but understood by none.

The air was heavy with the smell of incense and, behind him, Ichiro could hear the fervent muttering of sacred words, the occasional sucking of breaths, and a distant sob or two. Sitting up straight, he could see the profile of her heavily-powdered, cold, stony face protruding above the rim of the casket. It was a nice casket, but he still couldn't understand why his father had insisted on the four-hundred-dollar light-blue one when the two-hundred-fifty-dollar gray one would have sufficed. He hadn't argued. The old man seemed to know what had to be done.

He felt his father turn slightly toward him and he met his gaze.

The round face oozed with insuppressible excitement. It had been that way ever since the news of the mother's death had gotten around and the few close and many distant friends had crowded into the tiny store to offer assistance and condolences and to sit around and talk and drink tea and eat cookies and cake. Many were strangers whom he had no recollection of ever having met and yet they had filled the store during all hours of the day and night until this very evening. In the midst of it all, his father had been flushed without touching a drop, drunk with the renewal of countless friendships and elated by the endless offerings of sympathetic phrases. Women were constantly hovering over the stove, cooking meals for the bereaved and the mourning, scrubbing the floor, and making the beds and keeping the children quiet while the men ate and drank and smoked and talked endlessly. It had been quite a show and this was the final scene. If it all added up to something, he had missed it. He wanted very much for all of it to come to an end.

And, now, his father said excitedly to him: "Plenty people, Ichiro. A good funeral for Mama."

He felt the disgust creep into his face, but the father had already turned away and was again sitting with head slightly bowed and shoulders softly slouched so that he must have presented a grief-filled figure to his audience behind him.

Bringing his chant to a close with a series of well-timed blows on the gong, the priest rose and faced the mourning flock. He bowed to the widower and his son and ran a rosary-draped hand contemplatively along the front of his black robe with the wide, gold-embroidered collar.

His shiny, bald head bulged at the temples, the pink skin stretched tight as if ready to burst. Small, black eyes peered out of a round, massive face that might have been frightening had one unexpectedly confronted it, but which radiated only understanding and generosity to those who viewed it and knew that it was the countenance of their good priest. His voice was pitched too high and, attempting now to speak as one mourner to another, had lost the resonance and rhythm with which the holy chanting had been done. What he did, virtually, was to announce the funeral, giving the names of the deceased and the immediate members of the family, and then, gazing sympathetically upon the grieving father and son, he offered them words of courage.

Ichiro squirmed, looking neither left nor right and feeling the presence of his father beside him like a towering mass of granite. After the priest, there were others who spoke, embarrassed old gentlemen in ill-fitting Sunday suits who had been requested to speak of the deceased. They were like grade-school orators with badly prepared speeches, agonizing the audience with futile gestures and excruciating pauses and hopefully offering shaky grins, which merely heightened the general discomfort. They said fine things about the dead woman in fine language which none ordinarily used but heard more frequently only because the number of funerals seemed to be increasing. And it was the large man who had caused the blunder about the telegrams who gave, in a fairly shouting voice, the biography of the deceased. As he shouted, Ichiro listened and, it was as if he were hearing about a stranger as the man spoke of the girl baby born in the thirty-first year of the Meiji era to a peasant family, of her growing and playing and going to school and receiving honors for scholastic excellence and of her becoming a pretty young thing who forsook a teaching career to marry a bright, ambitious young man of the same village. And as the large man transported the young couple across the vast ocean to the fortune awaiting them in America, Ichiro no longer listened, for he was seeing the face of his dead mother jutting out of the casket, and he could not believe that she had ever been any of the things the man was saying about her. Then he looked at his father, who was hungrily devouring each meaningless word of praise and was so filled by now with the importance of himself that he held his head high and smiled pleasantly for all to see. First, he felt sick and wanted to get out of there. Then, he had an urge to laugh, so funny the whole affair seemed, and he made himself turn back to look at his mother's face to sober himself. And he kept looking at her until the service was over and the men from the mortuary in tails and striped trousers came up to close the casket. They wheeled it slowly down the center aisle to the long, black Cadillac hearse waiting at the curb. He got into the limousine behind the hearse with his father and waited for other people to get into their cars. A uniformed patrolman waited alongside his motorcycle, impatient to get the caravan to its destination and earn his extra pay.

"Pa, I feel sick," he said.

"Ya, Ichiro, but pretty soon. Not much more, now." He was looking out of the window and acknowledging the bows of passing people.

"What's next? I've had enough."

"Not much. We go to the funeral parlor. Then a short service by the priest, put the casket in the oven, and then to eat."

"Eat?"

"Yes, it is custom. We feed the people who were so kind as to come. It will be at the Japanese restaurant since home is too small. Everything is arranged."

"For crissake," he moaned, and at that instant he spied the face of Freddie hastening behind the limousine and cutting diagonally across the street to a parked car. He watched, seeing the little coupe billow forth a cloud of smoke, then begin to maneuver its way out of a tight spot. He jumped out of the limousine and raced across the street. Freddie was just getting ready to pull out into the street when he reached the car and jumped in.

"What the hell!" swore Freddie and, as quickly, was purposefully brandishing a huge pipe-wrench.

"It's me. Take it easy." He thrust his face closer.

Freddie blinked in amazement and repeated softly: "What the hell."

"Move. Come on," urged Ichiro.

"Sure." He shot the car down the street and sped away from the church and the people and the funeral.

I shouldn't do this, he thought to himself. I ought to go and see the thing through properly. I owe her that much. In a way, she did a lot for me, a lot more than most mothers. Looking at it from her side, it was a helluva lot. She meant well. She was all wrong, all crazy and unfeeling and stubborn, but she thought she was doing right. It wasn't her fault that things didn't go right. It wasn't she who wished the war on all of us and got the Japs thrown off the Coast and stirred up such a mixed-up kind of hatred that no one could think or feel straight. No, in her way, she was right and I'm still wrong, but I mustn't admit it. I want to stay here and find a place where I can work and eat and laugh a little sometimes. Is that asking for too much? I am right. She made me do wrong, but I am right in knowing what must be done. I will find work somehow, somewhere, and I will eventually learn to laugh a little because I shall want to laugh for feeling good all over. Time, how slowly it passes. I will hope and wait and hope and wait and there will come a time. It must be so. She is dead. Time has swept her away and time will bury my mistake. She is dead and I am not sorry. I feel a little bit freer, a bit more hopeful.

The car swerved hard, squealing around the corner and jarring him away from his thoughts.

"Goddamn," swore Freddie, "didn't see that red light. He gripped the steering wheel with both hands and drove recklessly with an almost frightened determination.

"What's the hurry?" he said alarmed.

"You askin'?" He kept his eyes straight ahead.

"Yes."

"For crissake. He's askin'."

"Well?"

"You told me. 'Take off,' you said."

"You can slow down now. I didn't mean it that way."

Braking the car hard and suddenly, he threw it to a stop against the curb. "Make up your mind, for crissake. You can do better, you drive." He fumbled for a cigarette underneath his coat and, poking it into his mouth, jabbed at the lighter. He waited nervously, pulling out the lighter too soon and sucking uselessly on the cigarette. He tried to get it back into the hole but his hand was trembling too much.

Ichiro took the lighter from Freddie and, after replacing it, struck a match for him. "What's eating you?" He remembered how quickly the wrench had been in Freddie's hand.

"Nothin'. You got me nervous, that's all."

"Why?"

"Why? 'Take off,' you said. I took off didn't I?"

"I thought you were going to slug me with that wrench."

"It was a mistake."

"What's got you so scared?"

"Nothin', dammit. I ain't scared of nothin'." As he gestured with his hand, he knocked the head off the cigarette. For a minute, he pawed furiously at the glowing embers on his coat. Then he was sucking busily on the stub, which wouldn't rekindle. He crushed it between his fingers and threw it against the dash. "Jeezuz," he moaned, "don't ever do it again."

"What's that?"

"Scare me like that. Goddammit, don't ever do it again or I'll shove a knife right between your balls." Heaving a long, drawn-out sigh, he slumped down and let his head rest on the steering wheel.

"Thanks for coming to the funeral," Ichiro said.

"Sure."

"Want me to drive you home?"

"No. I'm okay."

"Who did you think I was?"

"One of them guys."

"What guys?"

"I'm sorry about your mom. It's tough."

"Better this way."

"Sure. Still tough, anyway."

Lighting a cigarette, he tapped Freddie on the shoulder and put it in his mouth. Freddie sat up, no longer trembling.

"Who's after you?"

175

"Some guys."

"What for?"

"I cut him."

"Who?"

"Eto."

"Oh."

Freddie started to laugh, then said defiantly: "He asked for it. He come up to the bar and started diggin' at me. I told him to beat it. He wouldn't go. He kept needlin' me. The guys were laughin'."

"Everybody?" He had to know.

"No. Some of them were tellin' him to lay off. He wouldn't. Then he said shit like me wasn't good 'nough to spit on. I told him to try it. He did, but he was drunk. The stuff just dribbled down his chin. God, I hate the bastard."

"So you used your knife."

"I said I would. I was mad."

"Bad?"

Freddie laughed. "In the ass. When I went for him, some guy behind him pulled him off the stool. It swung him around and I got him in the ass."

"And then?"

"The Chinaman stopped it, the one who runs the place. He wasn't fixin' to lose his license because a couple of hotheads wanted to mix it up. He made us shake hands. What could I do?"

"Then it's all right."

"Sure, fine. Just fine. On the way home, they tried to run me down."

"Coincidence, that's all."

"I was on the sidewalk, way inside against the buildings, and the car didn't miss me by more than an inch."

"Oh."

Starting the car, Freddie eased it out into the street. He was smiling, fully recovered from his recent flight.

"Bastards," he muttered. "Think they own the country. They better keep outa my way."

They drove for a little while in silence until they came to a drive-in restaurant. Freddie ordered hamburgers and coffee for the two and tried to make time with the carhop.

"What have you been doing?" asked Ichiro.

Freddie frowned. "You're in a rut. You asked last time."

"I guess I did."

"Well, I'm still havin' fun, boy. Livin' it up."

"Still have your poker sessions?"

"Interested?"

"A little. A guy's gotta do something."

"That's tough," said Freddie, not unhappily. "I knew you'd come around, but you'll have to fix it up yourself. I don't play no more."

"Games getting too rough?"

"It's never too rough for me. I like 'em rough. I can't stand them guys." He spit through the window. "They're all chicken."

The carhop came back and hooked the tray to the door. Freddie ogled her shamelessly. The bill came to eighty cents. He tossed a dollar twenty-five on the tray and told her to keep it. She smiled.

"I'll make it yet," he said, handing over a hamburger and coffee to Ichiro.

"Nothing like trying."

"Boy," said Freddie, "she'd be a nice change from the fat pig."

"2-A?"

"Yeah," he replied defiantly, "you got one good memory. You should be a professor."

"Your luck's holding."

"Itchy-boy, you don't know the half of it. I got a silver spoon up my ass. Her old man likes me. Can you beat that?" He indicated the car with a sweep of his arm, throwing bits of relish on the dash. "This is his. 'Use it,' he says, 'any time you want.'"

"Doesn't he know?"

Freddie bit his lip, suppressing a chuckle. "Sure, I'm doin' him a favor. 'I go bowling on Wednesday nights,' he says to me. 'Saturdays I get together with the boys for a little game. Don't get home till real late. I like movies too,' he says. 'I go a lot to movies. I let you know when I go to the movie,' he tells me. 'You can run me down and use the car. No use lettin' the car sit outside while I'm in a movie.' He don't say he knows, but he knows all right. She was killin' him before I moved in. He's a nice guy. Timid, you know. Don't say much, but he's one good Joe."

"Screwy."

"Huh?"

"Sounds to me like he's screwy."

"He's not screwy enough. That's his trouble." He laughed loudly, enjoying his own joke immensely.

The conversation made him feel a little sick. He stuffed the rest of his hamburger into the coffee cup and reached past Freddie to set it on the tray.

"Don't like it? I think it's good."

"It is. I'm just not very hungry."

"Yeah," said Freddie with an obvious effort at sympathy, "it's tough. Guys like you take it hard."

"Wouldn't you?"

"Nah."

"How's that?"

The question seemed to embarrass him for a moment. He twisted uneasily in the seat. "Ah, they're old country," he said. "They shoulda never come here. They had no right to come here and born me and try to make me old country too. All that crap about Japan. Japan this, Japan that, hell, after what they done to me, you'd think they'd learn, but, no, the stuff they dish out is still the same. Like an albatross 'round a guy's neck. That's what they are. They sure screwed me up right."

"Why don't you move out?"

"What? I told you I'm livin'. No rent to pay, plenty to eat, money to spend, a car, a woman—I ain't givin' all that up. Besides, their line of crap don't faze me no more. Let 'em talk. They got nothin' else to live for."

"You make a lot of sense, Freddie. I never quite thought of it that way."

"That way about what?"

"About their having nothing to live for except making enough so that they could go back to the old country and be among their own kind and know a little peace and happiness."

"No kiddin', I said all that?"

"I thought so."

"Maybe I'll go to school," said Freddie. "I'm not so dumb."

He looked at Freddie grinning broadly, and felt sadly cheated. On the surface, there was wit and understanding and even a rough sort of charm, but one made a mistake in probing underneath. He understood now why Freddie was so constantly concerned with living, as he called it. It was like being on a pair of water skis, skimming over the top as long as one traveled at a reasonable speed, but, the moment he slowed down or stopped, it was to sink into the nothingness that offered no real support.

"I'd like to go home, if you don't mind," he said to Freddie.

"Sure, sure. Don't blame you. It's tough." He leaned on the horn, ignoring the prominently displayed signs requesting patrons to blink lights for service. A different carhop scurried over and, eyeing him hatefully, quickly removed the tray. "Any time, honey," he hollered at her back.

Backing out of the slot, he gunned the car into the street and jarred it over the strip of raised concrete in the middle to avoid having to drive a block to make a U-turn. He drove like a man possessed with a desperate urgency to move fast, covering ground in a frantic pursuit which was being conducted for the sole purpose of running from reality. To stop and sit still would mean to think. Ichiro looked at Freddie and felt these things and was glad for himself that he was bearing the problem inside of him and making an effort to seek even a partial release from it. He could only imagine what Freddie's nights must be like.

"Take it easy," he said.

Freddie neither turned his head nor slowed down. "Sure," he said.

"Have you thought any about working?"

179

"Na. Ain't got time."

"You will eventually."

"I'll think about it then."

He waited for a moment before he asked the next question: "Any of the fellows working?"

"You want a job?"

"I don't have much choice."

"Go down that place by the lake. You know the one I mean. Christian Reclamation Center or something. They know about us guys. I went down there."

"You?"

"Yeah, just to see. Me and Gary. They put him on right away. Real nice them church guys."

"What about you?"

"I told 'em I'd think about it." He took one hand off the wheel to light a cigarette.

"Gary the only one?"

"Na, there's a couple others I don't know."

"They working anyplace else?"

"Mike's old man's got a hotel and Pat's driving truck for some cleaning outfit. Some of the guys are going to school. Just like old times, I tell you."

"Doesn't sound too bad."

"Sure. Same crummy jobs, same rotten pay. Before the war the Japs got what the white guys didn't want. Now, if we want work, we take the jobs the good Japs don't want. Gary had a good deal in a foundry. He lasted ten days."

"What happened?"

"He'll tell you."

"I don't expect to see him."

"You wanta work?"

"Sure."

"I said go to that Christian Center place. Tell 'em I sent you. You'll see Gary. He likes it there. It's nothin' but a big junkyard and the place is fulla drunks and dead beats and homos, but they don't bother you. They got problems of their own. Gary'll tell you. He likes it."

He didn't mean to sound disappointed, but he couldn't help himself. "Sure" was all he could manage, in a tone full of uncertainty.

Freddie seemed aggravated as he said: "You asked me, didn't you? You're not doin' me a favor. All I said was you wanna job, you got one there."

"I guess I'll give it a try tomorrow," he replied, and remained silent until Freddie let him off at the store.

There were no lights on and he felt his way to the kitchen, swinging his arm around until he found the pull chain above the table. His mother was dead and his father was probably now at the Japanese restaurant hosting the post-funeral supper and making the most of being the center of attention.

Enjoy yourself, Pa, he said to himself. If this is what makes you happy, I guess you've had it coming for a long time. And, then, you might be lonesome for her. What with all the people coming and going ever since she died, you haven't had much chance to think about things. Maybe, the grief is waiting. Or is it that the grief has finally come to an end for you? It has for me in a way, her being gone. We'll have to talk about it.

He set a pot of tea to boil and, while looking for a spoon, came across the old deck of cards with which Taro had been playing solitaire on the afternoon that he had gone from house and family. It was an old deck, limp and greasy, and he had to peel the cards off carefully one at a time. It was better than nothing. For the first time it occurred to him that there wasn't even a radio in the house. He recalled that he used to listen to the radio a lot when he had been going to school. His mother hadn't liked it. Quite frequently she would slip into his room where he was studying and listening to Glenn Miller or Tommy Dorsey and firmly switch off the set.

Then, when the fellows started to learn how to dance, he got a bit of the fever himself and started to buy an occasional record or two until he had a fair-sized stack. The phonograph player he would borrow and keep a few days or a week at a time. She hadn't approved at all and that was what had led to the big trouble. At least, it was big then when he couldn't afford the price of a player. He had spent a couple of evenings at home listening to records and she'd said a few things about wasting time on foolish pursuits. He hadn't paid any attention, of course. He enjoyed listening to the records and saw no harm in them. It was on a Saturday night that he had gone to a dance at the church gym. When he got home, the phonograph was methodically and thoroughly smashed to bits. Nothing had survived. She had even gone to the trouble of snipping each of the innumerable lengths of wire into short pieces no more than an inch or two long. She paid for the player and had the satisfaction of seeing that he borrowed no others.

He justly felt after all these years that she had been very unfair. A radio, a record player, even a stack of comic books were small enough concessions. Had she made those concessions, she might have kept her sons a part of the family. Everything, it seemed, stemmed back to her. All she had wanted from America for her sons was an education, learning and knowledge which would make them better men in Japan. To believe that she expected that such a thing was possible for her sons without their acquiring other American tastes and habits and feelings was hardly possible and, yet, that is how it was.

Tragic, he said silently, so tragic to have struggled so against such insurmountable obstacles. For her, of course, the obstacles hadn't existed and it was like denying the existence of America. If only she had tried to understand, had attempted to reason out the futility of her ways. Surely she must have had an inkling during the years. He couldn't be sure and, much as he wished to know where and how the whole business had gone wrong, he could not, for he had never been close enough to his own mother.

Thinking that he heard a knocking on the front door, he remained still and listened. It came again, faintly, hesitantly. He went through the store, wondering who it could be.

She had stepped back away from the door and with the street lamp behind her, shadowing her face, he didn't recognize her immediately. When he finally realized that it was Emi, he could only awkwardly motion her inside.

"I heard only tonight," she said. "Mr. Maeno read about it in the paper. I am very sorry."

"Sure," he said.

They stood in the dark and tried to see each other's faces.

"You know about Ken?"

"Yes. I'm sorry I didn't know about your mother in time to get to the funeral."

"It's just as well. You didn't know her." The bitterness wouldn't be kept out of his voice.

She turned and he caught her face in the half-light coming from the street through the window. What he saw made him intensely sad. It wasn't sorrow or despair or anxiety, but the lack of these or any other readable emotions. Her lovely face was empty, even immobile.

"I'm sorry to keep you standing like this. Do come in, please." Grasping her elbow firmly, he led her to the kitchen.

Emi sat down without removing her coat and watched as Ichiro glumly resumed his game of solitaire.

"I'm getting a divorce from Ralph," she said.

"Does he know?"

"He asked me to get one."

"I'm sorry."

"Why?"

"Oh, I don't know. Seems a shame, that's all. I guess Ken never got around to finishing that letter."

"I hardly think it would have done any good," she said.

"Don't love him any more?"

She uncrumpled a ball of Kleenex and dabbed at her nose. "It's been too many years to talk about love."

"Son of a bitch." That wasn't what he was feeling, but only what he thought. Yet, how was he to say to her that a girl like her deserved a better deal than the rotten one that she had gotten, that a lot of guys including himself would give a right arm for a woman like her? He said again, mostly in despair: "No-good son of a bitch."

"Please," she said and she was close to tears.

"Sorry," he said hastily. Then he added: "This is sure the time for being sorry. Sorry this, sorry that. Why'd you come?"

"I heard about your mother. I wanted to see you."

"I'm glad you came. I hadn't expected to see you again and, really, it's very funny because there's no one else I can talk to."

"Mr. Maeno asked about you. He's still looking for someone to work for him."

"No."

"Oh."

"I've got a pretty good line on a job. I'm seeing about it tomorrow." He raked up the cards when the game wouldn't come out, shuffled, and started to lay out a new game.

"Stop, please." She put a hand over his.

"Sorry." He grinned at the word, then used his free hand to enfold hers. "It'll be nice for the fellows to have you back in circulation."

"Really?" She didn't sound pleased at all.

"Sure. You're still young, pretty—no, you're more beautiful than pretty. You've got a lot to offer any man. Ralph's a damn fool besides being a son of a bitch."

"Don't."

"Okay, but he is."

Talking, she slipped her hand unobtrusively from between his and back onto her lap. "I've been lonely a long time, Ichiro. I didn't realize how much until that night you stopped in and gave me word about Ken and then hinted you might not be seeing me any more. Then when Ralph's letter came, I really began to suffer from it. I've got to do something or go crazy."

"It takes time," he said, knowing that it meant nothing.

"Come and see me," she pleaded.

"I'm no good for you. No good for anybody."

"Why? Why do you say that?"

"True, that's why."

"It isn't, it isn't, it isn't!" And now she was sobbing quietly.

He drew a handkerchief from his pocket and put it in her hand. Emi sniffled into it and wiped her eyes, trying hard to compose herself.

"I'll be going," she said.

Without looking at her, he started to lay out a new game.

"It was after Ken was dead and Ralph's letter had come and I was feeling so lonely," said Emi. "I was thinking then how nice it would be to go dancing like a long time ago. I was hoping you would come and take me out. You see how it is? Thoughts of a little girl."

"Let's go," he said suddenly.

"Where?"

"Dancing."

"But, your mother."

"She's nothing. I ran out on the funeral. That's how it is."

"No," she said stubbornly, "not tonight. It wouldn't be right."

"Nonsense. What's more right than two young people going dancing because they feel like it?"

He straightened his tie and hustled into his overcoat.

She seemed to want to protest further but said no more.

"Come on." Taking her arm in his, they walked together out of the store and to her Ford, parked at the curb. Once in the car and on their way, they felt relaxed and free and happy.

"Where to?" he said gaily.

"Wherever you wish," she replied.

The only place he could think of was the Trianon in mid-town and it disturbed him because it was likely that he might run into some people there that might know him. He drove slowly, trying to think of some other places. Then it occurred to him that he couldn't help finding some place by driving along one of the busier highways going out of the city. He headed south, feeling the snug warmth of Emi close to him and immensely grateful that she had come to offer her condolences.

They didn't say much either in the car or after they found a sizable roadhouse and started dancing to a smooth six-piece orchestra. He was enjoying it and he felt that Emi was too. This is the way it ought to be, he thought to himself, to be able to dance with a girl you like and really get a kick out of it because everything is on an even keel and one's worries are only the usual ones of unpaid bills and sickness in the family and being late to work too often. Why can't it be that way for me? Nobody's looking twice at us. Nobody's asking me where I was during the war or what the hell I am doing back on the Coast. There's no trouble to be had without looking for it. Everything's the same, just as it used to be. No bad feelings except for those that have always existed and probably always will. It's a matter of attitude. Mine needs changing. I've got to love the world the way I used to. I've got to love it and the people so I'll feel good, and feeling good will make life worth while. There's no point in crying about what's done. There's a place for me and Emi and Freddie here on the dance floor and out there in the hustle of things if we'll let it be that way. I've been fighting it and hating it and letting my bitterness against myself and Ma and Pa and even Taro throw the whole universe out of perspective. I want only to go on living and be happy. I've only to let myself do so.

Hanging close to each other until the last note was gone, they slowly returned to the table to sit out the next or until they should again feel like dancing. They smiled at each other, for there really was nothing to be said. Ichiro saw a man coming toward them as he lit his cigarette.

He was not a young man and was slightly drunk. A few tables away he bumped into a chair and had to apologize, but he didn't take his eyes from Ichiro and Emi and he kept on coming.

"Pardon my intrusion," he said, smiling affably.

"Yes?" The skepticism was heavy on Ichiro's face. He felt the heat rising within him as he tried to adjust himself to what he felt was coming.

"I saw you and want to buy you both a drink."

"There's no need, really," said Emi pleasantly.

"There is," he said, his voice rising suddenly, "because I want to. Is that a good enough reason, or isn't it?"

"Sure it is." Ichiro relaxed. The man was obviously all right.

"Fine. No, don't ask me to sit down. All I want to do is buy you a drink. Okay?"

"Okay."

Pleased, the man went back to his own companions and, a while later, the waiter came to take the order for the drinks. They sipped them, eyeing each other quizzically and looking once or twice at the table of the man, who, as far as they knew, didn't look at them the rest of the time they stayed.

"What do you think?" asked Emi.

Ichiro rubbed his finger over a wet spot on the table. "I think the man had a lot of Japanese friends once. Maybe he was a produce buyer or something and he misses the ones who didn't come back."

"That's no good," she said.

"I think," he started again, "he had a son in that outfit that got surrounded up in the mountains by the Germans and was finally liberated by the Japanese boys."

Emi smiled. "No good."

"I think he's a Japanese who's lucky enough not to look Japanese and feels sorry everytime he sees a Jap that looks like one."

"That's even worse."

He took the butt of his cigarette and knocked off the glowing end into the ash tray. "I want to think," he said soberly, "that he saw a young couple and liked their looks and felt he wanted to buy them a drink and did."

"You keep on thinking that. That's how it was."

They rose, embraced, and moved out onto the dance floor.

"He probably had his eye on you," he said.

"Sure," she said, "other women they look at and undress. Me, they undress and put in bed. It's something about me."

"Keep talking," he said, feeling immensely full and wanting that moment to last a lifetime.

He didn't get home until three o'clock, but the kitchen light was on. The old man, quite sober, was busily tying up several large packages.

"Japan?"

"Ya, Ichiro. I send tomorrow."

He hung up his coat and sat and watched. "I felt sick. I just couldn't stay for the rest of the funeral, Pa."

"That is all right. Mama understands." He worked the heavy twine carefully around a brown package and motioned with his chin for Ichiro to lend a finger.

"You'll be lonesome Pa, huh?"

"Not so much. Mama was not well. It is better this way." He pulled vigorously at the knot, almost catching Ichiro's finger.

"You plan to keep the store?"

"Ya, it is just right for me. Maybe I fix up a little bit. Paint the shelves, a better cash register, maybe I think I buy a nice, white showcase for the lunch meat and eggs and things."

"That'll cost money."

"Ya, but I have. Mama was saving for Japan. She went for nothing. After a while, I go for nothing too." Sweating a bit from the effort of tying the packages, he wiped his brow with a clean handkerchief and sat down to pen the addresses. He seemed uncommonly contented for a man who had just lost his wife. He was still wearing the new blue suit as if he couldn't take the time to remove it before starting to work on the packages.

Ichiro watched his father, detecting an insuppressible air of enthusiasm and bubbling glee as he scratched in the names and addresses in both English and Japanese in several places on each package. There were four in all. The packages were the symbol of his freedom in a way. He no longer had just to think about send-ing them. It was his will to send them and nothing was any longer to prevent his so doing. He had no visions about Japan or about a victory that had never existed. While he might have been a weakling in the shadow of his wife, he was a reasonable man. He knew how things were and he was elated to be able finally to exercise his reasonable ways. Above all, he was a man of natural feelings and that, he felt, had always been the trouble with his wife. She tried to live her life and theirs according to manufactured feelings. It was not to be so.

"Do you ever think about life?" he asked his son suddenly.

"What?"

"Ya, that was too sudden," he said smiling. "I meant only to say that one must live in the real world. One must live naturally, not so? It is not always a happy life but, sad or happy, it can be a good life. It is like the seasons. It cannot always be fall. I like the fall."

"Sure, Pa. That makes sense."

The old man piled the packages neatly on the table and admired them. "You take time, Ichiro. There is no hurry. I do not understand everything that is troubling you. I know—I feel only that it is very big. You give it time. It will work out. After a while, maybe, you go to work or go to school if you wish. It can be done. You have a bed. There is always plenty to eat. I give you money to spend. Take time, ya?"

"Sure, Pa. I'm not worried."

"So? Good." And his lips trembled a little and Ichiro felt that it was because the old man was finally doing and saying what he should have long ago and knew that it was too late.

"I'm seeing about a job tomorrow," he said, heading for the bathroom.

"Ya, that is good. That is good." Sitting there contemplatively, he started to work the tie loose from his neck.

10

IT WAS THE SORT OF MORNING THAT NON-SEATTLEITES ARE always ascribing to Seattle—wet without being really wet and the whole city enveloped in a kind of dull, grayish, thin fog. The rain was there, a finely speckled spray which one felt against the skin of one's face and which clung to water-resistant garments like dew on a leaf. The temperature was around forty and the clammy chill of the air seeped through the outercoats and past the undergarments and sucked the warmth from the very skin.

Emerging from the stifling heat of the bus, Ichiro shivered and walked briskly down the hill toward the lake. Through the mid-morning haze, he saw the great length of yellow-painted fence proclaiming in red letters as tall as a man that everything beyond—the disreputable, patched-up, painted shacks and buildings, the huge pile of scrap, the freshly scrubbed trucks, the sad men and women—were of that charitable community known as the Christian Rehabilitation Center.

At the gate he inquired of a burly fellow sitting in a tiny guardhouse the way to the offices. The man pointed in the general direction of a cluster of garage-like, wooden structures. Ichiro stood there, showing by his expression that the directions weren't at all sufficient. The man pulled his arm out of the rain and sat down so that all Ichiro could see was the top of his head.

Walking close to the side of the roadway so as to benefit from the protection of the eaves, he ambled in the direction pointed out to him. There were stalls along both sides where the rejected items from a thousand attics and basements had been sorted out in a semblance of order and put out for the inspection of the bargain-hunting public. The junk was piled on tables, crammed into bins, hung from walls and ceilings, and pushed out into the drizzling rain. There were attendants to be seen, mean-looking men and women whose sole object seemed to be that of seeking out precious, overlooked cracks and corners into which more junk could be squeezed. They were like the junk, patched and refinished but with the wasted best years irrevocably buried. Neither they nor the antiquated, scarred, and barely salvaged items that they pushed about would ever see good days again.

Past the stalls was an expanse of open ground on which the junk was in the form and shape of yellowed iceboxes and ancient washing machines and huge stacks of iron beds and odds and ends of clumsy, rusted machinery and tangled heaps of pipes and one dilapidated two-and-a-half-ton army truck minus tires and wheels and a fender and the motor.

An old man in a long, black raincoat sat on the truck bed with legs dangling over the end. Beside him was a small pile of tools and he sat smoking his pipe as if he were out soaking up a bit of sunshine. His eyes, almost obliterated by bushy eyebrows and deep wrinkles, followed Ichiro's progress patiently.

"What'll you have?" he shouted.

"Nothing, pop."

"Got some fine refrigerators dirt cheap. I know. I fix 'em.

"I'm not buying today."

"How 'bout a washing machine. Got one in yesterday that's a honey." Picking up a screwdriver, he pointed behind him.

"How much?"

"I thought you weren't buyin'."

"I'm not."

"Why you askin'?"

"For the hell of it."

"You're cute," replied the old man, his whole face wrinkling further into a big smile. "Don't happen to have a drink on you, have you?"

Not bothering to answer, Ichiro continued along his way. He had now reached the buildings which from the gate had looked like garages and was surprised to see that they were workshops. Through the windows, he saw men fixing and painting furniture, repairing tricycles and wagons, upholstering sofas, sorting rags and baling them into enormous, rectangular bundles, and groups of women sewing and cutting and patching and cleaning clothing and curtains and rugs and bedding. They all looked warm and comfortable and satisfied.

There was a sign on the end of one of the buildings saying "Administrative Offices" with a red hand pointing over to his right. He took the corner and was mildly astonished at the sight of a new one-story brick building with plenty of glass and surrounded by a border of young bushes. Pausing at the door, he fought the urge to turn back and forget about the job. He brushed his shoes across the large rubber mat and saw that the woman behind the desk in the lobby was smiling at him. He took his time, walking in slow, deliberate steps and concentrating on the smile so as not to get nervous. By the time he was close enough to speak to her, he was quite fascinated by the smile, which had remained precisely the same all the while he had been watching it.

"Yes, young man?" She spoke quickly, almost sharply.

It was then that he saw that her eyes were not smiling and that the smile on her mouth was caused by a scar on one side of her face that tugged at the corner of her mouth so that she had not really been smiling at all.

"I came about a job," he said.

She pushed one of a half-dozen buttons on a brown, plastic box and lifted the phone to her ear. Waiting no more than a few seconds, she spoke: "Are you available for an interview, Mr. Morrison?"

A pause, then: "A young man. Japanese, I think."

"Down the hall to your left," she said, pointing with one hand and replacing the phone with the other. "Mr. Morrison will see you."

"Thanks." He walked down the hall, passing several unmarked doors. Confused, he halted and looked back at the woman. She was looking straight ahead and he couldn't see the smile because it was on the other side of her face.

"Over here, fella," Mr. Morrison called, stepping out into the hallway a few yards still further down. He was tall, blond, and wore a smart-looking blue suit. He motioned Ichiro into the office, saying: "Have a chair. Be with you in a minute."

There was a desk, a filing cabinet, a typewriter on a metal stand, and two chairs. He sat down on the one in front of the desk. It was several minutes before Mr. Morrison returned.

"I'm Morrison," he said with arm extended.

Thinking that the man couldn't be much over thirty, Ichiro took the hand and said: "Mine is Yamada. Ichiro Yamada."

"Ichiro Yamada," repeated the man fluently. "How do I pronounce it?"

"Good."

"Ought to," he said with obvious elation as he skirted around the desk to his chair. "Spent fifteen months in Japan. Ever been there?"

"No."

"Too bad. Go if you ever get a chance. Fine country. Fine people. *Nihongo ga wakarimasu ka?*"

"A little bit."

"I speak it pretty good myself. Only way to get to know the people is to learn the language, I say. I learned it and I got to know them. I was there before the war, thanks to my dad. He did a lot of business there." He offered Ichiro a cigarette and put one in his own mouth. "Now, tell me something about yourself."

"Not much to say. I need a job. I heard there might be one here."

"Someone who works here?"

"No. A friend of a fellow who works here. You know Gary?"

"Sure thing. Gary's a fine worker, a real artist. He does the signs on our trucks." Opening the center desk-drawer, Mr. Morrison withdrew a five-by-seven card and neatly lettered Ichiro's name on the top. He asked the usual questions concerning parents, address, education, special abilities and noted the answers in the same neat manner on the lines below. Then, since the question which needed to be asked wouldn't come out quite as easily as he had hoped, he made a pretense of studying the information on the card. Ichiro squirmed and Mr. Morrison smiled reassuringly and studied the card some more. Finally, he said: "Gary has a problem, you know."

Ichiro looked up, not quite understanding at first, but quickly grasping what Mr. Morrison was trying so hard to make as painless as possible for both of them. "My problem is the same one," he said in a very level voice.

"I see." A look of disappointment crept over his face. To erase it quickly lest Ichiro notice, he tried to smile, but, failing, rose hastily and turned about to gaze out the window. "Nasty day," he said emptily.

"I know," said Ichiro, sharing the man's discomfort.

"I'm sorry," said Mr. Morrison, settling back into his chair. He smiled but with a weariness which made him appear for the moment an old man. "If the question is impertinent, say so, but tell me, if you will, why you didn't comply with the draft."

"That's a good question."

"Don't you know?" He sounded almost angry.

"Not exactly, Mr. Morrison. The evacuation, the camp, my parents, all of it, and then some, I guess."

"Have you any regrets?"

"Yes."

"You're sorry then?"

"Yes."

"Sure you are." He slouched in his chair and folded his hands under his chin thoughtfully. "I like my work, Ichiro. I like it because I'm working with people and for people who need help. Drunks, morons, incompetents, delinquents, the physically handicapped. I've helped them all and it gives me great satisfaction. But you and Gary, there's nothing wrong with you. You don't belong here. All I can do for you is to give you a job and hope. That's what makes it tough. Hope is all right, but it's so much nicer when you can help it along. I can't do that for you. I've thought about it a lot. Ever since Gary came. Youth, intelligence, charm, a degree in fine arts, health—he's got everything. So have you. Makes me feel damned useless. Both of you could step into a hundred jobs out there in the city this very minute and do a more competent job than the people in them. Unfortunately, they never told me about a therapy for your kind of illness. Well," he said, straightening up suddenly, "no point in adding my woes to yours. How would you like to work with Gary?"

"I guess that would be all right."

"It pays thirty-five a week. A little more later on maybe."

He thought of the two-sixty a month offered to him by Mr. Carrick in Portland only a week before. I should have taken it, he thought; if Ma had been dead then, I would have. It would have been work that I would have liked. It could have led to something. Mr. Carrick would have been nice to work for. A lot of things could have been, only they weren't. Morrison isn't to be blamed for being young and disturbed. He means well. He's doing the best he can. "That's enough for me," he answered.

"No need to say yes right this minute, of course."

"Well, I would like to think some about it."

"Sure. Let me know in a few days."

"I will."

Mr. Morrison rose and came around the desk to shake his hand once more. "Stop by and chat with Gary long as you're here. He can tell you more about the job than I can."

"Fine."

"Take the side door to your right. You can't miss him."

"Thanks, Mr. Morrison, I'll let you know."

The man held on to his hand all the way out to the hallway. It seemed as if he were reluctant to let Ichiro go, for not having done more. He seemed to be searching for something adequate to say. Finally, shaking his hand vigorously a last time, he said with great enthusiasm: "I know you'll like working here. Maybe the three of us can find a solution to your peculiar situation. There's an answer to everything, you know."

"Thanks," he said again and walked down the hall to the door.

He found Gary up on a stepladder, working on the last *i* in the word Rehabilitation, which was being painted on a huge, green van. With deft, sure strokes of the brush, Gary applied the red paint, filling in the outline of the letter, which he had made with equal care. Not until he had completed it and leaned back to appraise his own work did he seem to notice that he was being watched. Still, he did not turn immediately. Brush in hand, he dabbed carefully twice before he looked satisfied. Then he turned toward the entrance and, recognizing Ichiro, frowned thoughtfully.

"Hello," said Ichiro as Gary climbed down and came toward him.

"Nice to see you, Itchy," said Gary.

They shook hands and Ichiro noticed that Gary still wasn't smiling although he seemed friendly enough.

"I was just in to see Morrison. He thinks he can fix it up for me to work here with you."

"Fine," said Gary, "fine." It occurred to him then that he was still holding the brush in his hand, and he walked to the back of the shop to place it in a can. He lingered there, fussing around with jars of paint and rags and shoving things into a semblance of order.

Ichiro, slightly disconcerted by Gary's cool behavior, walked up to the truck and examined the lettering. "You're good. That's all right," he said.

Gary turned abruptly, and he suddenly grinned broadly. "What the hell," he exclaimed. "You ought to kick me in the ass. Let's try again." He extended his hand once more and shook Ichiro's vigorously.

"If this is treatment number two, I like it better," said Ichiro, greatly relieved.

Gary took cigarettes from his shirt pocket, shook one half out of the pack, and offered it to Ichiro. They lit up and sat on a couple of boxes against the wall.

"I heard you were out," said Gary.

"Out?" grinned Ichiro. "If this is what it's like being out, I wouldn't have been so anxious."

Standing up, Gary walked up to the truck and studied the unfinished job of lettering. He wasn't tall, but slender with wide shoulders and strong, graceful arms and legs. He ran both hands through his thick, wavy black hair and stood poised for a moment with palms clasped behind his neck. "Maybe it's a little easier for me," he said softly as if to himself and, with back toward Ichiro, no longer aware of his presence. "I am a painter—that is, I think I am. I want to be a good painter, an artist. I'm painting now, but it wasn't always that way. Before, it was talk. Sitting over cold cups of coffee covered with cigarette ashes and talking about life and sex and philosophy and history and music and real art and getting so all-fire worked up that I was ready to run out into the black night and splash paint all over the side of a building in a burning frenzy of creation but never moving and continuing to talk and dream and sit like I had a lead weight in my hind end. It wasn't once in a while. It was all the time. Weeks, months, years, talking and squirming—and maybe working on canvas once in a long while, but only because you suddenly ran up against a day or a night when absolutely nothing was going on—and not being able to paint because the lead weight in the behind was sniffing around for the chair that wasn't there. If I had spent the time painting that I did talking, I might have had a painting now, a real painting. I wasted a lot of time. God, there's so much time that I've wasted." Fingers tightening about his head, he squirmed as if in agony.

Ichiro drew quietly on his cigarette and watched as the youthful figure worked the tension out of itself and started again to speak.

"It was good, the years I rotted in prison. I got the lead out of my ass and the talk out of my system. I died in prison. And when I came back to life, all that really mattered for me was to make a painting. I came home and said hello to the family and tried to talk to them, but there was nothing to talk about. I didn't stay. I found a room, next to the sky, a big, drafty attic atop a dilapidated mansion full of boarders who mind their own business. Old friends are now strangers. I've no one to talk to and no desire to talk, for I have nothing to say except what comes out of my paint tubes and brushes. During the day, I paint for my keep. At night, I paint for myself. The picture I want is inside of me. I'm groping for it and it gives me peace and satisfaction. For me, the cup is overflowing."

He turned and the peace he spoke of was clearly written on his face: "What was unfortunate for you was the best thing that ever happened to me."

"Sure," said Ichiro, as he looked deep into his friend's eyes to detect the fear and loneliness and bitterness that ought to have been there and saw only the placidness reflected in the soft, gentle smile.

"I'm not crazy," said Gary.

"I wasn't thinking that," said Ichiro reassuringly.

"It's just that I'm finally on the right track. If that makes me crazy, I won't argue about it."

"If it's right for you, that's all that matters I suppose."

Going back to the worktable to get his brush, Gary ascended the ladder and resumed lettering. "I've got to get this out before lunchtime," he said.

"I might as well run along, anyway," answered Ichiro.

"Stay and watch, if you like. It won't bother me."

"It was nice seeing you again." He started to walk out.

"Wait."

Gary jumped down off the ladder and walked up to Ichiro. "I'm sorry if I made you feel unwelcome when you came. It wasn't that at all. I'm just forgetting how to be sociable. I think we could get along very nicely working together."

"Thanks, but I think my mind was pretty well made up before I came here. You can tell Morrison that I've decided to pass up his offer. Maybe I'll see you around."

"Sure."

As he started out, he remembered Freddie's having mentioned Gary's brief period of employment at a foundry. He paused and, standing at the entrance, called back: "Gary."

He was beginning to climb the ladder, but stopped on the third rung and waited.

"What happened at the foundry?"

"Happened?"

"Yeah. Freddie said you had a good deal there."

Gary smiled. "Fine fellow, that Freddie. He didn't tell you?"

"No."

Descending to ground level, Gary came close to Ichiro. "I'm glad he didn't, seeing you have to know. He would have made it sound worse than it really was. It was a good job, a good deal as far as the money was concerned. The work was hard, of course. With overtime and all, I was taking home close to a hundred a week. There were a number of vets in the same shop, even a couple I'd known pretty well at one time. They steered clear of me. Made it plain that I wasn't welcome. But, hell, I have to eat too. I guess they spread the word around because, pretty soon, the white guys weren't talking to me either. Birdie knew about it too, but it didn't seem to matter to him. Birdie's a colored fellow. He took a liking to me. He let everybody know that anyone wanting to give me a rough time would have to deal through him. I heard he used to spar with Joe Louis some years back. I had plenty of protection. I should have left then, I guess, but I figured if I got killed accidentally by a falling sewer pipe or had my brains mangled by a crowbar, maybe it was something I had coming to me. As

I've said, I feel like a guy that's come back from the dead. Living on borrowed time, you know. Makes one a bit anxious, of course, but there's a peace about it that takes away all the ordinary fears of getting hurt or dying. I kept on working, ignored but not minding it. Really, it didn't bother me one single bit. Birdie pretty near got into a couple of fights over me, but only because it seemed to bother him for some reason. I kept telling him not to go to bat for me, that I didn't mind not being spoken to or being called names, but he couldn't see how that could be. He was suffering for me, really suffering. There's still plenty of good people around, you know."

Ichiro nodded, thinking of Kenji and Emi and Mr. Carrick.

"There isn't much more to say," continued Gary quietly. "I knew, if I stayed on, that something would happen to me. I could feel it building up in the awful quiet that kept getting bigger and meaner every day. And they sensed that I wasn't frightened and that seemed to make it all the worse. Again, I say I should have left like a sensible individual, but I didn't. There was no guarantee that I wouldn't run into the same sort of thing someplace else. The way I saw the whole thing was that the worst they could do to me was to kill me and, since that didn't make one bit of difference to me, why should I give up a good income? It was all too simple. Somebody was smart enough to figure that I'd probably show a little more concern for someone else."

"Birdie?"

"Yes, the bastards. They loosened the lugs on his car. He lost a wheel going fifty miles an hour and rolled over three times." He added, with a voice full of emotion: "Not a scratch. He got out clean."

"They don't know what they're doing."

"I shouldn't say that. They know too well what they're doing. Go for broke, you know. You've heard it."

"Sure."

Gary rubbed the wooden tip of the brush thoughtfully against his cheek. "This is a bad time. Bad for us, that is. The atmosphere is full of emotion. Too much of the heart and not enough of the mind. Makes bastards out of good guys. Later on, things will soften down. Reality will make them lose some of their cocksureness. They'll find that they still can't buy a house in Broadmoor even with a million stones in the bank. They'll see themselves getting passed up for jobs by white fellows not quite so bright but white. They'll take a trip up to some resort, thinking this is God's green land of democracy for which I killed a dozen Krauts, and get kicked in the face with the unfortunate mistake about the reservation story because he'd signed the letter Ohara and the guy at the resort thought it was good old Irish O'Hara. Tough to have a name like Ohara and feel that maybe when they made up the batch of orders upstairs one of the Lord's workers neglected the apostrophe and so the guy turns up in the U.S.A. a Jap instead of an Irishman. That's beside the point, however. When they find out they're still Japs, they'll be too busy to be mean to us."

"You really think there will come a time when what we've done will be forgotten?"

"I didn't say that. They'll forget. Some of the guys who have it real tough might even envy us secretly. Time will make them forget, but I'm not so sure that we will. Right now, I say the situation is highly emotional. They've gone all out to prove that their blood is as red as Jones's or Torgerson's or Mayo's or what have you. They've just got through killing and being killed to prove it and I don't blame them one bit for not hesitating to kill us. You and I are big, black marks on their new laundry."

"What if it had turned out the other way?"

Gary smiled. "You run along home and talk to yourself about any if's and but's about the thing. I only know what is. That's what we've got to live with."

Ichiro stretched out his arm and grasped Gary's hand firmly for a moment. "I'll think about what you've said. Makes sense."

"Good luck."

"Thanks."

He walked out of the garage and past the new building and around the workshops and up toward the gate without seeing the old man still sitting on the truck that would never run again. The fine drizzle had turned to a steady rain and, waiting for the bus, he shivered slightly and noticed that he hadn't buttoned up his raincoat. With groping fingers, he worked the buttons into the holes as he gazed back down the hill at the shabby collection of buildings which he had just left. The rain pelted his head, worked into his hair, and dripped down the back of his neck, but he was like a man whose mind was momentarily detached from his physical being.

He was thinking about the apostrophe, the topside comma, the period with a tail on it. It was the little scale on which hinged the fortunes of the universe. It was the slippery, bald-headed pivot on which man hung, unborn and unnamed until suddenly he found himself squirming on one side or the other. It made a difference, of course, which side he chose to fall off on but, when a fellow can't see for the heavy clouds down below, he simply has to make up his mind in a hurry and hope for the best. Was that the erratic way of the Almighty? Ohara, O'Hara. Lock up the apostrophes for a while. We've got too many Irishmen.

He heard the bus but wasn't quick enough to leap back as the wheels sloshed against the curb. The blackened spray clung to the front of his raincoat and he made it worse by rubbing his hand over it.

Getting on, he deposited his token and settled down in a seat next to a dozing man.

It wasn't his fault. Neither was it the fault of his mother, who was now dead because of a conviction which was only a dream that blew up in her face. It wasn't the fault of the half a billion Chinamen who hated the ninety million Japanese and got only hatred in return. One only had to look about to see all the hatred in the world. Where was all the goodness that people talked about, the goodness of which there was never quite enough to offset the hatred? He recalled how he'd gone to a church in Idaho with

Tommy, who was always reading a Bible. Tommy would say grace before he ate a lousy peanut-butter sandwich out in the choking dust of the sugar-beet field when all the other guys were cussing and bitching and stuffing the bread into their dirty faces. They gave Tommy a bad time. Freddie had been with them, too. He was the one who claimed he heard Tommy thanking God for the Sears-Roebuck catalogue one day while squatting over the hole in the outhouse. Tommy didn't seem to mind. He just smiled as if he understood it all. That's why he'd gone along with Tommy that day instead of playing poker in the bunkhouse. If Tommy had the answers, he wanted to know about them. They had slipped into the church, where Tommy had already gone for several Sundays. The service being in progress, they sat in the back. He sensed immediately that they weren't welcome. Tommy seemed not to notice at all the furtive glances and the unguarded whispering. He had been glad to get out of there and, as they walked to the bus depot, the car had pulled alongside of them.

The man leaned out of the car: "One Jap is one too many. I told them: Two Japs today, maybe ten next Sunday. Don't come back."

He'd gone back to his poker games and Tommy didn't go to town until they moved on to another farm. After several weeks Tommy, short and squat and studious looking, approached him in the showers. "There's an excellent church in this town," he said, "a true, Christian church where they are glad to have us. Why don't you come with me this Sunday?"

"Shove it," he had said and immediately wished he hadn't when he saw the hurt look in Tommy's eyes.

"Just this once, please," he pleaded, taking a step forward. "I'm quite sorry about the other time. I'd like to make it up to you for having given you such a poor start."

In the end he had agreed and it seemed that Tommy was right. It was a small church, but filled to capacity and, after the service, the congregation had displayed their friendliness to the extent of keeping them standing outside for an hour asking questions and conversing endlessly, as though they were old friends. By the third Sunday they were having dinner with Mr. Roberts, who had six children but still insisted on their coming. Ichiro was delighted and Tommy was beaming.

It was the sixth or seventh Sunday, he couldn't remember exactly. What with the heat and the crowded benches, he started to squirm out of his jacket, twisting as he did so, and he saw the white-haired Negro standing in the back. He wondered then why the usher hadn't gotten out one of the folding chairs which were often used when bench space ran out. He was comforted when, a few minutes later, he heard chairs being rattled in the back. He took another look after the minister had finished his sermon and the Negro was still standing. The chairs had been for the Kennedys, who had arrived late, and they were sitting only a few feet away from the Negro.

There was no whispering, no craning as there had been in the other church. Yet, everyone seemed to know of the colored man's presence. The service concluded, the minister stood silent and motionless on the stage. The congregation remained seated instead of disintegrating impatiently as usual into a dozen separate chattering groups. Very distinctly through the hollowness of the small church echoed the slow, lonely footsteps of the intruder across the back, down the stairs, and out into the hot sun. As suddenly, the people came to life like actors on a screen who had momentarily been rendered inanimate by some mechanical failure of the projector.

He had gone straight back to the bunkhouse by himself. He was mad and it hadn't helped any when he couldn't get into the poker game right away. It was almost an hour before someone dropped out and, when they quit late that night, he had dropped his earnings plus a week and a half's wages still to be earned.

A few days later Tommy, reluctant to lose one who had appeared such a promising recruit, tried to justify the incident. "The ways of the Lord are often mysterious," he had said. "There are some things which we cannot hope to understand. You will feel better by next Sunday."

"Save the holy crap for yourself," he had replied. "Seems to me like you goddamned good Christians have the supply spread out pretty thin right now."

And then Tommy had revealed himself for the poor, frightened, mistreated Japanese that he was. "Holy cow!" he had exclaimed in a frantic cry, "they like us. They treat us fine. We're in no position to stick out our necks when we've got enough troubles of our own."

"Good deal. You hang on to it, will you? Son of a bitch like you needs a good thing like that."

When he left him to join the others whom Freddie was entertaining with his inexhaustible stock of filthy jokes, he thought he heard a whimper.

That happened before I had to make the choice, he thought. That was when we were in the relocation camp out in the God-awful desert and it seemed like living to be able to be free of the camp for brief periods working for peanuts on a sugar-beet farm. That was all before I made a mess of everything by saying no and I see now that my miserable little life is still only a part of the miserable big world. It's the same world, the same big, shiny apple with streaks of rotten brown in it. Not rotten in the center where it counts, but rotten in spots underneath the skin and a good, sharp knife can still do a lot of good. I have been guilty of a serious error. I have paid for my crime as prescribed by law. I have been forgiven and it is only right for me to feel this way or else I would not be riding unnoticed and unmolested on a bus along a street in Seattle on a gloomy, rain-soaked day.

Through the front of the bus, he saw the clock tower of the depot. He could have ridden a couple of stops further, but he rose and pulled the cord. He stepped out into the rain, turning the short collar of the raincoat snugly up around his neck. Here was the bus station, the same stretch of concrete walk on which he had stood with his suitcase that morning he had first come back to Seattle and home and, yes, friends too. He was young still, but a little wiser. Perhaps he was a bit more settled in heart and mind.

205

And the rain, it was appropriate. "After the rain, the sunshine," he murmured. It wouldn't be quite as easy as all that. It could rain forever for all he knew. Still, there had been a lot of goodness that he had not expected. There was room for all kinds of people. Possibly, even for one like him.

I've got to keep thinking that. I will keep thinking that. It's only a thread, but how much it seems in a life where there might have been nothing.

He walked up to the depot and turned up Jackson Street, and, while he waited for the light to change, the cluster of people at the bus stop hardly gave him a glance.

11

HE LAY ON THE BED LISTENING TO THE OCCASIONAL NIGHT noises which drifted through the walls of the old frame building which was both business and home. There was, now and then, the gentle whir of rubber tires speeding over concrete, the foggy blast of a semi's air-horn far off in the distance, the muffled rumble and jar of trains being switched not too far away. It was a time of quiet, but, for Ichiro, the uneasiness prevailed.

The telephone rang out in the store. He listened to its ringing. Once, twice, three times—ah, he got it.

"Ichiro."

"Yes?"

"It is for you. The telephone."

Throwing his legs over the side, he fumbled his feet into shoes.

"Ichiro," called the father with a bit more insistence.

"Yes, yes, I'm coming." Trailing laces which clicked along the floor, he hurried out. Behind the counter, the old man was holding the receiver out to him. "Who is it?"

"I do not know. Somebody who wishes to speak with you," said the father with a shrug.

"Hello," he said into the phone.

"Itchy?" It was Freddie.

"Yes."

"This is Freddie." He sounded like a little kid.

"Hello, Freddie."

"Hi. Let's do somethin'."

"What?"

"Whatcha mean what? Somethin'. I got the car. You doin' anythin'?"

"Taking it easy."

"What the hell. You gotta get out and do somethin'. I'll pick you up, huh?"

"Well . . ."

"I'll tell you what. I'm gettin' me a shine and maybe fixed up. You remember where that place what used to be a cigar store is? On Jackson up from where the movie was. You know, that place where all the guys used to buy the dirty comics."

"Yes, I remember."

"Great. It's a shine parlor now. I'll see you there in fifteen, twenty minutes. Check?"

"Well, I . . ."

"Goddammit, you gotta get out and live, I told you. If you ain't shown when I get there, I'm comin' to your place."

"Okay, okay," he said with more irritation than willingness.

"Great. Fifteen, twenty minutes like I said."

He put the phone down and reached for a package of cigarettes.

The old man was thumbing through a catalogue of store equipment with a satisfied look on his face. "Who was it?" he inquired without looking up.

"Freddie."

"Akimoto-san's boy?"

"Wants me to go out with him."

"Ya. That is fine. You go and have a good time." He punched open the register and handed his son a couple of bills.

"Christ, Pa," he blurted out, "I can't keep taking money from you."

"Pretty soon you get a job," his father said softly. "It will take time, I know. It is all right. I want you to have the money. I want you to have a good time."

"I don't know. I'm not a kid any more."

"Take," he urged, "it will make me happy. Mama gone, Taro someplace else, only you and me now. We will find a way." His face puffed up as if he were going to cry.

"Okay, Pa, if that's how you want it." He slipped the money into his shirt pocket.

"Ya," said the father as he walked to the front and locked the door and began to turn off the lights, "I'm going to fix up a little bit. Buy a few things for the store. You can go to school and help me sometime maybe. That would be good."

"Sure." He sensed that his father was, perhaps, beginning to feel a bit lonesome. In the semidarkness he appeared very much like a frightened, lonely man and not at all the free and expansive soul he had seemed so short a time before. "Sure, if a job doesn't turn up, I might go to school and help you out here, Pa."

"That would be nice, Ichiro. Mama would like that."

"Great," he said curtly, and was immediately sorry. She's gone now, he thought. I don't have to fight her or hate her any more. It will take Pa a little while to get used to being without her. "I can give you a hand around here until something comes up or I decide to go back to school," he said soothingly.

The old man nodded agreeably as he walked to the kitchen with the catalogue.

Freddie was up on the chair getting his shoes shined by a white-haired, scrawny Negro who whipped the polish rag expertly over the now gleaming shoes.

"Itchy boy," shouted Freddie, "pull up a chair."

Ichiro climbed up next to his friend, surveying the dingy narrowness of the place, which was garishly dominated by a multicolored, giant juke box standing in the back.

"How 'bout it, Rabbit?"

The Negro looked up without breaking the whipping rhythm of the rag and, in marked contrast to the celerity of his arms, uttered lazily: "Not tonight, boy. Tomorrow maybe. All my gals are booked, I tell you."

"What the hell! My buddy here's been stirrin' for two god-damned years and he can't wait till tomorrow."

"Yeah?" He craned his neck to appraise Ichiro. Then he looked at Freddie: "Same deal?"

"Yeah, yeah. Same as me."

"Good boy. If they had come for me, I would of told them where to shove their stinking uniform too." He finished off the shoes with several long, slow swipes. "Shine?" he asked Ichiro.

"No thanks."

Rabbit ran the rag lightly over Ichiro's shoes and straightened up.

Freddie hopped down and put a hand on Rabbit's shoulder. "C'mon, Rabbit. Fix us up."

"Sorry. It's like I told you. I want to help, but that's how it is."

"Shit!" said Freddie, stepping back angrily. "Always tellin' me you can get a guy anythin' he wants. Big talk, that's what."

Rabbit smiled calmly, "I got you that nice Elgin real cheap."

"So whattaya want me to do? Go to bed with it?"

"You're small enough all right."

"All right. All right, wise guy. I got your number now. Ain't nothin' but a bag of wind. C'mon, Itchy. Let's blow."

Quickly, Rabbit stuck out his hand. "Two bits for the shine, mister."

Freddie dug up a quarter and slapped it into the outstretched palm.

"How's about a nice radio cheap?" said Rabbit.

Without bothering to answer, Freddie stalked out with Ichiro close behind. They walked down the block to the car and got in. Lighting cigarettes, they sat and smoked in silence.

"Well, that screws that," finally said Freddie.

"What's that?"

"That damn Rabbit. Always talkin' big. 'Any time you want a gal,' he's always sayin' to me, 'Rabbit's the boy to see.' The guy's full of crap. From here on in, this boy's shinin' his own goddamned shoes." He rolled down the window and flipped the cigarette at a passing car. "How 'bout some pool?"

"Well . . ."

"You shoot pool?"

"Yes, but . . ."

"But what? Do you or don't you?"

"Yes, I do."

"Well?"

"Sure."

Freddie got out of the car and Itchy followed. They walked back up the block past the shine parlor and around the corner to a pool hall. There were three tables, all empty. Freddie said "Hi" to the sleepy-looking Japanese man behind the cigar counter.

"Hello, young boy," said the man in unschooled English. "Take table way in back and don't make trouble." He was a heavy man of around fifty with rumpled slacks and shirt.

"Like hell I will. We're usin' the good table." He went to the first table and, slipping the rack over the neatly set-up balls, proceeded to jiggle them back into position.

The man, his face hardening perceptibly, grabbed Freddie's arm and pulled him firmly away from the table. "I say back table. I see you play before. That one good enough for you. If you no like, get out."

Freddie glared back at the man, his hand reaching out to curl menacingly over the cue ball.

Ichiro moved quickly between them. "Come on. It isn't worth blowing your stack about." He jostled him lightly. "I thought you were going to show me a good time."

"Aghh, friggin' Jap. Always out to give me a bad time." He threw the rack on the table and said flippantly: "Okay, let's have a ball." Still glaring at the man, he sauntered toward the last table.

The man restrained Ichiro momentarily with a tug on his sleeve. "That one, he no good. I know. Always trouble."

"Sure, sure," said Ichiro, "he'll be all right."

Shaking his head, the man went back to his stool behind the counter.

Freddie was pulling cues off the wall rack, holding them up against his eye for alignment, brandishing them like swords for weight, and testing them for balance on a finger. "Hell, gimme a broomstick," he said exasperatedly. He tried a few more and finally selected one. "Flip for break, Itchy boy." He tossed a coin high into the air.

"Heads," said Ichiro, his back toward his companion as he examined the cues against the wall.

Freddie snatched the falling coin and, without a glance, put it back in his pocket. "You lose. My break."

Cue ball in hand, he spent many deliberate moments spotting it for the initial shot. He settled on a location close to the bank of the table and crouched to make the break. Jiggling the cue, sighting, jiggling the stick some more, shifting his feet, moving his buttocks, he finally pulled back and plunged the stick forward. There was a faint click as the cue flailed up and away from the felt. The white ball, rolling askew, banked against the side and rolled easily into the neat pyramid, merely distorting it a bit. "Son-of-a-bitchin' cue."

It all happened too quickly for Ichiro to intercede. The stick flashed up and down with a resounding whack against the table. A piece flew up and against the wall.

"All right, boy. All right, boy. You ask for it." The crimson-faced man was hurrying toward them.

"Rotten Jap." Freddie plucked a ball and threw it at the furious proprietor, who sought cover behind one of the tables. The ball crashed into a case of empty pop bottles. "Beat it!"

They ran for the door, Freddie managing to toss a few more balls in the general direction of the enemy, and Ichiro running blindly with only the desire to get away. There was no further pursuit, but they ran all the way to the car.

Once again they sat in silence, waiting until they regained their breath and then lighting cigarettes.

"You're crazy," said Ichiro.

"Agh, he won't do nothin'."

"He might."

"Let him. Who gives a damn." Freddie punched his butt against the dash, letting the burning crumbs fall to the floor of the car.

"This what you call living it up?"

"Better'n nothin'. You got somethin' better to do? Give."

"I could be sleeping."

Freddie chuckled, then stared blankly ahead. He looked much more haggard than he had in the apartment that day which seemed such a long time ago.

Ichiro felt deeply sorry for his friend who, in his hatred of the complex jungle of unreasoning that had twisted a life-giving yes into an empty no, blindly sought relief in total, hateful rejection of self and family and society. And this sorrow, painfully and humanely felt, enlarged still more the understanding which he had begun to find through Ken and Mr. Carrick and Emi and, yes, even his mother and father.

He turned to Freddie, who stared ahead now with the face of a tired, old man. "Freddie." There was no response. He tried again, a little louder this time: "Freddie."

"Yeah. That's me."

"We can go to my place."

"What for?"

"Talk."

"We're talkin' now."

"Okay. What's bothering you?"

Freddie looked thoughtful, then defiant. "Nothin'. How come you ask?"

"Seems to me like you're out to lick the system singlehanded."

"I ain't, but if I am, so what? I'm just livin'."

"Take it easy, Freddie."

"Aw, can it." Anger pulled his face taut as he yelled at Ichiro: "I didn't ask you out to give me no lecture. I get my belly full at home. And that fat pig. Soon's I line me up a real babe, she's done. I'm gettin' sick a her."

Ichiro wondered if he should try again to get Freddie to go home with him. He didn't enjoy being with him, but, now that he was, he felt some reluctance about leaving him alone. "There's beer and whisky at my place," he said. "Why don't we go?"

"Nuts. We're gonna do somethin'."

"What?"

"Who gives a damn. Anythin'."

Thoroughly disgusted, he replied evenly: "Fine. Have a good time." He pushed open the door and started to get out.

"Wait a minute, wait a minute," shouted Freddie, "we'll do somethin'."

Ichiro sat down. "All right. Name it."

"Sure," Freddie thought for a moment. "Let's go have a drink. Someplace nice, with people around, but not jumpin'. You know."

"No, I don't."

"You know, for crissake. You know what I mean."

"Yes, I know just the place," he replied with heavy irony in tone and expression. "The Club Oriental."

"Naw, what the hell you—" he started. Then, brightening mischievously: "Why not?"

"Wait a minute," he objected hastily. "You're not taking me seriously?"

"Free world, ain't it?"

"Sure, but—"

"Chicken?"

"No, no, but there's no sense in asking for trouble."

Freddie was starting the car, his face aglow with devilish excitement. "Ain't nobody tellin' this boy to stay on his side of the fence. I got teeth and hair like anybody else."

"I thought they were laying for you."

214

"So what? I ain't scared no more. You and me, we can take 'em."

"Oh, no. I've got more brains than you think." Ichiro heard his voice rising with the mounting anger. "What in hell is the matter with you? We've got troubles now. What good is it going to do to look for more? You're in real bad shape if you think—"

Freddie raised his hand defensively. "Whoa, whoa." He smiled impishly. "A drink. That's all we want—a nice, quiet drink. We're goin' there and have a peaceful drink, maybe two. No trouble. No fights. Anybody says anythin', I'm headin' for the door. Okay?"

"If you really mean it, sure."

"Okay, that's how it's gonna be. First sign a trouble, we blow. Check?"

"Fine."

"Double check." He shoved the lever into low gear and, with tires screeching, abusively whipped the car away from the curb and up the street.

Wanting to protest, wanting to get away from Freddie and his madness, Ichiro sat silently trying to resign himself to the situation. Freddie was much too erratic to be trusted. Still, there was a hint of logic in his stubborn defiance. It was a free world, but they would have to make peace with their own little world before they could enjoy the freedom of the larger one. Maybe Freddie is on the right track, he told himself; but he found no comfort in his thoughts.

Freddie drove up the hill past the dingy stores, the decrepit hotels, the gambling joints, looking for an opening big enough for the car and not finding one. He cursed a steady stream of violent oaths all the way around the block. Finally, he turned into the alley, drove up to the door of the club, and parked under a sign reading "Absolutely No Parking."

"You're asking for a ticket," warned Ichiro.

"So what? Ain't my jalopy." He got out and waited for Ichiro.

"We aren't being very sensible. I'd rather not, you know."

"Can it. We're here, ain't we? Nothin's goin' to happen."

"I have your word?"

Freddie yelled: "I give you my word, didn't I? You want I should cross my heart on a stack a Bibles or somethin'?"

He started toward the entrance without answering. Hitting the buzzer, they waited for the release to buzz back. Ichiro looked at Freddie, who for the first time, appeared a bit apprehensive. It comforted him to know that he was on the defensive. Perhaps there wouldn't be any trouble. They both grabbed for the door as the buzzing started, and then they were inside. The place was dim, smoky, and crowded.

"I guess we picked a bad night," said Ichiro hopefully.

Freddie nodded silently. He looked all wound up, his face tense and watchful instead of arrogant.

"Shall we go?"

Freddie shook his head, not looking at his companion, but keeping his eyes roving vigilantly over the crowd. "We're in," he said finally, pointing to the bar, where a couple was preparing to leave. They hurried to take over the stools.

Hemmed in, as it were, on both sides and with his back to the people at the tables, Ichiro felt oddly secure. He lifted his glass and said: "Here's to Kenji."

"Who's he?"

"A friend who asked me to have a drink for him."

"Some guy in stir?"

"No, a friend."

"Okay, to your friend, wherever the son of a bitch may be."

"That wasn't necessary." His voice was low and firm.

"Jeezuz," said Freddie startled, "I didn't mean nothin'. I'm drinkin' to him, ain't I? If the guy was a real son of a bitch, I wouldn't waste the price of a drink on him. If he's a friend of yours, he's okay with me, I'm tellin' you. To him, your friend." He raised his glass.

At that moment it occurred to Ichiro that he and Ken had been talking in a very similar vein when they had sat at this very bar. It seemed appropriate. He smiled and raised his glass toward Freddie's. The glasses never met, for suddenly, Freddie's shoes banged against the bar as he shot straight back off the stool.

Ichiro turned and felt sick at his stomach. Bull, grinning hideously, held Freddie helpless by means of a beefy fist which gripped the victim's coat collar twisted tightly against his back.

Freddie struggled. "Let go, you stupid bastard."

"Make me, Jap-boy." Bull looked to the crowd for appreciation.

"Let him go," said Ichiro a little nervously.

"Make me," said Bull with the meanness in his dark face. "This little shit's been askin' for it."

"Cut it out, Bull," said a voice out of the crowd.

Jim Eng was pushing his way to the disturbance. "All right, all right," he kept repeating in an agitated squeak.

Bull shoved Freddie around and pushed him toward the door. Someone grabbed at his arm, saying "Leave him alone." He shrugged off the hand angrily. "Anybody wants to butt in, I'll bust his balls for him."

The crowd opened up for Bull and Freddie. Ichiro, close behind, was momentarily restrained by a hand pulling at his sleeve. He turned, ready for the worst.

"Stay out of it, fellow. It won't do much good." The one who spoke was a pleasant-looking youth with a black-gloved hand hanging with awkward stiffness at his side.

"I haven't got much choice."

"Let me buy you a drink. You're not the brawling kind."

The door slammed, and Freddie's loud protestations were cut off. Ichiro pushed his way out to the alley, where Bull was trying to propel his undersized opponent away from the illumination around the club's entrance. He ran up to the pair and took hold of Bull's arm.

"Let him go," he pleaded. "We won't come back."

"I'm makin' damn sure of that. You goddamn Japs think you're pretty smart, huh? I wasn't fightin' my friggin' war for shits like you."

217

Freddie, sensing his chance, drove an elbow sharply into his aggressor's stomach. Bull grunted, momentarily relaxing his grip, and Freddie wrenched himself free and sprawled forward.

Ichiro, seeing Bull lunge to recapture his prey, threw his shoulder against the solid mass of flesh and muscle. They rolled down the alley, clawing at each other and straining muscles to seek a victory in the senseless struggle. When they stopped rolling, Ichiro managed to gain the top position. Straddling the infuriated Bull, he shoved his face against the hate-filled countenance of the one who chose to speak for those who had fought and died.

"Please," he screamed, "please, don't fight."

And Bull cursed and strained and heaved with the strength which could not be restrained much longer. Driven by fear, urged by a need to fight this thing which no amount of fighting would ever destroy, Ichiro raised his fist and drove it down. He saw the eyes flinch, the head trying to avert the blow, and then the nauseating gush of blood from nose and mouth.

"I'll kill you." The words, spoken with icy fury, gurgled out through a mouthful of bloody sputum.

And Ichiro looked into the angry eyes and saw that to quit now would mean to submit to that unrelenting fury. He raised his fist again, sick with what he was having to do. Before he could strike, however, he felt himself being pulled off.

"That's enough," said someone.

"Break it up," said another.

Bull was up on one elbow, his hate-filled eyes intent upon Ichiro. "Okay," he grunted, a hint of a smile showing cruelly through the streaks of blood.

"Bull, no more!" a voice said authoritatively.

"Yeah? Who says?" He wiped a sleeve across his mouth and started to push himself off the ground, his eyes never for a moment wavering from Ichiro's.

Ichiro watched, not wanting to fight, and making no effort to run from the hands which held him only loosely. There was a sudden clatter of footsteps, and he saw Bull, not quite in a sitting position, raise both arms defensively as he fell backward.

In that instant, Freddie plunged his heel into the stomach of the fallen opponent. Bull gasped with pain, swore mightily, and seemed almost to throw himself upright. Startled by the speedy recovery, Freddie stood stock still for a moment. Not until Bull had taken steps toward him did he make a frantic dash for the car.

Bull, clutching at his mid-section with one arm, managed half a dozen steps before stumbling to his knees. He cursed continually, the hateful sounds painfully strained. Again, he rose to his feet and progressed erratically toward the car, which Freddie was furiously trying to start. Just as it roared to life, Bull pulled open the door. He reached in and grabbed at Freddie, who squirmed away and countered by swinging a wrench, which caught Bull on the side of the head.

The car jumped forward, throwing Bull roughly aside. The motor coughed. There was a hectic jiggling of the gas pedal, and the car screeched through the alley. A pedestrian, about to cross the alleyway, jumped out of the way with comic haste.

"Crazy damn fool," said a voice behind Ichiro.

Ichiro watched the car plunge out across the street. The next instant there was a muffled thud. The car which Freddie drove seemed to jump straight into the air and hang suspended for a deathly, clear second. Then it flipped over and slammed noisily against the wall of the building on the other side of the street. Not until then did he notice the smashed front end of another car jutting into view.

Someone was running to the overturned car. There was an excited shout and another and, soon, people were eagerly crowding toward the wreck from all directions. He stood there alone for a long while, feeling utterly exhausted, knowing, somehow, that Freddie would have to fight no longer.

Over by the club's entrance, Bull was sitting with his back against a trash can; his head hung between his knees.

He went up to him and said: "Bull."

"Get me a drink," he moaned without stirring.

"Sure."

"Damn."

"What?"

"That son of a bitch. I hope it killed him."

The club door was open. Inside, the juke box was playing for one couple at a table and a solitary figure at the bar who was too drunk to move. He went behind the bar and grabbed a bottle.

A Japanese youth, probably about Taro's age, came running in. Flushed with excitement, he exclaimed to Ichiro: "What a mess! Didja see it? Poor guy musta been halfway out when the car smacked the building. Just about cut him in two. Ugh!" He hastened into the phone booth.

Ichiro took a drink out of the bottle and made his way back out to where Bull was still sitting.

"Here."

Bull moaned, but made no move to accept the bottle.

He took hold of his hair, pulled him straight, and shoved the bottle against the bloody mouth. Bull drank, coughed, and drank some more. Then grabbing the bottle away from Ichiro, he let his head drop once more.

"They say he's dead," said Ichiro gently.

"So what?"

"Nothing. Just that . . . that . . . I'm sorry."

Bull swung his face upward, his eyes wide with horror, the mouth twisted with rage yet trembling at the same time. The throaty roar was mixed with streaks of agonized screaming verging on the hysterical. "Yeah? Yeah? I ain't. I ain't sorry one friggin' bit. That little bastard's seen it comin' a good long while. I ain't sorry. You hear? I ain't sorry. Damn right I ain't. I hope he goes to hell. I hope he . . ."

The words refused to come out any longer. Mouth agape, lips trembling, Bull managed only to move his jaws sporadically. Suddenly, he clamped them shut. His cheeks swelled to bursting, and the eyes, the frightened, lonely eyes, peered through a dull film of tears and begged for the solace that was not to be had.

"Agggggggghh," he screamed and, with the brute strength that could only smash, hurled the whisky bottle across the alley. Then he started to cry, not like a man in grief or a soldier in pain, but like a baby in loud, gasping, beseeching howls.

A siren moaned, shrieked, then moaned to a stop with a screeching of brakes. A door slammed. Official voices yelled at the crowd. The murmur of the curious filtered through the alley.

Ichiro put a hand on Bull's shoulder, sharing the empty sorrow in the hulking body, feeling the terrible loneliness of the distressed wails, and saying nothing. He gave the shoulder a tender squeeze, patted the head once tenderly, and began to walk slowly down the alley away from the brightness of the club and the morbidity of the crowd. He wanted to think about Ken and Freddie and Mr. Carrick and the man who had bought the drinks for him and Emi, about the Negro who stood up for Gary, and about Bull, who was an infant crying in the darkness. A glimmer of hope— was that it? It was there, someplace. He couldn't see it to put it into words, but the feeling was pretty strong.

He walked along, thinking, searching, thinking and probing, and, in the darkness of the alley of the community that was a tiny bit of America, he chased that faint and elusive insinuation of promise as it continued to take shape in mind and in heart.

AFTERWORD

IN SEARCH OF JOHN OKADA

I'M BACK IN SEATTLE AND NOT WHAT I WAS WHEN I LIVED here. Seattle isn't the city it was when I lived here. The only yellow motion then was lanterns in Chinatown. The yellow mouth in town was Ruby Chow blowing blowing sweet'n'sour hoochie koochie and a vision of the continuity of Chinese culture in the Pacific Northwest that was pure Jack London science fiction, all bunk, and totally believed by gah gah non-yellows who eat out Chinese to get away from real life. If they couldn't disappear into Shangri-la and passive immortality, they could put a fantasy in their stomach.

Ruby Chow's was loud and fancy with Chinamans out of the movies and funny papers, as if the "Chinese Americans" were the most accomplished, the best, the pioneering of the yellows here. I lived and worked here writing as if the greatest Asian American writer who ever wrote had never lived here. John Okada was Japanese American, Nisei, born and raised in Seattle. His first and last novel, *No-No Boy*, about a Japanese American who served hard time for refusing to volunteer to be inducted into the army in WWII, is set in Seattle. To Asian Americans outside of Seattle, John Okada is the proof of our yellow soul. I never heard of John Okada the four years I lived here.

Think of being born to a people who have no culture, no literature, no writing, no writers, except in some past across an ocean. In 200 years and all your generations of white people living and creating new American experience and know-how, not one word, not one joke, not one book.

What if there were no whites in American literary history. There is no Melville, no Mark Twain, no Kay Boyle, no Gertrude Stein, no Tom Robbins, not even a Rod McKuen. A white American writer would feel edgy if all the books ever written in America were by blacks, browns, reds, yellows, and all whites had ever published were cookbooks full of recipes for apple pie and fried chicken.

That's what I grew up with. A literary tradition of cookbooks and autobiographies by the children of Christian converts and Pochahontas yellows whites call progressive for marrying out white. I grew up told no one knew anything else about yellow writing because there was nothing else to know. In our 150 years, nine Chinaman generations, four Japanese American generations, three Filipino, two Korean, not one of us had an urge to say what's what and who's who about ourselves. In all that time all we had to look to was some dumpy plastic lanterns swinging in Chinatown like fat men strung up by a lynch mob to bloat.

I'll tell ya right now. I never won a fistfight in my life. I don't know kung fu or karate. I'm not a fast runner either. If I can't talk my way out of a fight, I've had it. I'm not known for being brave or especially savvy. I'm proof that the urge to self-expression is nothing special and writing isn't an act of courage. It makes no sense to me to be thought of as the first yellow writer of anything, much less plays, in the history of my people. To believe that I was the first to write was to believe Asian Americans were less than gutless all their history here.

224

I didn't want to be the first yellow to write. I didn't want to be the first yellow to write in Seattle. I didn't want to be a freak and I didn't want the responsibility for being deep and true that comes with being the first of your people to do it with words. For me, the discovery of John's 1957 novel was like a white writer feeling gloomy and alone in a literary history, discovering Mark Twain. *No-No Boy* proved I wasn't the only yellow writer in yellow history. The book was so good it freed me to be trivial.

Back in 1957 John said things Asian Americans are afraid to think, much less say today. Things that every yellow feels. I've known all my life that I am not Chinese and I am not white American. I was brought up to believe there was nothing else for me to be but a Chinese foreigner or a fake white American, as if there were nothing for whites to be other than British subjects or American colonists. Sometime 200 years ago, whites declared they were neither British subjects nor American colonists. They were "Americans."

Asian Americans have been wandering round the self-pity and pompous theories of the so-called "Asian American identity crisis" since the massive missionary effort to convert us to the notion that civilization is founded on religion, and the best religion is the one that worships one god. Christian missionaries controlled our population by denying us access to our women and allowing only Christian converts to marry. The twenties produced a generation of Asian Americans who didn't know who they were. We still don't. John Okada shows the "identity" crisis to be both totally real and absolutely fake in a book that is still too strong for many yellows to read.

Ichiro comes back to Seattle from prison to a home full of loonies. His brother despises him for refusing to serve in the war and joins the army to make up for Ichiro's disgrace. Ichiro's father is a slobbering lush terrorized by his wife, who believes Japan has won the war and the papers are holding back the bad news from the whites. She looks to Ichiro as an ally and accomplice to her madness and says, "Think more deeply and your doubts will disappear. You are my son," and triggers a spinning, running internal monologue that is one of the most powerfully moving passages in Asian American writing:

> No, he said to himself as he watched her part the curtains and start into the store. There was a time when I was your son. There was a time that I no longer remember when you used to smile a mother's smile and tell me stories about gallant and fierce warriors who protected their lords with blades of shining steel and about the old woman who found a peach in the stream and took it home, and, when her husband split it in half, a husky little boy tumbled out to fill their hearts with boundless joy. I was that lad in the peach and you were the old woman and we were Japanese with Japanese feelings and Japanese pride and Japanese thoughts because it was all right then to be Japanese and feel and think all the things that Japanese do even if we lived in America. Then there came a time when I was only half Japanese because one is not born in America and raised in America and taught in America and one does not speak and swear and drink and smoke and play and fight and see and hear in America among Americans in American streets and houses without becoming American and loving it. But I did not love enough for you were still half my mother and I was thereby still half Japanese and when the war came and they told me to fight for America, I was not strong enough to fight you and I was not strong enough to fight the bitterness which made the half of me which was you bigger than the half of me which was America and really the whole of me that I could not see or feel. Now that I know the truth when it is late and the half of me which was you is no longer there, I am only half of me and the half that remains is American by law because the government was wise and strong enough to know why it was that I could not fight for America and did not strip me of my birthright. But it is not enough to be only half an American and know that it is an empty half. I am not your son and I am not Japanese and I am not American.

John Okada was not No-No boy. He served in WWII hanging out of an airplane over Japanese-held islands asking their occupants in their own language to give up. When I came to Seattle to look for John Okada I learned he was dead. I got the impression his family was ashamed of the book. They thought of me as a "yellow activist," a troublemaker, for even bringing the book back to their minds. They had put him in his old uniform, buried him in Seattle and forgotten the book. John's widow, Dorothy, stayed away from the funeral and won't come back to Seattle.

John died in February 1971 of a heart attack. He was 47. I'd missed meeting John by a few months. If only I'd read his book sooner, I might have gotten together with Lawson Inada, the Sansei poet, and gone driving down to L.A. looking for John sooner. As it was, his family in Seattle said they'd talk to us only if John's widow would talk to us. I broke out the old suit I'd worn at my high school graduation, and Lawson and I drove to L.A.

"I wish you had come visiting when John was alive," Dorothy said. "He would have liked to meet you." In the 15 years since Charles Tuttle of Tokyo had published the novel, not one yellow had come up to John to say, "Hey, John, I read your book and I think it's pretty nice."

We asked her about John's second novel. Charles Tuttle had sent me a copy of a letter John had written him saying, "I am now at work on a second [novel] which will have for its protagonist an immigrant Issei rather than a Nisei. When completed, I hope that it will to some degree faithfully describe the experiences of the immigrant Japanese in the United States. This is a story which has never been told in fiction and only in fiction can the hopes and fears and joys and sorrows of people be adequately recorded. I feel an urgency to write of the Japanese in the United States for the Issei are rapidly vanishing and I should regret if their chapter in American history should die with them."

John wrote that in 1956. Dorothy said he'd almost finished a first draft before he died. Then she told us something that turned our blood to puke in our veins. After John died she offered all of

John's manuscripts, notes and correspondence to the Japanese American Research Project at UCLA. John Okada was then and still is the only known Japanese American novelist. His *No-No Boy*, the only Japanese American novel. He belongs to Japanese American history and American literature, but the Japanese American Research Project refused to so much as look at the Okada papers. These champions of Japanese American history encouraged Dorothy to destroy the papers. Lawson and I looked around her little apartment for signs of John. "I had to move," Dorothy said. "I could not afford to keep the house and put the children through college. I didn't know what to do with John's things. Nobody had any use for them. Nobody wanted them. I burned them."

"Everything?" I asked.

"Everything," she said, and I wanted to kick her ass around the block. I wanted to burn UCLA down. Instead we stayed up late talking about her life, talking about her marriage to John, keeping her up and asking every now and then about a letter, a story, a scrap of paper. But the answer was always the same. "Burned."

Back in Seattle again, the family agrees to see us. The brothers don't look like the heavies of the piece. They're proud of the book, talk freely and feed us sushi. Fredy, John's father, is 84 and is lying down in the next room. "Old age sickness," he says when I step in to shake hands and say hello. "A little stroke awhile ago," he says.

Out his window Robert and Roy point toward Pioneer Square. "John was born in the old Merchants Hotel. Upstairs," they say. They point down toward the International District to a bit of grey between the top of Puget Sound Hotel and the top of another brick building. "That was the old Yakima Hotel. Our father owned that," and they point out the other hotels in sight that Fredy owned. They talk about growing up in the Merchants Hotel, and spill bits of John Okada that could mean anything to Sumida the scholar, Inada the Sansei poet and me, the only Chinese American in the room. John was born in a hotel room with the help of a Japanese midwife, in September of 1923. He went to Bailey Gatzert Elementary and Broadway High. He might have collected stamps.

Roy says John had always wanted to write something about the Issei, the first generation. They didn't know if John had actually started writing that book. I tell them what Dorothy told me. He wrote it. He died. It's gone. Burned. No one looks at anybody else. Steve Sumida looks out the window to the King Street Station clock tower. I look over the empty chair between Roy and Robert to a picture on the wall. A family portrait.

After a while I ask about the family and learn the Okadas are remarkably artistic. Roy, the oldest son, is a graphic designer, John was a writer, Frank, a younger brother, is a well known painter. We are finally talking about the book again. "The clock tower, the Wonder Bread factory, all the landmarks are in the book," Robert says.

"Yeah," Roy says. We all laugh. We've all been to Seattle. We've all read the book.

John's brothers, and Frank Ashida, John's old fishing partner, Doris Mitchell, John's boss at the Seattle Public Library all remember John's brains, his brilliance, his "bright shining eyes," Doris Mitchell says. She's retired, neat, powdered and carries a white handkerchief tucked under the cuff of her left sleeve. She lives in one of those awful places where old people make friends out of other old people come to die here under discreet and watchful eyes. The place is air conditioned, piped and wired like a hospital. It's burglar proof. The front door seems off a bank vault. Lawson Inada and me stepped in to talk with her about John like other people talk stick 'em up for money.

She had the complexion of cabbage. She had all the facts of John's education, residences and employment memorized. She recited John's resume so affectionately, I couldn't watch her, so reverently, I was afraid to touch her when I thought she was crying. Of all the people we'd talked to about John, only Doris Mitchell effortlessly, deeply, unabashedly tried to bring him back to life right before our eyes. Dorothy was surviving John when we met her. The brothers felt close to John but didn't know that much about his business. Doris chanted the facts and figures, the dates and places of John Okada from the letters and cards he'd sent her, first week after week, then month after month, then once every six months, then Christmas cards once a year and an occasional letter. In an act of librarian's passion, she catalogued the facts of the man from about who knows what.

Neither me nor Lawson asked to read John's letters to her. Not that we have dirty minds, or are afraid of finding out something we don't want to know, or are code of the west about respecting privacy. We thought of asking. We just never asked. We were no longer visitors come to interview someone who had a line on the John Okada who wrote *No-No Boy*. We were participants in an old white woman's seance. There's old mellowed emotion cooking in her voice that makes the facts sound deep, with John's presence. But without her voice, they're just facts.

He went to Bailey Gatzert Elementary, Broadway High, Minedoka, Scottsbluff Jr. College with Frank Ashida, volunteered for military service with Ashida. Ashida went his way in the service and John was discharged a sergeant in 1946. He graduated from the University of Washington heavy into English lit, and, in John's words, "narrative and dramatic writing, history, sociology." M.A., Columbia U. 1949. He met Dorothy there, brought her back to Seattle, got a B.A. in Librarianship at the University of Washington, then married her. Or vice versa.

John Okada worked as Doris Mitchell's assistant in the Business Reference Department of the Seattle Public Library, moved to Detroit to take a job for more money and hopefully more time to write at the Detroit Public Library. The work was long hours, no growth and unrewarding. The neighborhood Christian church didn't want Japanese Americans in their congregation. John became a technical writer for Chrysler Missile Operations of Sterling Township, Michigan. He wrote Doris Mitchell he had no time to write his new book and he felt Dorothy and the children were unhappy. As part of his plot to leave Detroit he prepared a resume and autobiographical essay. Dorothy hadn't destroyed everything after all. The bits of John folded and tucked away in her books, left in pockets, in the bottoms of drawers began to find their way back into Dorothy's hands. The resume and profile he wrote to get him and his family out of Detroit in 1956 is the only writing by John Okada on John Okada we've seen:

> At age 33, I am a married man who feels that he is uncommonly devoted to his wife and unusually fortunate in having two wonderful children, a son approaching five and a daughter who recently touched six. Normal feelings for a normal husband and father, one might say, but I choose to think that my family is quite special. Perhaps, I have been endowed with a larger capacity for normalcy than most people.
>
> Next to my family, and of somewhat lesser importance, is my personal writing. Reduced to an avocation, though a disciplined one, my writing finally seems to be making headway. A novel completed a year ago is scheduled for distribution this coming June or July. A second is in the works and progressing sporadically.
>
> My health is good (two days lost because of illness in the past five years); I make an effort to be consistently punctual (both a four and nine-inch snowfall combined with a 16-mile drive proved somewhat time consuming this past winter, however); and I do not mind working under pressure or digging my way out from under a mountain of material (no objections to overtime, homework, or disrupted vacation plans).

The facts of his life, school, college, camp, service, more college, marriage, kids, movement across the country following jobs, nothing extraordinary, nothing revealing about Okada the man or the writer. Maybe his feeling "endowed with a larger capacity for normalcy than most people," is a clue. I wonder about the writer who can resist mentioning the title of his novel on the eve of its release. If he needs time to write, I wonder about his begging for overtime, homework and disrupted vacation plans. This is all that's left of John Okada: his one novel, *No-No Boy*, Seattle, the few memories of him a few Seattleites still keep. His family. A few friends. And his grave.

This month Asian American writers and word punks like me from all over the country are coming to Seattle to meet each other here because Seattle's special. A lot of our history's here. Several pioneer Asian American journalists and writers come from here, James Sakamoto, Monica Sone, Bill Hosokawa, Jim Yoshida. But John Okada is the only great one. I'm back in Seattle to say, "John, I read your book. I like it a lot."

Frank Chin
Seattle, June 1976

CLASSICS OF ASIAN AMERICAN LITERATURE

America Is in the Heart: A Personal History, by Carlos Bulosan,
with a new introduction by Marilyn C. Alquizola
and Lane Ryo Hirabayashi

No-No Boy: A Novel, by John Okada,
with a new foreword by Ruth Ozeki

Citizen 13660, drawings and text by Miné Okubo,
with a new introduction by Christine Hong

Nisei Daughter, by Monica Sone,
with a new introduction by Marie Rose Wong